CASTRO'S DREAM

by the same author
LOST

LUCY WADHAM

Castro's Dream

faber and faber

First published in 2003
by Faber and Faber Limited
3 Queen Square London WC1N 3AU

Typeset by Faber and Faber Limited
Printed in England by Clays Ltd, St Ives plc

A CIP record for this book
is available from the British Library

ISBN 0–571–21637–4

2 4 6 8 10 9 7 5 3 1

For my sisters Louise, Catherine,
Amynta and Rosie and my brother Tom

Author's Note

Part of this story takes place in the Basque Country (Euskal Herria), on both the French and Spanish sides of the border but mostly in the province of Gipuzkoa, around San Sebastian. Anyone familiar with this troubled region will know that it is difficult to consider the place without considering the violence therein and the role of the armed group, ETA. It will become clear, however, that the story is not about ETA, nor indeed about Basque politics. It does not attempt to shed any light on ETA's present formation. Certain characters in the story are linked to a now extinct movement known as ETA-PM (a schism of ETA-M, which survives today). After Franco's death the 'Poli-Milis', as they were called, abandoned the armed struggle in favour of political action. To this extent the story examines the effects of long-term violence on those who are looking for a way out.

Euzkadi, Euskadi: the Basque Country
Donostia: San Sebastian
ETA: Euskadi ta Askatasuna (Basque Homeland and Freedom)
In Basque the letters 'Tx' are pronounced 'Ch', so the name 'Txema' is pronounced 'Ché-ma', 'Itxua' is 'Itch-ua'.

Acknowledgements

My thanks to Sarah Ferguson for all her support and encouragement; to Dr Sophie Cohen for answering all my questions; to Dr Jorge Cardozo for letting me watch him work; to Gerard Toupier at the Pasteur Institute; and in loving memory of Professor Jean Julvez, without whom this story would never have been invented.

Castro's Dream

ONE

On the morning of Mikel's release Astrid expected to have another episode. She dressed slowly, carefully stepping into her clothes, as though afraid that any sudden movement might act as a trigger, making her mind short circuit.

You may not have any symptoms, the neurologist had told her. *There's rarely any warning that it's about to happen. If it's going to happen, it'll just happen.*

Of course he had not addressed the fear. Fear brought its own symptoms and as Astrid well knew, it was not the thing itself so much as the fear of it that was dominating her life. The symptoms that assailed her now, as she stepped out of her building into the Paris dawn; the palpitations, sweaty palms, dry mouth and the sensory distortion, were the products of an over-active adrenal gland: knowing this did not help. She stood on the kerb, the object world swimming before her, stiff with terror.

Behind her, the heavy glass door slammed shut, sending an unpleasant ricochet of sound waves through the spaces in her body. She took deep breaths, focusing on the horse chestnuts that grew out of the pavement on the other side of the cobbled road. The dark bitumen, buckling from the roots growing beneath, looked soft and foamy. She closed her eyes. The air was too thick, the birdsong too slow.

Look at me now, Lola. Your calm, rational sister. Look at what a wreck I am.

The vision of Lola dancing around her flat in her shell-pink nightie helped Astrid step off the kerb onto the cobbles. As she walked down the hill she began to hum 'Gracias la Vida', their favourite song. Sticking to her part, the alto, she imagined Lola's fine voice singing out the soprano harmony she had invented to go with it.

Up the hill towards her came a youth astride a square, fluorescent green motorcycle, trailing behind him the piercing sound of the vacuum sucking up dog shit from the pavement. Astrid walked steadily towards the man and the machine. As they passed her she did not flinch but gave a victorious smile. The youth was busy with his next target and did not see what she suddenly realised was closer to a grimace.

While she waited for her bus, Astrid noted the slow return to normal of her metabolic function. She breathed deeply as she studied an advertisement for a vitamin supplement on the side of the shelter. A middle-aged woman with a youthful smile, aided by an invisible trampoline, had been caught in mid-air, just at that moment before her skirt flew up and gravity pulled her back. Astrid stared at the ecstatic smile and wondered at the circumstances that had brought the woman to such indignity.

She looked down at the water running in the gutter at her feet. This habit they had of flushing the gutters with clear water every morning was one of the things she liked about Paris. They would never dream of doing something so munificent in a Spanish city, or an English one.

The bus hummed as it approached. The doors hissed open and shut behind her. She validated her ticket in the machine beside the driver, waiting for the sound that always reminded her of her stepfather Josu's abattoir gun. Then she made her way to an empty seat at the back of the bus and sat down.

She looked out of the window at the dawn sky, the electric-blue and pink tinted purple by the brown glass. Her first malaise had been brought on by a conversation with Lola. She had been standing in her lab, watching the new machine that had been hooked up to a baboon's liver. Lola had called to tell her the news of Mikel's release. When Astrid picked up the phone Lola was already crying.

He's getting out. They're letting him out. Lola had started laughing through her tears. *I'm so happy, Astrid. I don't deserve to be so happy.*

Astrid had not been able to reply. This time it was not guilt that had prevented her from speaking, but a sense of loss that took her breath away. She had stood there watching the baboon's blood in the tubes, gripping the phone until she could feel nothing but her tight fist around the phone and herself trickling like sand through the fist, onto the floor. She had intended to go for a walk and had called out to Vincent, the lab technician, to watch the baboon,

4

then she had passed out where she stood. When she woke, her head was in Vincent's lap and he was stroking her hair ineptly.

Now, as usual, nausea followed the other symptoms, and a numbing in the upper body, but as the bus crossed Paris from north to south Astrid noted an improvement in her state. By the time they crossed the Seine at Austerlitz she was feeling better.

She entered the hospital compound. The doorman in his glass box beneath the porch looked up from his paper and nodded. She noticed that today he had white tape on the arm of his spectacles. She made her way along the narrow concrete path towards the lab, breathing in the smell of dew on grass, her senses tethered again.

She opened the lab and stepped inside and turned on the ceiling lights one by one. She took her lab coat from its hook and put it on. She thought of Lola lying awake in her dirty little flat, waiting for her lover's call.

Astrid fetched her mobile phone from her handbag and laid it on the workbench where she could see it.

Lola would be waiting for the call in that shell-pink nightie. She had bought it in the flea market near her flat. It was made of shiny, synthetic material, cut on the bias that clung to her shape. She wore it all the time indoors. Often she wore a bedjacket over it made of Easter-yellow ostrich feathers.

Astrid took a tray of new test tubes from the supply cupboard and broke open the cellophane. She pulled a tube from its holder, setting her teeth against the squeak of the polystyrene. They needed more bleach. She made a note of this on the wipe-clean noticeboard beside the fridge. She sniffed the pleasant smell of the felt-tip pen, then replaced the lid.

She put on her gloves and fetched her utensils from the sterilising unit and laid them out on the trolley, one by one.

Lola had only ever had one persistent ambition: to be a woman. At boarding school she had drawn hair with black biro onto her bare pubis and Astrid had watched her cry as their house mother, Sister Theresa, had slapped her face. Wicked girl, she had called her. Astrid wanted to believe that she had been filled with compassion at the sight but she suspected herself of having felt a first flicker of that pleasure, so dangerous, in being the good one.

Astrid lifted the white rat from its cage. She held it expertly in

5

one hand, its head in a delicate clamp between her index and middle finger, and carried it to the slab. She did believe that guilt had brought on the first attack, made her mind cut out as the neurologist had put it. Thomas Meydenburger was an old friend. He told her that the EEG showed delta waves, indicating a lesion.

It's just scarring. Probably from an old fall. Did you fall as a child?

Constantly.

He nodded, smiling at her with his mouth closed. His face was tanned, although it was winter and his blue eyes were pink around the rims.

Is that it? she had asked.

It's not a very precise science, I'm afraid.

Does that bother you?

He contemplated his biro, which he turned between his well-padded finger ends.

Not really. I wasn't cut out for science. I prefer ideas. And people.

Is that why you decided against surgery?

Surgery was for the macho, people who need action.

She raised her eyebrows.

I'm macho then.

I think you're a woman of action. I've always admired that in you.

Astrid clicked her tongue, a Spanish habit, out of place here.

Will you have dinner with me? he asked.

I don't have dinner. I'm virtually married.

How is the great man?

He's fine. He's seventy next year.

Thomas smiled. His lips were dry and chapped. Astrid thought it must be the air conditioning.

He looks good for seventy, he said.

He does.

They're all like that, the great surgeons. Go on, have dinner with me. Please.

I'll come if you can tell me what's wrong with me.

Next week. I'll tell you at dinner next week.

What, you'll have made something up by then?

You're a hard woman, Astrid. Then he must have caught her expression. I'm joking, he told her. I like it. You always reminded me of one of those Latina freedom fighters.

6

Astrid looked into her handbag:

You're right, Thomas. I am hard. She looked up. How much do I owe you?

But he had refused payment and replaced the lid of his biro with a resolute click. As they stood by the door, he had put a soft, manicured hand on her cheek.

Don't frown, he said. I didn't mean to upset you.

And she had told him that she did not believe him about the old fall.

What can I say? he said. It's an ictus. Transient global amnesia. The mind cuts out. No one knows the aetiology. Do you have migraines?

I did. For a while a long time ago. Bad ones. Then they went. He nodded slowly. She could see the questions crowding in his mind. They started when I was in prison, she added.

Clearly, he said, there can be psychological factors.

Clearly, she said.

He had smiled an apology and told her that there was unlikely to be a sequel and that she should try not to worry.

Should I stop operating? she had asked.

No. Listen to me. You know how you can drive somewhere for hours, thinking about things, listening to music? You may not remember a single thing about the drive itself, about how you got from A to B but that doesn't mean you weren't concentrating on your driving. You were just on automatic on some level. Do you see?

But I didn't remember anything, Thomas. Not a single thing. Four whole hours completely gone. All I know is that I had a case of wine in the back of my car and when I got home it was gone.

Are you sure?

Yes. Chastel put it there.

Maybe you drank it with a group of Brazilian transsexuals in the Bois de Boulogne.

Astrid smiled distractedly.

They had said goodbye and hugged and he had not mentioned dinner again. In that moment by the door she felt him retreat from her. It was not hard to understand why. She remembered a date with him in their first year of medical school. They had been to a cramped Chinese restaurant near the faculty. She had tested

7

him on the endocrine system and then he had taken her back to his tiny maid's room that smelt of stale yogurt. She remembered sitting beside him on a small, lumpy sofa and becoming aware that he was very nervous. She was deliberating as to whether or not she should kiss him and get things started when he suddenly put out his hand and gripped her breast hard and with such suddenness that she uttered a cry of alarm. The gesture had been entirely without eroticism and he had begun to apologise immediately. I'm sorry, he had said, shaking his head. I'm so sorry. She had not minded but Thomas had been mortified and never invited her back to his flat again.

She sighed at the memory, made an incision into the sedated rat's sternum and drew the scalpel in a neat line to its pubis.

TWO

Lola was lying on her side staring at the red digits of the alarm clock and still the buzzing sound, when it came, pierced her poor heart. She drew an arm from beneath the sheet and stopped the noise. Lola's heart was her weak organ. It murmured, Astrid said, and because of this murmur would never be fully reliable. When Astrid told her this, the cold stethoscope pressed against the freckles on her chest, Lola had watched her long dark lashes from above and smiled to herself. This was her sister's first diagnosis and Lola was proud of her, even if she was telling her something she already knew, that her heart was weak and unreliable.

Yes it's a heart murmur, Astrid had said, pulling her head away from Lola's chest, wrapping her brand new stethoscope around her hand. Don't worry, Lolita. It's not serious. We just have to watch it.

And Lola had buttoned her shirt and gone to get some beers from the fridge for them both and they had clinked bottles as though they were toasting this new task they had in common, to watch her heart.

The alarm clock displayed 06:31.

He had been let out one minute ago. It would take that long just to draw in some of the dawn sky from all around him, the blue of an exotic butterfly above him and the gold of lager on the horizon behind him, and then to take a pack of cigarettes from his pocket and light up his first free man's cigarette in twenty years.

Lola closed her eyes and saw her beloved standing there on that arid plain with the high walls of the prison behind him; standing as he always did with his feet apart as if the earth might shift beneath him at any moment.

Smoke, Mikel. Smoke, she said. And she rolled over and buried her grin in the pillow.

She was stupid. She rolled over and looked up at the ceiling. She had not been thinking clearly. It would take time to get to the nearest call box. He would have to wait by the side of that lonely

9

road for a truck travelling from Ciudad Real to Cuenca. He would climb up and greet the driver and in that greeting alone there would be something at once warm and commanding that would make the driver want to be liked by him. All men wanted to be liked by Mikel. She turned and looked at the clock: 06:46.

Of course: the first call box would have been vandalised; perhaps by an inmate, just freed, sour from captivity and looking to poison the next man's freedom. But Mikel would gently replace the receiver and step out of the phone box and climb back into the truck without a word. The mystery of this man who had been locked away for blood crimes was that he was quiet and meek in all his actions save those that were part of what he used to refer to as The Work.

But this, Lola did not like to think about.

Call me, call me, call me, she said aloud.

She put her hand between her legs to distract herself and closed her eyes but the phone was bound to ring now and he would catch her after all these years and he would tease her, saying that she could not leave her bizcocho alone for one minute. But the telephone stayed quiet and Lola knew that it was the old Mikel she was imagining, he would not tease her now. She could not remember when she last saw him laugh. He no longer tried to get into her pants during visits and even in the last place, a model prison, where rooms were made available for sex, he had not wanted her. She had stopped weeping and begging because she did not want to drive him away. Lola was afraid of life without Mikel.

She kicked off the sheets. After all this time, she could still feel the precise weight of his hands on her body and smell that faint smell of damp on his skin. She remembered Astrid talking about a well-documented regressive sexual disorder, and had thought she recognised herself in the pathology. It had something to do with the primary sexual experience and never being able to get over it. There was a name for it that Lola had forgotten.

She looked again: 07:15.

She wanted to call Astrid but did not dare use the phone in case he should call. She climbed out of bed and went to the window and drew the curtains. Astrid hated it when she stood naked like this in the window.

What if there's some pervert watching?

I don't care if there is.

Astrid was never naked.

Lola looked out over the railway lines and the glazed canopy of the Gare du Nord, glowing orange in the dawn. Lola was never awake at this time and she knew why; it was so sad. Astrid was up every morning in this. Lola imagined her moving through the empty streets on her way to work, her heels echoing too loudly on the pavement, passing the zombie folk who functioned at this hour and to whom the world, in spite of the saying, definitely did not belong.

Lola turned away, baring her magnificent bottom to the thankless dawn, looked again at the mute phone and went into the kitchen. She remembered that Astrid was sometimes naked, but her nakedness had a terrible, vulnerable quality to it that was the opposite of sex: naked as a worm, their mother would say. Lola opened the fridge but it was too early to eat so she went back into the bedroom and turned on the tape recorder. As the tape hissed, Lola positioned herself in preparation for the opening bar.

THREE

Astrid watched the open rat's beating heart. She was accustomed to being in control. Unlike Lola she did not like narcotics or alcohol. Her personality was organised in such a way that she was rarely taken by surprise. She was rational but not rigid, she had taught herself to expect variations. Nothing however had prepared her for the first time she saw a team of surgeons wilfully stop a human heart for the purposes of transplantation. She knew the protocol, she had learned every step but she was not prepared to see that great, red muscle slow and stop its beating, lose its colour and turn pale as the preservation fluid flowed in and replaced the blood.

Astrid ran to her phone and picked it up.

Yes, Lola. Yes. Speak slowly Lola. Oh my Lolita no. Don't cry. Please.

Astrid held her hand over her mouth and listened.

It was 8.53 and Mikel hadn't called her.

Astrid listened to Lola sobbing.

The lab assistant walked past her to the fridge, averting his eyes. She clicked her fingers at him and he stared blankly at her for a moment, then understood and left the room on squeaking shoes.

I'm coming over now. I'm taking off my lab coat now and I'm coming over. Don't move. I'm coming now. Keep talking. It's alright, I'm on my way. I'm leaving right now. Hush Lola. Don't cry, my heart. I'm coming.

Astrid yelled, Vincent!

He came to the door, his tired eyes wide. Lend me your car. Please. It's an emergency.

I can't.

What?

I would but I didn't bring it today.

Shit. I'm sorry. I'm taking the day off. It's OK. I'll call Chastel. Don't worry. I'll tell him myself.

The lab technician smiled with relief.

I'll help you get a cab, Mademoiselle Arnaga.

It's OK, Vincent. Put my rat on ice. I'll finish tomorrow.

She ran out.

The assistant, who loved the way she pronounced his name, with a soft 'sh' sound in place of the 'c', closed the door behind her.

It was already hot. When Astrid wound down the window of the cab the driver glanced remonstratively at her in the mirror. Perhaps this was why he decided to take the *périphérique*, Astrid thought, watching helplessly as he pulled up behind the congested traffic.

I'm in a hurry. Do you think we should cut through Paris?

The taxi driver huffed out a sarcastic laugh.

You must be joking. At this time of day? He paused, letting her take stock of the absurdity of her idea. Then he added, What do you want to do? Take the Grands Boulevards, L'Opéra maybe? He smiled bitterly at her in the mirror. After another pause he added with disgust, La Madeleine?

I just thought. It's not moving here.

The driver shook his head, deciding that this was not even worth an answer. Instead he turned on the radio. Canned laughter tumbled out. A French comedian with a smoker's voice was telling an elaborate joke about a gorilla and a barmaid. Soon the driver was in a state of weeping hilarity.

The traffic was moving but very slowly. Astrid looked out of the window. She looked at Paris laid out below her and at the Sacré-Cœur, shining on a hill in a bar of sepia smog. Mikel was out. It seemed to her that the world had undergone a slight shift, leaving her unsafe. She tried to remember Mikel's speaking voice but could not.

Accident, the taxi driver told her jauntily. The three-tone siren of an ambulance was indeed coming towards them. In its wake a black BMW threaded its way through the dispersing traffic. Filthy Arab, the taxi driver said.

I'm sorry?

Arabs in dealers' cars.

Astrid felt herself flush red.

Where are we? Porte de Vincennes. You can let me off here.
You said, Porte de Clignancourt.
This will be fine. How much do I owe you?
The driver reached out lazily and turned off the meter.
Seventy-three, he said, checking his teeth in the mirror.
Astrid gave him a hundred-franc note.
The driver sighed as he counted out the change.
You shouldn't assume that everyone thinks like you do, she told him.
I wouldn't want to think like you, lady. I bet your mind's a sewer.
Astrid climbed out as if the cab was in flames. She slammed the door hard.
Fascist!
As he drove away, nonchalantly and without turning round, he gave her the finger.

FOUR

Lola picked up the phone on the first ring.

Oh Astrid. Where are you?

Astrid's voice was calm but Lola could hear she was upset. Astrid was no good with abusive men. Her righteous indignation just spurred them on to greater and greater obscenities.

It's alright. I'm not going anywhere. Oh Astrid, don't even think about it. You're a surgeon, my love.

Lola herself could send a man crawling for cover with her insults.

I'd come but I can't leave the flat. Just get on the Metro. Don't talk to anyone.

Lola hung up and lay back on her unmade bed. Her back was wet from physical exertion. She had danced for twenty-five minutes without stopping, whirling around her sitting room, dripping with sweat and tears until she fell panting on the phone and summoned Astrid. She ought to make up the bed, otherwise Astrid would start tidying up as soon as she arrived. She got up and began clearing the morning's debris off her bed; the tray with her coffee cup and her bowl of half-eaten Special K, the tape recorder, the pile of travel catalogues. She had plenty: the Jet Tours catalogues of Tunisia, Malta, Sicily, Vietnam and the Framtours magazines with pictures of the Antilles and the Seychelles. Every time Lola passed a new travel agency she went in to get catalogues so she could dream about taking Mikel to the hotels that featured in them. She smoothed the bottom sheet with her hand, making the bed as carefully as Astrid would. Poor Astrid who had never, as far as she knew, been able to dream about anything. She went to exotic places for medical conventions but never got away from the coffee machine in some modern hotel on the outskirts of town. As a child Lola had wanted to be Astrid, had wanted her black hair and the dimple that appeared on her left cheek when she smiled, had been jealous of Astrid's qualities and the respect

15

they brought. Now these qualities seemed only to set her apart from people.

They had fought hard all through their childhood. Astrid had a cruelty in her then, the memory of which still shocked Lola. She remembered hiding under the three stone steps that led up to the front door of their house, listening to Astrid coaxingly calling her name.

Come out Lolita. I won't hurt you. Bring the eggs if there are any. (Because since their mother had lost her grip on things, the hens had started laying anywhere they chose.) But Astrid had Josu's cattle prod in her hand and Astrid had said that one touch would fry her brains in her head.

Lola looked at the neatly made bed with the mauve counterpane crocheted by their mother. It was ugly but she liked it because crochet was about the only thing their mother could do now. In complete ignorance of her daughters' lives, she sent them crocheted coasters and crocheted antimacassars.

Apart from routine masturbation, the bed was chaste. In the ten years she had been living here, Lola had always had sex outside the flat. She had shared the bed with no one but Astrid, who would sometimes spend the night when she needed a break from Chastel. Jacques Chastel was, Lola believed, the principal impediment to Astrid's happiness. An angry obituary began to take shape in her mind:

Astrid Hamilton Arnaga moved to Paris when she was twenty-three. She came to join her younger sister, Lola, who was in the final year of her training with the Opéra de Paris. Against all the odds, Astrid had managed to complete the first two years of a degree in medicine; this while serving a five-year sentence in a Spanish prison for logistical support of ETA, the armed wing of the Basque separatist movement. (Lola could still not bring herself to call them terrorists.) When she was released after completing two years of her sentence, it was into a climate of euphoric camaraderie between the new socialist governments in France and Spain. This brief interlude of political idealism contributed to the decision by the examining board of the École de Médecine de Paris to accept Astrid Hamilton Arnaga, Basque political prisoner, into the second year of its course. Astrid's beauty and her romantic background soon made her a prized curiosity for the medical establishment at their dinner parties. It was at one such evening on the thirteenth floor of the new tower overlooking the Seine at Grenelle, during a dinner organised by the very short cardiologist, known as much for his voracious sexual appetite as for his considerable talent with paediatric cases, that Professor Jacques Chastel, the famous liver surgeon, had first met the lovely Astrid Arnaga. She already knew of him, of course, and deeply admired his work . . . (Lola remembered Astrid reading out bits of an early paper of Chastel's on the magical difference between the blood running through the vena cava and the portal veins. They had been sitting together, on a bright winter Sunday, in one of the love seats in the Jardin de Luxembourg. I swear I'll work for that man, Astrid had said, tapping the article with her finger. He's a poet of medicine.) Jacques Chastel (with luck, long dead at the time of writing) must have sensed that Astrid Arnaga would never be interested in stealing his light. With her past she would always be content to live in his shadow. At the end of her six-month internship in his department and before moving on to A & E at La Pitié, Astrid and he began their long affair. From that moment she became his *eminence grise*. She moved out of the flat she was sharing with her sister on the Place de Clichy and set herself up in a miserably functional unit near Chastel's hospital in the eighteenth arrondissement. Astrid spent long hours in the laboratory for Chastel, tested new medication, attempted new surgical techniques, hooked rats to equipment that she invented and stayed up all night writing articles in his name for the *Lancet* and the *New England Journal of Medicine*. Soon she started accompanying him to conventions in foreign cities to coach him on her ideas in his hotel room so that the next morning he could shine before the greatest in his field . . .

Lola stamped into the kitchen and pulled up the roller blind, letting the sun flood through the dusty window. The old man munched Astrid's brain and made summary use of her body, fucking her sporadically and Lola suspected, badly. Lola dreamed of revenge but Chastel was untouchable. Sometimes the three of them had dinner together and Lola would watch him eat, his big jaws crunching, the veins standing out on his great lion's head as he chewed and she would search her mind for words to devastate him. Chastel thought her picturesque and stupid, Lola knew this. But Mikel would cut him down to size. Mikel was afraid of no one. A man who had no fear of anything, not even death, cut a man like Chastel down to size by his very presence.

Call me. Lola said aloud. Call me please.

She opened the cupboard in time to see a small cockroach disappear into a hairline crack behind the Nesquik. Once she had called in the fumigator. Never again. For some reason the insects had crawled out in their thousands to render up their lives in a pile on the kitchen floor. Lola had been unable to bear it. She had called Astrid who had come round and swept them up.

There was no coffee but Lola would not leave the flat. In a saucepan on the stove was some coffee from the night before, already reheated from that morning. Lola inspected the pearly meniscus that was breaking up into platelets. Then she turned on the gas and heated it a third time. She was just transferring it into the glass jug of the coffee machine when Astrid rang the doorbell. It was not just the subterfuge with the coffee but habitual guilt that made Lola jump out of her skin.

FIVE

Lola cried in Astrid's arms. This done, they sat at the kitchen table and drank coffee. Lola looked at Astrid over the rim of her mug.

I've always done this, haven't I? Spilled myself all over you. There's never any room for your feelings.

Astrid put down her mug.

It suits me. I don't know what to do with feelings when I have them.

How are you? Lola asked, looking about her for cigarettes. Wait.

She stood up and went next door to retrieve the pack from beside her bed. Astrid sat alone, her face raised to the frosted window that gave on to a blind courtyard. She noticed the filth surrounding the extractor fan high up in the wall.

So, Lola said, sitting down. She drew deep on her cigarette. Tell me.

What?

Are you OK? The memory thing.

Fine. Everything's fine. I'm a little tired.

Come with me. Lola smiled broadly, leaning across the table. Come down with me. Take a holiday. Spend some time at home. She took another drag.

I can't.

Why not?

I've got a convention.

When?

Early September.

Come until then. Prepare for it down there.

I can't.

You haven't taken a holiday since Mummy came out of the clinic and that wasn't a holiday.

Lola stood up and leaned against the sink, watching Astrid, one arm folded across her chest, the other occupied with the business of smoking.

I can't go home, Lola. I'm not ready.

19

I think Chastel's making you ill. He's responsible for the ictus. He's made you so unhappy, Astrid.

Astrid looked at her sister's knees, purple with cold. She smiled at her.

Oh Lola. Have you ever considered the possibility that I've chosen my life? I chose Chastel. It may be that I'm not interested in happiness.

That's rubbish. You want happiness as much as I do. You're just not very good at it. But you could be.

Lola turned and threw her cigarette into the aluminium sink. It hissed out. She stepped over to her sister and enfolded her head in her arms, pulling Astrid's cheek to her stomach. To Astrid Lola always smelt like towels soaked in milk. She relaxed a moment, closing her eyes.

I'm so scared, Lola said.

Astrid pulled away.

Why?

Lola looked down at her.

It's been such a long time.

You haven't changed, Lola.

But he has. Why did he ask me not to come? Why would he not want me there when he came out?

He's afraid for your safety. He thinks he might be a target. It's obvious.

Lola gave her the unseeing look she sometimes gave when she was thinking.

I'm not scared of the organisation. I'm not even scared of being killed. What I'm scared of is that he stops loving me. Lola stepped back and leaned against the sink. She raised a hand to her throat. Her eyes filled with tears. He's changed, Astrid. Hasn't he? You changed in prison.

Astrid looked down at Lola's poor, battered dancer's feet.

Astrid?

Astrid did not want to discuss how Mikel had changed. She leaned forward and picked up a curled cornflake from the floor. Lola held out her hand for it. Astrid watched Lola drop the cornflake into the sink. Lola would never be tidy. Perhaps, Astrid thought, she had tidied up after her too much when they were children.

Tell me, Astrid.

You know he's changed, Lola. You've seen it happening. For a start, he doesn't believe in all that shit that he used to believe in.

I'm not talking about his ideas.

Astrid could not meet Lola's eye. She looked at the scar on the bridge of Lola's foot. She had caught it on a barbed-wire fence near their village as Astrid was lifting her over.

What is it, Astrid? Aren't you happy for me?

I'm happy if you're happy.

I think I am. She looked at her sister and her face brightened. Come with me, she said suddenly. We'll find him together. He always speaks so fondly of you, Astrid. He knows you don't like him but he loves you.

I don't dislike him.

You think he's bad for me.

He was.

Lola smiled.

Do you want some more coffee?

No thanks. I should go.

Please don't. Tell me how you think you were changed by prison.

Astrid disliked talking about prison only a little less than she disliked talking about Mikel.

I suppose I learned how not to be affected by my environment, how to cut myself off.

Lola pointed at her:

That's what scares me.

I meant cut myself off in order to work.

But Lola wasn't listening.

I'm so scared, Astrid. Please come with me. I need you there. She covered her eyes with her hand, ashamed of her tears.

Astrid stood up and faced Lola. She wiped her sister's tears away then gathered her thick blonde hair into a ponytail and held it tightly.

Listen to me. Mikel is free. Soon you're going to be in his arms again. Focus on that.

Lola nodded.

Astrid let go of her hair.

I have to go.

21

Are you coming with me?

Astrid picked up her bag from beneath her stool.

I can't.

She could feel her throat tightening. She had to get out of the flat and walk fast along that bridge that crossed over the railway lines. She had to breathe deeply. Lola was going away. She would get on a train and go south to find Mikel, her beloved, who had been locked up for twenty years for something he had done and for which he had been rightly punished.

Please, Lola was saying.

But Astrid was heading for the door. She was thinking of a letter Mikel had written to her from prison. It was the letter that had pulled her in:

I dream of a simple life with you, Astrid. I want to build you a house.

Lola was standing by the front door, smiling at her. She tugged one of Astrid's curls and released it.

What's the name of that syndrome you told me about?

What syndrome?

The one about regressive sexual behaviour.

Astrid stepped out onto the landing and pressed the button to call the lift. The machinery clanked into motion. Her face was flushed and she could not look at her sister.

It's not a syndrome. I've only ever read about it in French. They call it *le fantasme masturbatoire originaire*.

Why *masturbatoire*?

It's a kind of debilitating nostalgia for the first sexual experience, which is generally auto-erotic. The idea is that when you masturbate for the first time there is a flash of recognition, a total recall of the mother's fusional embrace. People with addictive tendencies . . .

Like me, Lola interrupted.

I don't think so. These kinds of people are said to be prone to a quest for an ultimately unreproducible kind of ecstasy.

Lola reached for her sister's hand and kissed it.

Mikel was my first sexual experience, she said. I was fourteen. Not masturbating. I didn't masturbate until after he went to prison. I was *fourteen*, Astrid.

I know.

And I've never got over it.

Astrid watched the lift approaching, her hand on the gates.

Do you remember our first march, in Donostia?

Astrid nodded. It irritated her that Lola still gave San Sebastian its Basque name.

It was a students' march, Lola said. Remember? It was the summer of 1976. Yes, Astrid said. I remember.

The lift slammed to a halt in front of her. She wanted to open the door.

It was so exciting, Lola said. Mikel was wearing a red scarf over his mouth to hide his face. I remember watching him throw a Molotov cocktail. I remember seeing that arching motion, the power in his arm and I fainted. Remember? You took me to a bar but the owner wouldn't let us in, so we sat on the step. You thought it was the crowd that had made me faint, or my asthma, but it wasn't. It was the sight of Mikel throwing that thing. I fainted from love. That was ecstasy, Astrid. I thought it was politics but it was love.

Astrid felt the tears rise in her throat.

He killed people, Lola.

Yes, but it was a different time. And Mikel was never like the others. You know that. Only the military, the police or the judiciary. No innocent bystanders. Mikel always condemned random targets.

Astrid could hear Mikel's old voice coming through her sister's words. But he did not speak like this any more. Astrid looked at Lola's lovely face. It had not changed as far as she could see. Mikel would still find that insolent look in her eyes, that sweet, soft mouth. She still moved her hair out of her eyes with the same childish gesture. She still beamed when she caught sight of you in a public place and threw up her arms or waved vigorously. And every time Astrid saw her, every single time, she felt a moment of joy, but then when Lola hugged her and sat down with her, stealthily the feeling would creep back in, the persistent nausea, as though somewhere inside her, a lift with severed cables were plunging.

Astrid grabbed her ringing mobile from her pocket. It was Chastel's secretary. She slid open the lift gates and backed in.

Lola was mouthing at her: *Please come*. Astrid held the phone to her ear like a talisman against her sister's plea. She let the lift gates slide shut. Lola was cut into diamonds on the other side. Chastel wanted to meet her at the Brasserie Lipp that evening at eight.

I'll be there at eight, Astrid said.

Lola shook her head vehemently.

Yes, Astrid said. I'll have the article.

She pressed the button and watched Lola slide upwards. By eight Lola would be on the train to Irún.

SIX

Kader Benmassoud threw the first shovelful of earth onto his dead dog's body. He was struck by the hollow sound made by the earth falling upon the drum of his belly. El Niño's tongue was lolling from his mouth, which was pulled back into a smile. But, thought Kader, You've not had the last laugh – not yet, boy.

Kader went on shovelling earth onto his beloved dog until he was completely covered, then he paused and leaned on the head of his spade. He looked across the valley to the Pont de Bezons and the Eiffel Tower beyond. In the foreground were the shining white tower blocks of the Cité Pablo Picasso. His estate had no doubt been named in the seventies by some well-meaning bourgeois, wanting to bring art to the masses. Kader knew that it was pollution making the dawn sky so magnificent, but its beauty still did him good.

He patted the earth with the flat of his spade and then marked the initials E.N. across the top of the grave with pieces of gravel, which he had gathered from the path along the canal. Then, without looking back, he crawled under the wire fence into the dump site. The scorched piles of rubbish smouldering here and there made the place look like some volcanic planet. Burning refuse, smelling of soot and rubber, stung his nostrils. In the distance he heard the first siren of the day.

El Niño was killed by a flashball, a weapon invented by the Americans for riot control. The French police got hold of a few in the mid-eighties, sold cheap by the FBI who had stopped using them: an internal note had indicated that the flashball was generally left behind on the weapons table and was considered pansy by US law enforcement. The French found the weapon useful for immobilising ringleaders. The rubber ball, fired at high velocity from a metal tube, could knock a man to the ground at twenty metres without inflicting much damage except perhaps a broken rib or two. Fired at a dog at close range, it could cause internal bleeding which would lead, sooner or later, to death.

The gates of the dump were now open. Kader pushed the shovel back into the pile of sand behind the portacabin at the entrance, then he drove his hands into the deep pockets of his tracksuit and jogged through the gates. A shout went up but Kader kept moving, stepping lightly over the ground, weaving through piles of rubble, down the hill to the railway line. He could hear the TGV but not see it. He ran across the tracks, feeling a tightening in his bowels as the train reared up from nowhere. The rush of air being displaced as the train passed blew his tracksuit top over his head. Kader shook it off and continued at a walk. Someone had once put cement breeze blocks on this track and the train had run straight over them, crushing them to rubble without derailing. Kader wondered what kind of deranged individual would do a thing like that. For months, the bearded on the estate had been persecuted by the police but Kader knew the imams were not behind the act. It was not their style.

He walked along the high wire fence beside the Renault depot. They were all Twingos: ugly cars thought up by men to make women drivers look stupid and designed by some weirdo who never got over kindergarten. Kader thought of his own kindergarten. He remembered Mademoiselle Anne. She was dark, could even have been Arab but wasn't. She was a Catholic from Brittany. She smiled constantly, even when he cried. And as a kid, he cried all the time. He cried when his mother left him. He sat all day watching the swing doors with snot all over his face, waiting for her to return. When at last she came through those doors, he jumped to his feet and hid behind her legs while she talked politely to Mademoiselle Anne who just kept on smiling as if nothing was wrong. After kindergarten when he had to give up crying, nothing had ever gone right and his mother went on talking respectfully to the teachers, year in year out, as though it were enough that she could stay respectful, even if her son was a delinquent.

Kader walked past the recycling plant, past huge piles of some indeterminate by-product, in different shades of grey, like sludge. Occasionally, Caterpillars came and took chunks out of the hillocks, leaving behind marks like a fork in butter. A friend of his had had a job here once. He should have asked him what the stuff was. There were a number of questions like this one, which he wanted to ask but did not. That was one of the first things he had learned, never to ask questions. Ever. Not at school and not in the street.

El Niño had taken three days to die. The vet had refused to operate. When he turned down his cash, Kader had threatened him.

Listen, mister. If you don't save my dog, I'll pick up your daughter from school tomorrow.

Look, young man. I could operate, I could take your money off you but your dog's going to die anyway. I suggest you take him home and make it easier for him. Help him through it.

The vet was a good man.

Kader quickened his pace as he approached his friend's block. It was a high-rise like his own but facing east instead of west, so poor Amadou got the sun in the morning. It came through those terrible windows that you were supposed to be able to slide open but which never slid. One pane was transparent and the other smoked-glass so the block looked like it had hundreds of black eyes. Kader had left the piece under Amadou's mattress because his own mother cleaned out his room ten times a day. Amadou's mother, on the other hand, cleaned the toilets at Roissy airport for a living, so her hygiene standards were not as high.

As Kader ran up the stinking stairs to the tenth floor, he recalled the sight of Fabien Leman standing on the doorstep of his café with his mates. Fabien Leman had once employed Kader's father as a plasterer and had never paid him. He was often seen at the National Front's annual festival. Kader had hated him before he killed his dog. He now realised that Fabien must have borrowed the flashball from his cop brother with one idea in his shaven skull, to use it on his pit bull. Kader remembered smiling in disbelief at the sight of Fabien standing there with two clowns, jeering at his new trainers. In the moment that Kader had unleashed El Niño, he had seen Fabien's triumphant expression and sensed a trap. But it was too late. His dog lurched forward and sprang, haunches gathered beneath his compact little body. Fabien had already pulled the weapon from thin air and taken aim. Kader could still hear El Niño's yelp being knocked out of him as he hit the ground.

Amadou was waiting for him in his room. He was lying on his bed, his hands behind his head, listening to his Discman. There was a large photo of Lilian Thuram on the wall above his bed. It was the shot of Thuram during the France–Croatia World Cup semi-final. He had just scored, running as he did, like a gazelle up from the defence, and he was on his knees, his finger pressed to his lips in a gesture of mock perplexity. Thuram was Amadou's role model. Thuram was a superior man: strong, smart, witty and always in control.

Amadou grinned at Kader and held up a hand. Kader swept Amadou's rough palm and dropped into the white plastic bean-bag on the floor. Amadou took off the headphones. Kader rubbed his eyes.

I'm tired.

Did you sleep?

Kader shook his head.

You should of.

You on tonight?

Yep.

What shift?

Ten till six.

How's the old man? Kader asked.

Amadou raised himself up onto his elbows.

I dreamed I left. Earlier, before you came I dreamed I gave in my notice. The man broke down and wept. His face was dripping with Turkish tears, man. I swear to God.

Amadou spoke with his hands. He had big hands with long fingers. He smiled as he talked and his black skin made his teeth whiter than white. Kader could see why the women loved him. All, that is, except one, the woman of his heart, who happened to be Aisha, Kader's elder sister, a stuck-up, fundamentalist bitch. But Amadou was not wrong. Aisha was in a category of her own. There was no other woman in the whole of Nanterre who came close to her. But it was a lonely business, being in love with the Queen of Sheba, and Kader tried to encourage Amadou to break his vow of chastity because he was afraid it was damaging to his health.

You're going to walk out? Kader asked him.

Amadou clicked his tongue in a negative. He swung his legs over the edge of the bed and rubbed his thighs. He was wearing a pair of black satin Adidas shorts. Amadou only ever wore

Adidas. He was a one-woman, one-brand man.

It was a good dream, though, Amadou said. We were standing in the warehouse and there was a whole shipment of shower-heads to be loaded. Eighty-four boxes. I took off my gloves and handed them to the old man and he started swearing at me. You know, as he does.

Kader remembered; the Turk was eloquent.

Then suddenly the sound went and I watched his mouth moving under that moustache and I remember thinking in my dream, I wish this happened in real life, and I just left and I knew as I walked away, through all the boxes, that I had somewhere to go. Somewhere good.

Kader raised his eyebrows.

Oh yeah?

Can't remember where, Amadou said.

Course you can.

Amadou hid his smile, reaching for the remains of a joint in the ashtray by his bed.

I saved this for you. Thought you might need it.

He handed his friend the joint. Kader lit it and breathed deep.

You sure you don't want me to come with you?

Kader swallowed the smoke and looked at Amadou, his eyes watering, and his mouth bitter.

No. I'm getting out of here afterwards. You're not. It'll be bad enough for you as it is. I'm scared his brother will have you down the *commissariat* in your underpants.

Amadou was watching him. Kader took another toke and offered it back.

Finish it, Amadou said.

He moistened his lips.

You still taking the gun?

Kader shook his head as he held the smoke in his lungs. Amadou's smile was one of relief.

When I buried El Niño it became clear it wasn't appropriate. I was throwing dirt on the little fellow and I saw his mouth. You know how he can look like he's smiling? Well he was smiling and I knew that shooting the bastard wasn't the answer. I'm going to beat him so hard, though, he's not going to know who Le Pen is any more.

I'm coming.

You can't come. You come you'll be a dead nigger. Someone's got to look out for Aisha.

How long are you going for?

I don't know. But if it's good down there I'll call you and you can come and join me.

Amadou had gone dewy-eyed.

It's sunny down there, right? he said.

Yeah. Marseille's sunny. Not all year round maybe. Not in January. But it's not pissing down, so I hear. The sky's blue pretty much all the time. But it can get nippy. Like in Casa at Christmas, say.

Like Casablanca?

Pretty much.

Have you been to Casa?

No.

But you know, right?

Kader gave a resolute nod.

You mean sea and sun and football?

And sex, Amadou. Don't forget sex.

Amadou grinned and Kader stood up to leave.

Here, Amadou said, unhooking the headphones from around his neck. He held out his Discman. Take it for the journey.

No man. I'm not taking that off you. You need it more than I do. To block out your mum for a start.

Take it, man.

Amadou shoved the Discman at him. Kader took it.

I can get another one, Amadou said with a grin.

Suddenly Kader wanted to get out of the way of Amadou's smile because it made him weak.

Amadou held up his hand and Kader swept it with his palm, then placed his hand on his heart. They faced each other a moment like two knights before combat. Then Kader turned and left the room where he had spent almost every afternoon since his twelfth year. As he ran down the concrete stairs, the memory of tears assailed him like some fossil emotion that could still make him wretched. He descended through a miasma of piss and told himself that he was leaving for all of them. Not just for himself but for his friend and his mother and his haughty bitch of a sister who was as clever as it was possible for a woman to be but who was heading for nothing better here than to be the wife of some bearded fanatic who would tie her to a sewing machine and feed her until her young body was hidden for ever beneath folds of fat and a shiny pink djellabah. In Marseille his sister could be one of those beautiful Arab women who wore suits: like the woman in a little jacket and skirt and high-heeled shoes he had once seen standing with a clipboard in the lobby of the Hotel Mercure where he had made a delivery for the Turk. He was leaving for Aisha and Amadou, to find a place for them where they were free to love each other.

As he burst out into the sunshine Kader broke into a run. It was two blocks to Fabien's café. He pumped around the first corner on his fantastic new running shoes. He was a whirlwind, a desert storm, a simoon, a Bedouin sword . . .

As he rounded the second corner, he inclined his body into the curve and then took the last straight line at a sprint, bringing his knees up high, carving the air with the flat blades of his hands, and he closed in on Fabien who was setting out the tables, his back to Kader, a rag in the back pocket of his jeans. And Kader once again saw El Niño springing at the racist but on this occasion there was all the time in the world.

SEVEN

Astrid sat waiting for Chastel at his favourite table on the left of the revolving door. Chastel liked it here: one, because he could see people come and go without being seen, and two, because this table was only ever given to the illustrious. Only those in the know turned their heads as they came through the door to look back at the occupants of this table. Sollers sat here and Finkhielkraut and the great Glucksman.

The whisky was still burning the walls of Astrid's mouth. She had stood at the end of the platform watching Lola's train leave, watching the beautiful undulation of its flank, the orange sunlight on the windows blinking on and off, and listening to the echoing clatter even after it had disappeared from view. She stood there a moment, aware that it had taken with it something vital of herself, and then she turned and walked her zombie remains back along the platform and up the escalator to the bar on the upper floor. She had sat down at a table in the corner and drank two whiskies, one after the other, mechanically raising the glass to her lips and closing her eyes to the bitterness. When it was time to leave, she caught a bus from Montparnasse to Saint Germain, gripping so tightly to the vertical bar that she could hardly uncurl her fingers. It was only when she came through the revolving doors into the bright light of the brasserie and let André help her out of her raincoat, that she felt like crying.

The whisky had deposited its light moss onto all her senses. As she sat waiting for Chastel, she allowed herself to think of Mikel crossing La Mancha in a truck, his dark eyes wide in the fading light of that vast, empty plain. He would be trying to discover if the change that had come about in the world since he went inside was discernible in the landscape.

A flurry preceded all Chastel's comings and goings. His bearing commanded attention. André, as usual, fawned; the cigarette girl hovered, smiling coyly, and a new waiter was arrested for a moment in his progress to the kitchens by the sight of him. Even Astrid found herself rearranging her hands on the table. Chastel sat down beside her, took her hands and pressed his lips to them.

How are you?

Fine, she answered.

Hungry?

Not very.

I'm starving.

Astrid smiled. Chastel's appetite was a point of honour to him.

Let's order, he said. He nodded at André who started towards their table. Did you have any luck with the anti-coagulant?

No. I'll have to do it tomorrow. Lola needed me.

Not another abortion I hope.

Astrid ignored this, turning her gaze to André, who was there, at their table, standing to attention.

As usual, Chastel ordered gigot and purée. There seemed to be a pact between the two men to behave always in the same way. André asked the professor what he wanted, though he knew because it never varied, and the professor never looked at him when he gave his order.

And for Madame?

Brandade please.

We'll be in among some decent laundry, Chastel said as André slid away. Malinski and Karl will be there.

Karl?

Karl Bopp, said Chastel. He says he has something new on prions.

He was talking about the conference.

Chastel liked to sit side by side in restaurants. He liked to hold her hand in her lap. I don't need to sit opposite you, he had told her years ago. It's distracting. Generally, Chastel did not like to face Astrid. His favourite position for making love was on his side with Astrid's back to him. Again, he could look without being seen. This suited Astrid, who had never been able to look into her lover's face anyway.

Chastel took her hand.

Are you alright? You seem distracted.

I feel a bit strange. I put Lola on the train home. Mikel got out today.

Good God. How terrifying.

She asked me to go with her.

She would.

I nearly did.

Come now.

It's true. I nearly went. This evening when I put her on the train I wanted to jump up after her.

What on earth for? You hated being there the last time.

I don't know.

Careful Astrid. You remember the tone of that lunatic's letter. You don't want to let those people pull you into their lives.

Astrid smiled. She had told Chastel about Mikel's first letter. The second letter she had kept to herself.

Astrid,

Do you remember when we first met? Lola brought me to meet you. It was a warm evening in June and you were watching Reál Madrid, Atlético Bilbao on the TV. The windows were open onto the street and people had pulled their chairs up to watch as your mother was the first in the village to have a TV. You were sitting cross-legged on the floor. Your sister said, this is Astrid, the brainbox. You had a bottle of beer in your hand and you glanced at me and raised it briefly. A brainbox who likes football, I said. You smiled but did not look at me again and I remember thinking, Look at me. Please look at me, but you went on watching the match. I see now what struck me about you. It was as if you needed no one.

Can we work tonight? Chastel asked. Or are you too tired?

No no. Let's work.

André brought Chastel's gigot and a side order of purée. He set about eating with the same precision and elegance and purpose with which he performed surgery. She stared at the elaborate fork patterns on the golden surface of her brandade, smelt the garlic and felt her appetite close down as fast as if she were in the morgue.

What do you think of Henri's paper?

I think it's brave.

Brave. Chastel went on eating. Why brave?

Because he's saying after all these years that he might have got it wrong.

34

Astrid could see from the way Chastel was slapping his purée with the back of his fork that he resented her praise of his former teacher.

It's easy for him to spit in the soup now he's retired. What is it? Aren't you hungry?

I feel a little sick.

She leaned back.

Chastel put down his fork and turned to face her.

She looked sideways at him, hardly moving her head, breathing shallowly, her face damp with sweat.

Chastel wiped his mouth with his napkin, put it on the table beside his plate and gently took her hand to read her pulse. His bedside manner was reverent.

I'll take you home, he said.

Chastel's car smelt of leather and his wife's perfume, which as far as Astrid knew had not changed in the ten years she had been his mistress. Laetitia Chastel was a woman of habit and of boundaries. She required of Astrid that she stay within a prescribed area. Only with time had Astrid learned where this lay. She could go with Chastel to Brasserie Lipp but not to the theatre. She could attend dinner parties at Professor Jean Daudet's but not at Dr and Mrs Patrick Berberian's. She could call him at home in the week but not at the weekends. And she could kiss Laetitia in public but never in private.

Frankly, I think Henri is behaving badly, Chastel was saying. Astrid looked out of the window at the Place de la Concorde lit up like a Russian ballroom. It's this new moral superiority that gets me. It's egomania and it's bad form. Like an old spy writing his memoirs. I think we should nail him at this conference. We'll do some work, study the statistics. What do you think?

Astrid was still feeling nauseous. She rested her head against the back of the seat and closed her eyes.

I agree, she murmured.

There behind her eyes is Mikel. He is young again. She is at a clandestine press conference being held in the hills behind her village. A black balaclava hides his face but she can see his eyes, which slant downwards a little at the corners and give him a gentle look. Journalists from all over Spain are gathered to hear him. He is a hero, an anonymous hero, a man of glory. He leans

35

forward and speaks into a microphone. He quotes Carlos Marighella:

> *To be a terrorist today is a condition that ennobles any man of honour, for it signifies precisely that attitude worthy of the revolutionary who takes up arms against the shameful military dictatorship in all its monstrousness . . .*

Astrid stands up to address the triumvirate of masked men behind the microphones. The world they speak of has disappeared, she tells them. No one wants glory any more, or freedom for that matter. No one believes in them. The people who join up today are not monks or warriors. They're outlaws, people fighting to live against the current. You are too old to be an outlaw, Mikel. You cannot survive on your wits any more. You have become slow. You are forty-three, your joints ache and you cannot run.

EIGHT

Lola rested her forehead against the cold glass. She could see her own reflection against the flat expanse of the Beauce that seemed not to flash past but to rotate slowly beside the train. She thought of the poor souls who lived beneath the weight of that enormous sky, now hatched with red. Their horizon gave them no opportunity for speculation, let alone dreaming. Lola closed her eyes and smiled.

I catch myself smiling like an idiot in the street at the thought of you, she had once written to Mikel. *I have decided that it would be a mistake to learn to drive. I would be a danger to myself and to others. Whenever I think of you I close my eyes. Behind the wheel I'd go sailing into the car in front.*

In the seat beside her a man had his table down and was cutting out newspaper articles. The man had long, thick sideburns and in his lap was a leather handbag that smelt strongly of goat. Lola felt a wave of tenderness towards him and towards the rest of the people in the compartment. He must have sensed it for he turned and smiled at her. She smiled back and returned to her reflection.

The Beauce was not unlike the landscape around Astrid's prison: the flat plain tied up with high-tension cables, the occasional concession to forest in a geometric plantation of pine trees. Every week Lola had taken the bus from Donostia to Madrid and then another bus to Henares where she would pick up one of the green vans run by the penitentiary. There was no talking in the van and Lola would sit with the other visitors, each hemmed in by the peculiar shame of having a loved one in prison. Boyfriends and husbands sat arms folded and faces closed. The men, she noticed, sat rigid while the women, the mothers and sisters clutching their shopping bags full of food, cigarettes and magazines, let their bodies sway slackly with the movement of the bus.

Lola still went on marches calling for the regrouping of Basque prisoners. The authorities scattered them all over Spain, making

37

it expensive for their relatives to visit them. She still received literature from the party and flyers put out by the youth movement to which she had once belonged. Astrid would not march and she would not read the literature. She would have nothing to do with anything related to Basque nationalism. Lola had once asked her to accompany her on a trip to demonstrate outside Mikel's prison and she had refused.

Why won't you do anything to help him?

He's paying, Lola. Everyone has to pay for what they do.

Lola was watching her pour the warm milk into the egg yolks for flan.

You paid and you'd done nothing.

Astrid stirred in the vanilla sugar.

I paid, she said. It wasn't much.

God, Astrid. Sometimes I think you're mad. You got put in prison for something you didn't do.

It wasn't that bad. I would never have got away if it hadn't been for prison. I'd be a family doctor in San Sebastian.

Astrid thought she was better off in Paris but Lola worried that if she left Paris Astrid would have no one. And she would leave Paris. Mikel, she knew, would never agree to live outside Euskadi.

I cannot say how I will be when I get out. I have changed, Lolita. I am not the man you fell in love with. I no longer like myself, for one. Your hero has lost the self-love that made him a hero. Perhaps this is what was meant by the word honour. It is an old-fashioned word but that is what I had and have lost. I believe it is something that cannot be retrieved.

Prison mail was slow. It had been months before Mikel received her reply. It had been the beginning of a new phase between them.

Mikel. You've forgotten who I am. I'm a woman now. I'm not a child. I don't need a hero. I need a man and I've chosen you. Everything I do, I do for you. I dance for you and sing for you, I wash and dress for you. I even fuck for you.

On her next visit Lola had found him changed for the better. He met her with his sad smile and held her face in his hands.

Yes, he had said. You're a woman. You're a woman who must make love. You would become ill if you didn't.

He had kissed her as he had not kissed her in years. When she left him, her mouth was red and sore.

At just before midnight Lola was on the new train from Hendaye to Donostia. The train was brightly lit with lavender neon. She sat alone in the carriage while Spanish pop music played loudly from the speakers. When the train crossed the border, she could feel the change in her that never failed to occur. It was as though she had been wrapped in an invisible cloak that impaired her movements and made her weak.

In Irún a young couple boarded. He was very drunk. She supported him as they made their way to the far end of the carriage. They dropped into a double seat facing her and began to kiss voraciously. She remembered kissing like that, her tongue turning relentlessly in Mikel's mouth. She remembered feeling drunk on Mikel's spit or perhaps dizzy from the apnoea, for she had never liked breathing through the nose. It could make her panic and trigger an asthma attack. The girl was pierced through the bridge of her nose and all along her earlobes. The boy creaked in his leather jacket. Both had long, dark, unwashed hair.

The journey took her through Renteria, the suburb where Mikel grew up. After his father died, his mother had moved into town to inherit her parents' joke shop but Mikel had never taken to Donostia and all his friends were from Renteria. Lola looked out at the same red-brick tower blocks, still spilling laundry, only now there seemed to be more of them and more tightly packed. (The speed with which housing blocks went up in this country was astonishing, and the speed with which they fell apart.) She looked down onto a group of kids playing football in a floodlit playground. When she had met Mikel there had been scrubland between the flats, patches of no man's land inhospitable enough to adults to serve as a sanctuary to the children. She remembered sitting there on a grassy hillock with him, watching a group of kids play rugby.

These kids will all feed the organisation, he had told her. Erakundea, he had called it. One way or another, their anger will serve us.

39

She and Astrid came from the hills. Their beautiful village, with its vast pelota court whipped by the west wind, had fed the organisation since it began and had provided many of its leaders. Unlike Astrid, Lola had always been proud of her roots. No one had ever bothered her about the fact that only her father was Basque. The other kids felt sorry for her, not because her mother was English but because she was a drunk.

When Lola came out of the station, she felt one of those hot breezes, laden with the smell of refuse that seemed to rise only on this side of the border. She could feel everything acting upon her, effecting the change, that pulled her back to her past self: the outdated graphics, the road signs, the dustbins, their shape and colour. And the brown: why so much brown everywhere? Surely the prevalence of brown was something worth fighting against. For brown was definitely the colour of Franco-ism and it was still everywhere. In this part of town, at least, nothing had changed since Franco: the hat shops, the umbrella shops, the toy shops, the glove shops and the numerous mar-ble-floored patisseries, frequented by armies of smart, fat ladies dressed in beige and brown and teetering on tiny high-heeled shoes.

She passed a café she remembered. It had always been full of Guardia Civil. Inside, a group of men stood at the bar in a sea of cigarette butts. She slowed to look at the faces. One of them looked straight at her. He was sallow with thick jowls and piscine features. He dropped his cigarette and stamped on it. Her heart jumped and she hurried on. But he was not Guardia Civil because she could have taken a clear shot from the door. They always made sure they faced the door, backs to the wall. She told herself to look at this town anew. It had been ten years. There was an autonomous government with its own police force. It was no longer occupied territory.

She lifted her face towards the bay. Even from this distance she could smell the sea. Ahead was the red neon sign of the Hotel Londres. The curling letters had always made her think of luxury and she longed to spend a night with Mikel in one of the rooms with balconies overlooking the bay. Nothing, of course, would make Mikel set foot in a place like that. Once, many years ago, she had had a drink in the bar by herself. The barman had given her a lighter with the hotel's emblem on it. She had thrown it away like an incriminating object.

She was ashamed of her love of luxury. Even now she was ashamed of her desire to go to that hotel and take a room just to bathe and wash her hair and blow-dry it properly and shave her legs. Mikel disliked all artifice and she believed he sniffed it out in her. This was one of the things that made her cleave to him. She believed he had the ability to see through to her essential self. No one else had ever given her this impression.

She hurried past the hotel and out into the wide promenade that lined the bay. The warm wind from the sea made her eyes water. She looked at the blurred lights of the Santander ferry on the horizon where the black water met the thinner darkness of the sky. The wind moved in the soft branches of the tamarisks and in their strange, hollowed trunks. A group of small boys ran across her path and down the steps to the beach. She admired the Spanish habit of letting the children play at night. She watched them chase each other, drawing illegible patterns with their foot-prints in the smooth, flat sand. She offered a wish then: a little boy. She wanted their first child to be a boy.

When she entered the narrow streets of the old quarter, Lola was finding it hard to breathe. She scrambled for her inhaler in the bottom of her bag but it did not help. It was the place that was oppressing her, assailing her with its own memories. She hurried on, averting her eyes from the now meaningless graffiti, from the posters – filled with new faces, new prisoners that she did not care about – hanging in shreds from the walls. She turned away from the bars open to the street and the faces, the sea of Basque faces. At his mother's joke shop she stopped, fighting for breath, and put down her bag. The coat of blue paint, the last Mikel had put on, was now peeling. The lettering, of course, was brown: Bromas y Regalos. She walked past the shuttered facade to the side door and rang the ground-floor bell. Mikel's mother opened the door. She was wearing a candy-floss pink dressing gown. Hungrily, she searched Lola's face. Then she burst into tears.

He was not there. Lola could not feel her arms or her hands. She was numb as she followed Mikel's mother along the dark, narrow hall. The place smelt of wax. In the bright kitchen the smell of cleaning fluids filled her nostrils. Manuela was still crying when she opened the fridge and took out a baking tray. When she turned and said, Rice pudding? Lola opened her arms. Manuela put down the tray and went to her. Lola had always towered above her, even at fourteen. She took Manuela into her arms and let her cry.

He's gone. I don't know where. I'm so afraid.

He had been here. Lola searched the kitchen for evidence of his presence. There was none but then there never had been. Lola held Manuela away from her.

What are you afraid about, Manuela?

But Manuela shook her head and sobbed. Lola watched her busy herself by serving a plateful of rice pudding.

Shall I heat it? Manuela asked, holding out the plate.

No no. Lola took the rice pudding. How was he? Did he say where he was going, what he might do?

Manuela just shook her head and looked sadly at Lola. Lola wanted to hit her.

Sit down, Manuela said. Eat.

Lola tried to eat the rice pudding. Manuela sat opposite her, clutching her elbows, watching. Lola was not hungry but she could tell that the sight of her eating was soothing to this woman. The pudding was very sweet. She noticed that so long as she ate, Manuela talked. When she stopped eating Manuela would be overcome again.

He arrived by bus at about two this afternoon. I was not napping. I knew he would come. I was just lying there ready. Oh Lola. He's so old!

Lola steeled herself. She did not want to be drawn into what felt like a ritual of grief.

I fed him and I told him about the visit that I had from the refugee committee.

Who? Lola's tone was harsh. Do you remember who they were? she asked, more gently.

I didn't recognise them. There was a young woman. Or perhaps she was not that young. A little older than you, perhaps. Her name was Lorea Molina. And a younger man with blond hair who called himself Anxton. I only know one Anxton and that's Mikel's old friend who they sent to Cabo Verde. They weren't rude but I didn't like the look of them. Especially the woman. She had a hard face. They wanted to know when his release date was and I told them I didn't know.

Well done.

Lola wished she had let Manuela heat the rice pudding. She took another cold, thick mouthful.

What did they want? What has he done?

He hasn't done anything, Manuela. He's paid and now he's a free man.

Manuela shook her head again. There was an irritating resignation about her, Lola remembered now. She watched Manuela pull a handkerchief from her dressing-gown pocket and blow her nose and it suddenly dawned on her that Mikel's mother was incapable of feeling anything unless she had an audience. She dropped the spoon into the bowl and leaned back in her chair.

How was he? Did he talk?

You know how he is. At least with me.

What are you afraid of, Manuela?

But Manuela said nothing. Here was a superstitious woman. She had crosses above all the beds in the house. She would not name her fears.

At last Lola offered her a cigarette, which she accepted. Lola lit their cigarettes and sat listening to the ticking of the same electric clock on the wall. On the face she remembered the words Ramirez, Madrid printed in gothic bold, as though it had been made in the Black Forest or something. It was one-thirty. The cigarette seemed to calm Manuela and the two of them smoked a while in silence.

I've made up the bed in Mikel's room.

Manuela shook her head and took another drag.

I'll sleep a few hours, then I'll leave, Lola said.

Where will you go?

Up to the village.

To see Txema?

Lola nodded.

And my mother, Lola said, putting out her cigarette.

Of course, Manuela said.

This was not a bad woman, Lola thought. Her only son had been locked away for all his youth. Perhaps she had simply come to the end of feeling.

43

I'm tired, Lola said, standing up. She leaned over Manuela and kissed her on the forehead. Thank you for the rice pudding.

Do you want a hot drink to take to bed?

No. I'm fine.

Shall I wake you?

Yes. At eight. I'll catch the nine o'clock bus.

Will that leave you enough time?

Seven-thirty then. Shall I leave you another cigarette?

Manuela shook her head. Lola picked up her cigarettes from the table and left the room.

She stood in the doorway of Mikel's bedroom. The posters had gone. She remembered the one of Che and of Jimi Hendrix and the red-and-black poster with the beautiful Basque word INSUMISOA. His books were gone, in the end he had them with him in prison. She looked for signs of him but the room no longer bore his imprint. It had been too many years. His smell too had gone, that close smell of mildew. Lola looked at his narrow bed against the wall. There had been a dip in the middle into which they had both fallen. At seventeen she had slept in his arms. She wondered if she could do the same at thirty-seven. She dropped her bag on the floor and went and sat down on the edge of the bed. The window behind the head of his bed still glowed yellow from the street lamp. Lola raised her chin and smiled. Mikel, she whispered. Where are you? Her heart was heavy in her chest but she had no wish to cry. Manuela had done all the crying. Perhaps, she thought, this is how Astrid found her strength, in the contemplation of her little sister's weakness. She took off her sandals. Her feet were streaked with dirt from the journey but she was afraid that if she showered she would lose this mood, so she lay back on the bed without getting undressed, folded her hands on her stomach and closed her eyes. Breathing in as much air as her asthma would allow, she felt obscurely that it was necessary for her to be strong this time, for Astrid. She had been seeking a way of paying her debt to her sister. Perhaps she would find it here, in this ordeal. Lola prayed: Give me strength. For once, give me strength.

NINE

Astrid read Chastel's note on her way to the kitchen.

Forgive me. I took advantage of your patience last night. You were tired and I left too late. I was wondering if you would allow me to go on taking advantage of you in all possible ways for another ten years.

Yours ever, J.C.

She scrunched up the note and threw it into the kick-flap bin. It fell among some dead carnations and ground coffee. In place of charm, Astrid's building offered a rubbish chute, washing facilities and a lock-up garage. The flat gave on to a triangle planted with horse chestnuts that blocked her light and referred to itself pompously as a square. The wooden roller blinds on the windows came into the bargain as did the glass-fronted fireplace in the living room and the aluminium clothes molly above the bath. The white Formica cupboards Astrid had personalised with red stick-on knobs but the rest of the flat was as untouched as if it had been rented by three terrorists casing a target.

Astrid poured water into the coffee machine and turned it on. Chastel teased her about her utilitarian attitude towards her home. His flat in an eighteenth-century building on the Île-St-Louis was all bibelots and scented candles. It was one of the apartments on the Seine that threw its curtains open every night to the liquid floodlights of the *bateaux mouches* so that the tourists could gaze up at the painted ceilings and chandeliers.

Astrid watched the coffee drip through. It had indeed been ten years. Perhaps this ictus business was merely a reminder to herself, a kind of metaphor, if metaphor is condensed meaning, for all those years lived in a state of somnambulance. Thomas was right: the motorway was an appropriate image. She had been on a motorway through her thirties, her only moments of consciousness prompted by letters from Mikel. Astrid loved service stations on Spanish motorways. Mikel's letters were like the

45

cafeterias which served tapas on Spanish motorways.

She took the coffee jug from the hotplate.

I can make tortilla. You do not know this about me but I believe it is important. When I get out I will make you a very good tortilla. Potato, green pepper, onion, chorizo and tomato or just potato and onion if there are any of these ingredients that you don't like.

She had believed that she was smiling at the simplicity of the wording but she should have been warned by the pleasure the letter brought her. Indeed it was shortly after his letter about tortilla that she had begun to dream about him. She never dreamed about Mikel at night, only early in the mornings, after Chastel had returned to his wife's bed. These were the days before guilt and the fear that came with it. Then just as she began longing for these dreams, they had stopped.

The night before she had told Chastel of her intention to take a holiday. She was sitting at the kitchen table with a cup of coffee in her hands. Before her lay a pile of articles in English to read and summarise. She was tired and Chastel too seemed to be slower than usual, rising to his feet as if he were moving in something thicker than air. He had turned in the doorway.

I'd like to take a couple of weeks off, she had told him.

Good idea. Where shall we go?

No. I mean I'd like to go home for a while.

Oh. When?

She looked steadily at him. This week.

He had made a face.

I'm afraid that's not very convenient.

I realise that.

Chastel plucked his earlobe.

You're on call for procurement.

I know.

We'll talk about it in the morning. Call me from the lab. We'll have lunch.

He did not pause for an answer but left so hastily he forgot his tie on the kitchen chair.

Astrid now sipped her coffee, her gaze sliding over the surfaces of her kitchen, as clean as her lab. There was a miraculous lozenge of sunlight on the black-and-white checked linoleum into

46

which she placed her bare feet. Mikel had been out for twenty-six hours. She washed up her mug then emptied the bread bin. She disposed of the rubbish, dropping it into the chute outside her back door. The smell of boiled fish came wafting up the back stairs, as did the guttural drone of the downstairs neighbour's Buddhist chant tape.

She put on the red linen suit she had bought with Lola but the sight of herself in the wardrobe mirror made her change. The skirt was, as she had always suspected, too short. There was her beige dress but she preferred not to go home in something that Chastel had bought her. In the end she wore her black dress with daisies on it; one of those that Lola referred to as her widow's weeds. She put on a large silver bangle as a concession to Lola's love of ornament and pinned up her hair.

She put Chastel's tie in a padded envelope and added the following note.

Dear Jacques,

I do not like to ask favours as you know. This one will be the first and I hope the last. I have not taken a holiday in all the years I have worked for you, not that I ever wanted one. I am leaving today. Vincent will hold the fort while I am gone. I will let you know when I am coming back and will work on the conference down there.

Fondly, Astrid

She reread the note. Her written French was still a disaster, full of spelling mistakes. She packed a small bag of clothes and filled a large leather briefcase with printed matter. Then she left the flat, double-locking the door, and took the lift to the basement. She threw her luggage into the boot of her car and climbed in through the passenger side as she had parked too close to the wall. When she turned the key in the ignition she jumped at the blast of classical music from the radio. She turned off the radio and drove out, aware that she was hugging the wheel like an old lady.

The *périphérique* was flowing smoothly. Her windscreen was soon covered with a fine coating of squashed insects which reduced visibility, forcing her to lean forward and peer through the gaps in a greasy film of chlorophyll and haemolymph. She stayed in the fast lane and for the first time took note of the season: the squashed insects, the coating of dust on the cars, the black shredded plastic washed up against the dividing wall like seaweed were all the signs of urban summer. Before passing beneath La Muette she glanced up at the egalitarian horse chestnuts, flowering here in the pellucid sunshine of the sixteenth arrondissement with as much vulgarity as those that bloomed in her own dingy square in the eighteenth.

TEN

Soon the compartment filled up and Kader was no longer alone. When a middle-aged woman sat down on the folding seat beside him, he shifted, leaning into the door of the train, careful to keep his shoulder out of contact. He drove his hands deeper into the pockets of his tracksuit top to still their shaking.

Fabien had crumpled on impact. The look of surprise on his face after Kader had brought the top of his forehead down onto the bridge of his nose had suggested that he was not accustomed to a fight. Kader had stood over him watching him rise, first onto his knees and then slowly upright, vertebra by vertebra, arms dangling, like some woman in a gymnastics class, until he was face to face with Kader for the second round; only this time Fabien's small eyes denoted not surprise but blurred vision. The second blow, to the solar plexus, had knocked the air out of him and the grunt that came from him had made Kader pause for a moment and consider. He believed it was this intrusion of thought that had been his downfall. The knife blade had appeared then, at the edge of his vision, and he had seen it glint like a silverfish before it struck him on the shoulder and it was his turn to be surprised at the sight of his own blood blooming on the sleeve of his T-shirt. He was then aware that he and Fabien were no longer alone. Fabien's voice rose up, indicating that he was a man again, one of an army of men, not calling for so much as acknowledging the reinforcements, and when Kader had jumped away from the knife someone behind him had grabbed him around the waist and his abdomen shrank from the blade all by itself and then he was whirling, spinning free of their grasp, his arms flailing and as he ran he was aware of their weight beside his, aware that he flew while they only seemed to stamp harder on the ground. But it had not been satisfactory. There had been no glory in the fight with Fabien.

There had been a time when he had dreamed of glory. As a kid he was the best footballer Nanterre had and his coach believed in a great future for him. When he was twelve he began to prepare for trials at the famous training centre in the forest west of Paris where he would have played football six hours a day. But he didn't grow. The other kids did; their voices broke, their muscles developed, dark hair sprouted from their nostrils. Time passed. He was still better than the others technically but the force of their kick so surpassed his own that he was made to play *piston*, an inglorious position that required much mobility and little efficacy. At fifteen, puberty had still not come. He began to deal and he got fed up with waiting. When it did come, the following year, he outgrew everyone. But it was too late; he didn't care any more. One evening his mother had asked him why he was back so early.

I left the team, he replied. I left like a prince.

His mother clutched her head.

Like a prince, she had moaned. Like a prince.

Kader looked out of the window of the RER. Years later the phrase was funny. Like a prince was what you said when you jumped before you were pushed. What he liked about Amadou was that he never needed such phrases. With Amadou, there was no posturing. He did not nudge his balls in public. He stood tall, his feet firmly on the ground. He did not play the *caïd* for women either. He had not started smoking with the other ten-year-olds in the class, nor had he ever racketeered younger kids. When anyone had tried it on him, it soon became clear that they would have to saw off his hand before he gave up his watch. Not that he squealed; he was just stubborn, sufficient unto himself. Like Thuram. But, thought Kader, as the train pulled into La Défense station, what would he know about a professional footballer who was probably worth over 300 million francs? What could he possibly know about a person like that? Thuram might be black but he was from another planet.

As the doors opened Kader felt a rush of fear in the face of Amadou's absence. Without Amadou there beside him he suddenly feared his own nature. Amadou was like his name, all love and gentleness, while Kader saw grounds for conflict everywhere. Amadou had left a CD in the Discman for him. It was Bach. Amadou liked classical music. He said it was the last good thing white civilisation had produced, that after all this time it had come into the public domain, so to speak. It's for everyone, he had said. And what people like us do with it, weave it into our music, is a healthy mixture of gratitude and revenge. Gratitude and revenge: Kader had liked that.

He put on the headphones and turned on the machine. The woman beside him was staring at him. He tried to ignore her and enjoy the music. But the hag was crowding him. He unhooked the headphones from behind his ears.

Want a listen? It's Bach.

But the woman made a tutting sound and turned away.

What is it, you miserable bitch? Don't you like Bach?

Just then Kader caught sight of the man standing in front of the nearest set of doors, saw him reaching into the pocket of his leather jacket, and his cop radar made him forget the woman. Just as the siren sounded to signal the doors closing, Kader upped and jumped off the train.

The next train came in no time. It was a miracle to him they did-n't crash into each other more often, just as it was a miracle that people didn't jump on the lines more often. Once Amadou had seen someone try. He had spotted the man a few metres away from him and he had known what the man was about to do as surely as if he had been holding up a sign. Luckily for the man, or unluckily, Amadou was there at his side, his long arm plucking him from certain death and total bodily disintegration; a detail in which the man, if he was a Catholic, would have no interest, since for him the body would be a useless envelope; not the case for a Muslim for whom, as Kader's mum had told him, the head was required for all valid applications to paradise. Still, Catholic or Muslim, as far as the head was concerned, there would have been no chance of retrieval.

Kader was decidedly not in the mood for Bach now. His arm was throbbing, he missed El Niño and he missed Amadou. He sat on the RER until Châtelet, then changed trains. He had forgotten the interminable corridor and the depressing conveyor belt that was like a sorting machine for passive and active human beings, those who stood still and those who walked. Kader always walked: in the event of an attractive woman coming in the oppo-site direction, he liked to be seen in motion. At the far end a group of Peruvian buskers blew into their pipes and stamped on the ground. He bounced past them on his trainers, the Adidas bag

Amadou had lent him over his shoulder; his mind already turned from this city that had never let him in anyway.

Except, he thought, for that brief moment the summer before, on the day after the World Cup final. That day it had been as if Paris had turned herself inside out, letting her dark lining show itself at last. He remembered how it had felt to take possession of the Champs-Elysées that day and how unlike those Friday and Saturday nights when he and his friends would sit on the low wall that surrounded the entrance to the Métro as if they were afraid to venture too far from the underground where they belonged.

That glorious day after the final was already a well-documented social phenomenon. The media referred to it as the World Cup effect. The newspapers had announced that the collective joy shared that day by France, her immigrants and her immigrants' children, was the death knell of the National Front. Pure bullshit, of course. The monster, Kader knew, was only sleeping.

Still, it had been a beautiful day. Kader remembered the girl with long silky hair the colour of wheat, tied back in a ponytail. She had creamy skin and greenish-brown eyes. Kader knew, as she bounced up and down on the balls of her feet in rhythm to the crowd's cries, that she was enjoying his presence beside her, was aware of every single move he made, and when the kids had started banging on their congas and they had all started jumping and she turned and threw her arms around his neck and let him dance with her in an apparently spontaneous outburst, he knew how planned it was and he was thrilled. And later when they had floated with the crowd down to the Place de la Concorde and he had slow-danced with her to the song 'We are the Champions', he had buried his face in her long white neck, breathing in the smell of her hair, which even smelt like wheat, like the wheat fields of France, and he was the conquering hero. He smiled now as he remembered looking at the piece of envelope on which she had written a phone number (not, it had turned out, hers) and at her name: Françoise.

When Kader came up into the bright sunshine of the Place de la Porte d'Orléans, he saw that the wound in his shoulder had started bleeding again. He put down his bag and looked about him. The entrance to the *périphérique* was on the other side of the vast square. He looked for a pharmacy where he might get a bandage for his arm but could not see one. Across the street beside the bus depot he spotted a series of benches in a row facing a patch of ragged yellow roses penned in behind a wire fence. His head ached and his eyes would not open properly in the bright sunlight. He walked over to the benches, made a pillow of Amadou's bag and lay down. He had been up all night with El Niño in his arms, watching him die, and he was exhausted. He gripped his shoulder to stop the flow of blood, which continued long after he had fallen asleep.

ELEVEN

Generally sudden in its onset, an ictus may sometimes be triggered by an emotional episode, by a hot or cold bath, by physical effort or by coitus.

Astrid smiled at the memory of the chapter in her French diagnostic encyclopaedia entitled 'Mnemonic Disturbances'. On the day of her ictus she had been running. She had jogged around the very lake that she was now passing on her way through the Bois de Boulogne where she had hoped to avoid the traffic. Instead she found herself stuck in the gloomy wood bestrewn with condoms, among fitful drivers being held up by nonchalant sex tourists in no hurry at all. She remembered now, running past the lake and thinking about the story her mother used to tell them about a group of ducks who, to spite a bloodthirsty landowner, had rolled his lake up like a carpet and flown away with it.

For the duration of the lacunal amnesia, the subject remains capable of performing complex activities: he may drive, carry out his work normally, play chess . . . The semantic memory is unperturbed as are all superior brain functions.

Beyond her thought about the ducks, Astrid remembered nothing.

It had been a week since she had been running. If Astrid did not run she found she lost much of her stamina in the operating theatre. When she stopped exercising, her legs ached after one hour instead of three.

Astrid turned on the radio. Bach's Double Violin Concerto was being played too fast. After a while she grew irritated and turned it off. A Latino transsexual in an electric-blue boob tube and red PVC miniskirt emerged from behind a clump of ash trees. He adjusted the strap of his handbag and straightened his skirt. Astrid could see his penis moulded beneath the red plastic. She looked away. This was surely a barbaric age in the history of medicine, the age of organ transplants and sex changes. These she was certain, would be looked back on as the dark ages. She drove past a group of Portuguese men, young and old, playing *boules* in a clearing. Then her mobile phone rang. She snatched it from her handbag.

It was Colette from Transplant Coordination. She wanted to know if she was on call for procurement. Organ procurement: it always struck Astrid as a dainty euphemism for the looting they did.

I'm sorry, doctor. It's not clear from the rota. Are you on call or aren't you?

Colette's manner was always slightly aggressive. Astrid did not generally hold this against her. She had a hard job for she had to deal with the families and seek their consent for donation. It was her responsibility to oversee the operation, to make sure the body was sewn up 'hermetically and aesthetically', in the words of article L771/11; to check, in the event of bone procurement, that the body was restored to its former rigidity; that the cornea was replaced by a glass one, 'respecting the initial colour of the donor'. Astrid knew how arbitrary the matter of consent was. She knew that people could rarely imagine before the event what it would mean to agree to hand over their loved one's body to be cut open and stripped of its organs. Often, she knew, people agreed simply because they were not troublemakers or because they did not want to disappoint the surgeon. Sometimes a mother, haunted by images of her child's body being carefully butchered, would come back to see Colette and sit drinking coffee in her office right next to the operating theatre, unable even to formulate the questions that would free her.

Your name is still on the list, Colette was saying, but when I called the lab your assistant told me that you had gone on holiday.

Chastel had not taken her off the list, either to punish her by rendering her responsible for a grave professional fault, or because he had simply not believed her, could not believe that she would do something contrary to his will. Indeed, it would be the first time.

I could call Dr Phung but it may cause problems for me afterwards, he not being officially on call and everything . . .

I'll call Professor Chastel and get him to call you.

I'm sorry, Dr Arnaga. It's just that I can't take the responsibility . . .

I understand.

Astrid called Chastel's mobile.

Chastel here.

I'm on my way out of Paris.

So you haven't gone.

She pictured his smile, the chipped front tooth that he had not repaired because he knew it made him look roguish.

I just got a call from La Pitié, she told him. They've got a brain-death. It's been an hour already. The kidney team is due to arrive in two hours. If you don't get Phung down there you'll have no transplant.

Phung's in Lille.

Well then you'd better do it.

Astrid. I'm not in a position to discuss this now.

He had company.

Jacques. I'm sorry. You'll have to do it yourself.

He was speechless. She helped him by hanging up.

As she pulled onto the motorway, she looked at the clock on the dashboard. It would take her eight hours to get to Saint Jean de Luz. She would be a few hours early. He had written:

We will do what you decide. We will tell Lola or keep it from her. You will choose. I will be at the bandstand in Saint Jean de Luz at 22h00 on Tuesday 22nd, the day after my release. We will catch the night train to Paris.

It had been the sure, conspiratorial tone of his last letter that had helped her decide not to go to him, a decision in which she had honestly believed, right up until the moment when she had watched Lola's train ripple away.

TWELVE

Lola stared trancelike through the window of the bus. Everywhere she looked, she saw her memories hung up like sad banderols: there was another, down below in the poplars beside the brown, sluggish water of the Bidassoa. It was the winter of her sixteenth year. She was crouching beside Mikel, leaning into him for warmth:

There he is. See him?

No. Where?

On the other side, left of the hut. There he's moving. See?

No. Oh Mikel, where?

A fine scout you'd make, little Lola. He's gone.

It was a member of a special Civil Guard unit that patrolled the hills. They were dropped off by helicopter and would patrol on foot, looking for people who had gone underground and were trying to cross the border. They wore camouflage and lived out in all weather for weeks on end. It was they who would catch Mikel two years later and yet to her shame she could not remember the name of the unit.

The morning sun was already scalding her cheek through the window. She stood up and went to the opposite side of the bus. Most people had descended at Hernani and only three seats were occupied as they began the climb into the hills. Lola was in the front row to the right of the driver. Three rows behind her sat a gypsy woman with henna-red hair and deep shadows under her eyes. In her arms was a big red-and-blue striped laundry bag filled to bursting. Sprawled out on the back seat lay a youth, fast asleep. From where she sat Lola could see only his heavy boots but she could hear his snoring.

Before getting on this bus she had wandered into a café in Donostia. She had had a cup of coffee and a croissant at the bar, then walked out and got on the bus before realising that it had been the very café where she and Mikel had come after they had planted their first bomb.

It had been a Sunday, so the archive library was closed. They were told it was a protest bomb, that the aim was zero casualties. They were to leave it on a window sill on the north side. It was spring and the trees in the square were laden with pink blossom. She was only fifteen but Mikel did not know that yet. She looked old enough to be his girlfriend. He had his arm round her. He was carrying the bomb under his anorak. She was not frightened because she was with him. She was watching his face. Everything in him was alert. She had little idea of what they were doing. All she knew was that he had his arm around her as if they were a real couple. They stopped beneath the window of the archive library. She could feel the bomb pressing into her ribs as he embraced her but she did not care. She knew he was scared because he was trembling all over but she was not because she was in his arms and he was pressing his lips to hers and she did not care if the bomb blew them up there and then. Then he had pulled away suddenly and taken the bomb from inside his jacket and placed it on the window sill.

When they were in the café they had heard the explosion. Lola was not thinking about what it meant. She was not considering the possibility that this so-called protest bomb might tear some-body's arm off as they were out on their Sunday morning stroll. At the sound of that explosion she was simply watching Mikel's face as though waiting for a signal. He had smiled at her and she had smiled back. The whole of her future could have been read in that smile of hers.

The bus had come to a halt halfway up a hill in what looked like the middle of nowhere. On both sides of the road Lola could see only pine trees. She looked for a bus stop or some sign of habitation but saw none. The gypsy woman hugging her voluminous bag stepped off the bus.

It was Txema who had briefed them for the mission at the archive library, the great Txema Egibar, Mikel's friend and mentor. Lola disliked Txema. It was not so much that he disapproved of women; he simply did not see them. In the old days she would go with Mikel, who liked to listen to the pearls of political wisdom that fell from Txema's mouth. Whenever Lola spoke Txema's eyes would flick over her and then back to Mikel as if she were a distracting noise. But the main reason for her hatred was that for all his blood-crimes, Txema had only spent nine months in prison and that had been in France. In 1982, when Mikel had been in a Spanish jail for three years, Txema had been released by the French authorities. As one of the three leaders of the Executive Committee, the Spanish government needed him to negotiate the disbanding of the military apparatus. Mikel had never been so full of hope. Txema had told him that his release would be one of the items on the agenda, that it was only a matter of months. Afterwards, when Txema had told her how hard he had tried, Lola had not believed him. Everything about Txema spoke to her of envy. He had been the first of their generation to go into mainstream politics. She was sure he did not want Mikel overshadowing him.

They were nearing the village. The bus swung round the hairpin bends. The driver's sleeves were rolled up and Lola could see his muscular arms working the steering wheel. She leaned forward to speak to him.

Do we stop at Vera?

He looked at her in his rear-view mirror.

Is that you, Lola?

Lola beamed.

Paco.

He held out his hand and she stood up and grasped it. He gripped it tightly and tugged her towards him. She kissed his cheek.

We don't stop at Vera, he said, keeping his eyes on the road. God, Lola. It's about time. How long has it been?

I came back about five years ago when my mother came out of hospital but I didn't see you. You were in Bilbao.

I got fired. You look lovely, he said, turning back to the road. How's that clever sister of yours?

She's well. She's a full surgeon now.

I knew that. And you? Your dancing?

I teach. Those who can't, teach, she said with a smile.

Not true. I teach singing and I sing alright.

She touched his shoulder.

You have a lovely voice, Paco.

Paco told her about how he had lost his job in the canning factory in Bilbao and about the long months of unemployment on the coast. Lola watched him. He had smooth, pale skin and very dark, watery eyes and full red lips like a woman's. When he spoke his cheeks flushed. Paco had been in love with her since they were at school together. He had never once showed any signs that he held this against her.

I just woke up one morning and knew I was not meant to be down there. I was meant to be in the mountains, Lola. That's what it felt like. I knew that down there it would always feel like I was short of air, so I just came back.

He told her how he loved his life in the village. He was choir-master now. He had ten boys and fifteen men. They sang polyphony in the churches north and south of the border. They had even sung in the cathedral in Saint Jean de Luz with a world-famous choir from the Philippines.

I hear Mikel's out, he said at last.

Yes.

Are you still together?

We are, Paco, but I don't know where he is. She lowered her voice. I think he's gone into hiding.

Why?

I don't know. A couple of people came looking for him.

Paco's face seemed to close. He shook his head.

Ask Txema. If anyone knows anything, it'll be him. He's in the village today. Tuesdays and Wednesdays he takes visits.

Visits?

He's mayor. Didn't you know?

No. Since when?

Since elections last November. Didn't your Mum tell you?

Mum doesn't say much these days. Lola was unsure of Paco's feelings about Txema. Is he a good mayor? she asked him.

He grinned at her.

Excellent. He made me choirmaster. He paused. Listen, I don't think he's any worse than the others.

A little more self-righteous perhaps, she said.

Paco smiled.

They had stopped. Lola watched a herd of goats crossing the road in a clamour of bells.

How's Maïté? she asked him.

She's well.

60

Are you married yet?

Paco held his hand up to the goatherd and drove on.

She married Koldo. They have a restaurant in Zumaya. It's in all the guidebooks.

Aren't you interested in getting married, Paco?

When Maïté left I realised that what I liked most about her was her quietness. Apart from you, Lola, I've never met a woman I want to spend more than twenty minutes a day with.

Lola punched Paco high up on the arm, hitting the nerve with her knuckle as he had taught her. Lola watched him to make sure she had hit the right spot. The pain always took a few seconds to declare itself. He smiled and rubbed his arm.

Good, he said.

Oh look! A playground! They were crossing the stone bridge into the village. Where the old bus station had been, they had built a playground. Look Paco, I can't believe it! There are so many children. Where do they all come from?

The village has changed. People are moving back. Txema managed to convince the Basque government to put the school for mountain guides here. God only knows how. The village has become a centre for what they call eco-tourists. You'll see them. They wear shorts and walking boots and they carry big packs on their backs. They come from all over the place: America, Italy, France. They have a lot of money but they like to rough it. He paused. Not everyone is happy. Txema has his enemies but the place is thriving.

Lola saw that the streets were busier. And the passers-by did not seem so languid. They hurried purposefully along the streets. Paco was right; it was thriving. Here was somewhere to bring up their boy. Then she thought of Astrid, alone in Paris, and her spirits sank.

Paco dropped her off outside the town hall. He made her promise to meet him for a drink that evening. With or without Mikel, he said. Lola waved as he and the sleeping youth drove on to the terminus at the school for mountain guides.

Lola turned the pages of a magazine in the waiting room of the town hall. Through the open windows came the cries of more children playing on the pelota court below. She raised her head to listen. She could hear the strange sonar of the swallows, ravelling

61

the children's call and pulling it with them into the deep mountain sky. Not long ago she had written:

> *I don't long for children, Mikel. I long for your children. It's a desire so deep in me that it's like knowledge. It can't be undone.*

But she had not sent the letter.

The magazine was a tourist guide to the region. She looked at the picturesque photographs of her village, of the surrounding valleys and hills where she had spent her childhood, and experienced no sense of recognition.

> *The listing of this unique region by UNESCO as a biosphere reserve has helped to maintain the precious equilibrium between biological diversity and economic and cultural development. Henceforth the Social and Economic Activity Harmonisation and Development Plan has enabled us to achieve our goal of 'sustainable development'.*

She turned over the magazine to see who 'us' might be. Eusko Jaurlaritza: the Basque Government. She tossed the magazine onto the table beside her and looked at the clock. It had been almost an hour. She stood up and opened the door and looked out into the deserted corridor. She followed the muted sound of voices and stopped outside an office marked Cultural Affairs. She knocked softly and opened the door. A woman was on the phone. At the sight of Lola she smiled and held up her hand. She had dark hair with a razor-sharp fringe. Her blue eyes were made up like Cleopatra's.

Lola looked at the posters on the walls and waited for the woman to finish. There was a large photograph of part of a Gothic arch, one of a heron with a fish in its beak and another of three fishermen unravelling their nets in some port, which she did not recognise. The woman hung up.

Yes? How can I help you?

I'm waiting for the mayor. It's been forty minutes. Does he know I'm here? The woman who showed me into the waiting room seems to have gone.

I'm afraid he's left. She looked at her watch, holding it delicately on her wrist. He had a lunch.

Suddenly Lola knew that this woman and Txema were fucking each other.

That's a pity. As I said, I've been waiting for some time. I came from Paris to see him.

The woman sat up a little straighter in her chair. She picked up a pen from her desk.

From Paris?

Lola nodded.

Can I help you at all?

I'm afraid not. It's personal. I'm an old friend. Can you tell me where he might be having lunch?

I wish I could.

What's your name? Lola asked pleasantly.

Now the woman was on her guard.

Lorea Molina.

Lola nodded slowly. Manuela was right. She did have a hard face.

Well, Lorea, she said. I won't waste any more of your time. She took a step towards the door.

And your name is?

Lola. Just say Lola dropped by. Tell him I'll be at my mother's.

Lola hurried along the corridor, down the wide oak stairs, and out through the main door. At the bottom of the stone steps, she stopped. A football rolled towards her feet. She kicked it back to the boys and walked on. Who was Lorea Molina? The name was familiar. Lola sat down on the stone wall that surrounded the pelota court. Here was recognition: the strange clarity in her head and the tingling numbness in her body that was fear. She stood up and walked on down the road to Txema's bar.

THIRTEEN

Kader stood under the hot sun facing the slowly shunting traffic as it edged forward onto the motorway. With his good arm he held up the sign he had made, unsure that he had spelt Marseille correctly. He wanted to pull the hood of his tracksuit over his head for shade but he knew he would never get a lift if he did. He stood swaying slightly in the dust and the fumes, trying to focus on the drivers' faces, his eyes closing against waves of nausea. His wound, now glued to his T-shirt, was banging in syncopation with the pulse in his head.

It felt good to fall. He saw the big blue sky rotate above his head and then shrink to the size of an aspirin and disappear. Throughout he never lost the sound of her voice. There was an accent. What was it: Italian? When her face came into view, he smiled. An Italian babe. Not young but a babe. She was looking down at him. He stared back at her for a long time, unwilling or unable to find his voice. He discovered that he could track her thoughts in the area around her eyes. There between her dark brows, he saw worry; then something was happening to her forehead, like a sheet being smoothed, and he saw relief. In the reduction of the space between her eyelids and her eyebrows he could see her making a checklist of some sort and there she was registering his gaze and a flicker of mistrust in her eyes and it was gone. He found himself wondering how this woman could go around like that with all her feelings plastered over her face for everyone to see. Kader noticed that he no longer felt sick. Indeed, he had not felt this good for a long time. She had her hand under the back of his head and she was lifting it off the ground and moving it a little so that his head felt like a balloon, light as a balloon attached to a string and floating and she had hold of the string.

Can you stand? You're alright.

Kader was enjoying the film. He had no wish to move.

Try and stand. You should get out of the sun. You're dehydrated.

What are you, a nurse?

She slid her arm under his back. He winced as he felt his wound split open.

What is it?

She was taking his arm out of his tracksuit top.

How old are you? he asked her. He could feel her fingers pressing on the skin beneath the wound.

Forty-two. When did this happen? she asked.

You look good.

Is it a knife wound? she asked.

Are you a cop? he asked.

The muscle has hardly been touched.

Kader turned his head and looked. She had pulled back the T-shirt and the wound was bleeding again. He looked at her and wondered if she were impressed by his arm. He wondered if she ever slept with anyone young.

I'll take you to the nearest hospital. They'll sew you up.

He had his hand round her wrist and was gripping tightly.

I'm not going to hospital. I'm going to Marseille.

This motorway goes to Bordeaux. Not Marseille.

Shit. You serious?

She nodded. A coil of her dark hair sprang free. She hooked it behind her ear.

Bordeaux, he said. I might as well go to Bordeaux. It's not a bad team. You going to Bordeaux?

I'm going to Spain.

You're Spanish. I thought you were Italian.

Try and stand please.

He let her help him into the passenger seat. In the wing mirror he watched her legs as she walked round to put his bag in the boot. He liked being in the passenger seat of this woman's car. Think what you liked, it felt good. He closed his eyes.

When he opened them again she was sitting beside him in the driver's seat, looking through a blue plastic box on her lap. In the box were first-aid supplies. He closed his eyes again. Spain: now there was a thought. Amadou and Aisha in Spain. He knew no one from Spain. He thought their music stank but they had beaches. He opened his eyes.

What's your name? he asked. His mouth was dry and his words sounded slurred.

She took out a roll of gauze.

I'll disinfect the wound and dress it for you. Then I'll drop you off at the nearest service station.

Kader did not argue.

I'm not running from the cops, he told her.

It doesn't concern me, she said, without turning. She was cutting through the gauze with a pair of large silver scissors. He liked the care she took. He watched her soak the gauze with pink liquid from a plastic bottle. He looked at the heavy silver bracelet swaying on her arm. He saw the long, lean muscle moving under her skin, which was a yellowish-brown colour, like his own when he was not tanned.

Give me your arm, she said. It won't hurt.

Kader watched her clean the wound with the piece of folded gauze. The pink liquid smelt of chlorine. Soon the gauze was brown with his blood. She had small hands and she kept her fingernails cut short. The clean wound was a perfect incision and looked to him like a thin slice of watermelon.

You'll have a big scar if you don't have stitches.

He grinned at her.

Cool, he said. But she did not look at him. I'm not running from the cops. I swear.

I don't care if you are.

I'm going to Spain.

Well I'm not.

Bullshit.

She cut another piece of gauze and applied it to the wound.

I've changed my mind, she said, tearing some tape and sticking down the dressing. I'm going to stop about ten kilometres further on from here. There's a service station just before the exit. You'll be able to get a lift from there.

Sure you've changed your mind. You're not looking for a delinquent Arab in your car. Am I right?

She looked straight at him. Her eyes were dark, darker even than his sister's, but shining.

I'm wrong, he said, holding up his hands. I see I'm wrong.

I'm going to give you some stuff so you can change the dressing. From tomorrow you can leave it open. You'll have your scar and you'll be fine. Hold out your arm.

66

He watched her as she wound a length of fine bandage around his arm. Her mouth was slightly open and he could feel her breath on his collarbone. A warm feeling was spreading upwards from his groin to his face. He did not dare to breathe in case he disturbed something. When she had finished she sat back in her seat.

Come on, what's your name?

Astrid.

What's that? Spanish?

I think it's Swedish but there's a famous Brazilian singer called Astrid. My father was a fan and he named me after her.

Well well, he said. Aren't you going to ask me my name?

She tidied away her supplies.

It's Karl, he said.

She raised her eyebrows.

Strange name for an Arab.

No stranger than Astrid for a Spic.

She looked down at her box to hide her amusement. He found he wanted to see her teeth but could hardly say, Show us your teeth, lady.

She leaned into the back and put the box on the seat.

Here, she said, handing him a bottle of water. You should drink.

Are you married?

Yes.

He watched her put her hand on the ignition key. He was in no hurry to go.

Where's your husband?

Just be quiet and drink.

Where's your wedding ring?

I don't wear one. I'm a surgeon.

Kader whistled.

If you're a surgeon, you can stitch me up.

I don't have my equipment with me. Now drink.

Kader tipped back his head and drank.

Astrid watched the Adam's apple move in the boy's neck. His skin was so smooth, she doubted he even needed to shave. He gulped until water dripped down his jaw and neck. When he had finished he handed her the empty bottle, which she threw into the back, then she turned on the ignition and pulled back onto the motorway. She was grateful to this boy. His appearance by the side of the road had woken her. She wondered at the moral stupor that had enabled her to desert her post, hang up on Chastel, and drive out of Paris. The idea that she might have driven, unchallenged by reality, all the way to Saint Jean de Luz, frightened her. Some arbitrary force had intervened. She now decided to go to Orsay and see Régis Aubry. She would ask him about his research on a new immunocompetent molecule. By the time he had finished telling her, she was sure it would be too late to meet Mikel.

She looked at her passenger again. She could see at least one break in the bridge of his nose.

Go on, Astrid, he said, without looking at her. Take me with you to Spain. I'm good company. I'll tell you all about my adventures.

There can't be many, she said. You're not old enough.

Guess how old I am, he said, striking his chest with the flat of his hand. Go on.

She glanced at him.

Seventeen? Eighteen?

Twenty-one, he said triumphantly.

You're lying.

That makes two of us then.

Why?

The husband, he said, sitting deeper in his seat. He began drumming rhythmically on his thighs. There isn't one. He's dead or divorced is my guess.

What about you, Karl? Have you got a girlfriend?

One or two.

He grinned at her. She saw that he had learned to use his smile, which was full-blown and generous. She noticed that his teeth crossed over slightly at the front. Perhaps, she thought, it was a smile that had come untainted from childhood.

Where are you from? she asked.

Nanterre.

And your parents?

Algeria.

Whereabouts?

Why, do you know it?

68

I know Algiers a little.

My Dad's from Algiers and my Mum's Kabyle from a village in the mountains.

Do you ever go back?

Why would I? Don't you read the papers? The place is a mess. People getting their heads taken off with chainsaws. Hooded cops kicking down your door in the middle of the night. No thanks. Where in Spain are you from?

A little village in the Basque Country.

He shook his head.

Never heard of it. Basque. Is that where the lobster soup comes from?

She looked at him in disbelief.

Bisque, she said. Lobster bisque.

He pointed at her.

You smiled. I know the Basques. They plant bombs. I don't know where or why, though.

Spain. They want independence from Spain.

Put it there, he said holding out his hand. We're both from oppressed races. Basques, Berbers, Kabyles. What's the difference?

She swept his palm but he caught her hand in his and looked at her. He had pale, honey-coloured eyes. She pulled her hand free.

Here we are, she said, pulling into the service station.

He sank down in his seat and drove his hands deep into the pockets of his tracksuit top.

Shit. You can't leave me in this dump. Look. It's a truck stop. I'll get raped.

Please, she said.

Her *please* discouraged him.

Tell me the truth. Where are you going, really?

The new pathos in his words set up an unwanted intimacy. She was in a hurry for him to get out of her car.

I'm going to the campus of Orsay University, to the molecular biology department. I'm going to talk to a colleague. Then I'm going to turn round and drive back to Paris.

All right then, Madame Astrid-the-Surgeon. Just tell me what kind of a surgeon you are, in case I ever need an operation.

Liver, she said.

And who should I ask for when my liver's falling out? Dr Astrid what?

Arnaga.

Cheers then, Astrid Arnaga, he said. It's been a pleasure.

And he opened the door and climbed out. Astrid drove away quickly to try and elude the desolation of his sudden exit. In the wing mirror she saw his tall, loping, delinquent walk. She shivered once and turned off the air conditioning.

It was two o'clock when Astrid walked across the main lawn at Orsay. A couple of students, each plunged in their reading, sat together in the parsimonious shade of the monkey puzzle that stood right in the centre of the lawn. Its spiked form was reflected over and over again in the smoked glass of the prismatic building that housed the research laboratories. As Astrid passed beneath the portico she too was reflected, but in a foreshortened version. A video camera, picking her up in the reception, righted her again.

A pretty young woman in a navy-blue suit smiled at her enquiringly from behind the reception desk. Astrid found she missed the former receptionist, a middle-aged man with the commercial flair of a museum guard who barely looked up from his crossword magazine when he handed over the visitor's badge.

Is Professor Aubry expecting you?

Régis was not, as far as she knew, a professor.

No. No, he's not.

The young woman opened her mouth and caught the tip of her tongue between her teeth.

I'll just call then, she said. Name?

Dr Arnaga.

She watched the young woman drag the rubber end of her pencil down the list of names.

And some form of identification please, the woman said, without looking up.

What was this place? Interpol? Astrid handed over her *carte de séjour*.

Thank you, she sang. Silly me, it's at the top isn't it? Here we are: Aubry. Extension 297.

The young woman cocked her head to one side and looked

wistful as she listened to the ringing tone. When Aubry told her he would come to the reception, she took this as confirmation of her suspicion that the woman before her was an interloper.

Just take a seat, please. The professor will be down when he can.

He's not a professor.

I beg your pardon?

Aubry isn't a professor. I'm sure he wouldn't thank you for referring to him as one.

The receptionist opened her mouth to protest, seemed to hold her breath for a moment, then smiled indulgently and returned with her pencil to some spurious notation of the list of names on her desk.

Astrid now felt sorry for her. She turned her back on the receptionist and looked out through a triangular smoked-glass pane at a magpie landing on the lawn. One for sorrow: she spat discreetly.

Astrid?

Régis's voice was always too quiet. Astrid turned round. He had his hands in the pockets of his lab coat, his narrow shoulders raised. This posture made it difficult to give him a hug. Astrid gripped his arm, just at the place where she had bandaged Karl, and smiled at him.

Régis.

A transactional smile was quite beyond Régis. His beady eyes flicked in their sockets.

Have you eaten? he asked her.

No.

Shall we go to the cafeteria?

As they left, Astrid gave a sober nod to the receptionist in an attempt to set the tone for their next meeting.

They walked back across the lawn to the main building. The students had deserted the tree. In the lift down to the basement Astrid felt compelled to tell Régis what she was doing there.

I was on my way south and I thought I'd drop in and find out how you were getting on.

Régis shrugged.

Oh you know. It's pretty slow.

Astrid nodded. Régis, she remembered, had no curiosity about anything relating to human behaviour. The lift doors opened.

71

We're seeing some nice occlusive endotheliolitis in the untreated mice, he was saying.

Nice was a strange choice of word for this slow death, Astrid thought. She followed him out of the lift. He kept talking as they walked along the white tiled corridor.

The molecule does its business. There's no doubt about that. It's just not clear what else it does, he told her as he pushed through the swing doors into the brightly lit cafeteria. Hot or cold? he asked, half turning as he made his way towards the trays. Do you want the salad bar or the dish of the day? It's hot.

Salad bar, I think.

They each took a tray and split up. Astrid made her way to the unit in the centre, a kind of mock manger, decorated with sheaves of wheat and filled with different salads. By the time she had paid, Régis was already seated and salting his veal Marengo. She sat down opposite him.

I don't know what you're expecting, he said between mouthfuls. The knockout effect works every time, though.

Astrid could tell from his tone that he had not carried out the research according to her recommendations. When she questioned him about the protocol she discovered she had guessed right. She was careful to hide her disappointment.

I was hoping you might take on board the Cambridge research and leave a window after the first rejection crisis, so we can focus on tolerance rather than rejection.

She regretted having used the word 'we'.

No one takes that very seriously round here. I personally haven't seen much evidence of what you call operational tolerance.

He was sulking now. Astrid always forgot how susceptible he was. She did not feel like arguing. Her mind wandered to the Arab boy at the truck stop.

So tell me how it works, she said.

And he was off. Astrid knew more or less how the new molecule worked. It had a beautiful simplicity, which she did not want marred with details, so she watched Régis's pious mouth for a while and began to eat her lentil salad, nodding at appropriate intervals. The canteen was emptying and she glanced at the clock on the wall behind him. It was only two-thirty. She began to experience an uncomfortable dragging sensation in her legs, which she recognised from childhood, a feeling that accompanied the longing to be somewhere else.

Kader took off his tracksuit top and tied it around his hips. He was overjoyed at the bandage she had made. He liked its cleanness, its whiteness against his skin and the fact that she had done it. As he walked along the road, he glanced at it from time to time, to make sure that it was not getting dirty. Ahead of him stretched the hot, straight road, sweeping down into a wooded gully and then steeply up again. At the top of that hill was her university. He had taken a risk leaving his things in her car but it was worth it. The only objects of value to him in the Adidas bag were the bag itself and Amadou's Discman. Kader regretted only one thing, that he had not kissed her. He was sure that if he had kissed her he would have got under her skin, but then an opportunity had not really presented itself: during the bandaging would have been ugly.

Kader looked at the heat waves dancing on the road, at the fields on either side of him brimming with yellow grass, at the cool woods below him, and he decided to sprint. He felt triumphant. It had been so simple to slip the noose from around his neck; so simple just to leave, leave the estate, his weeping mother, his weak and rigid father, his stubborn sister; leave the social workers, the pally karate master, the cops on foot, dragging all their stuff around – their cuffs, their gloves, their guns, their whistles, their batons – all on one belt, and the cops in cars (whom he disliked more than the underlings in blue because they had it easy, playing cowboys and Indians all night and drinking Chivas from plastic cups, but they were always moaning that their cars were too slow and their weapons were too old and they didn't have enough bulletproof vests). He hated them, with their buffoon moustaches and their leather jackets that went out some time in the last century and those terrible ankle boots they all wore because they all thought they were Alain Delon and their fucking blue lights that they loved slapping on the roof and the chase – you on a scooter and them in a ropy Peugeot, straining the engine (they didn't care; they might get a decent car if this one died on them) – and the interception as they called it with their stupid copspeak, when they slammed you against the car if they were feeling chipper or face down on the ground if they hadn't got their leg over that morning, and then insulted you – badly, because they had about as much repartee as a pit bull . . . And Kader remembered El Niño and slowed his pace. Truly, without his dog he was a poor man. To be honest, he was a nineteen-year-old Arab with no qualifications and a criminal record. But he gave thanks to his dog because he saw that it had been the loss of his dog that had enabled him to leave. It was fate and this surgeon woman was an angel.

Kader walked into the little hut at the entrance to the campus. He held out his bandaged arm to the uniformed guard:

I have an appointment with Dr Arnaga. Molecular biology. She's expecting me.

The guard looked puzzled. Before he had time to open his mouth Kader had walked out.

He found Astrid's car parked in a bay with five others next to a big lawn. Kader tried the boot. It was unlocked; anyone could have nicked his stuff. Kader looked about for signs to the Molecular Biology department but there were none. He considered climbing into the boot but decided against it. Instead he set off across the lawn.

When Astrid stood up to leave, the cafeteria was empty except for the staff. It was ten past three. Régis had explained the action of the new molecule with the help of a sprawling diagram of the kind that immunologists loved. It was drawn in black ink on a red paper napkin. Politely, Astrid folded the napkin and put it in her bag. In the lift they did not talk. Astrid looked at the ceiling and stifled a yawn and Régis looked at his feet.

As they approached the laboratory building, they heard cries. Astrid recognised the shrill tones of the receptionist. The glass door was flung open and out came Karl between two security guards; one looked like a child and the other like somebody's grandfather. Behind them came the receptionist who stood on the threshold of her domain, smoothing back her hair and trying to regain composure.

Don't touch the arm! Karl shouted. Astrid! What is this place? These people are morons. I said don't touch the arm! The young security guard who was holding him lightly by the elbow let him go. And you, Grandad.

74

The old man looked at Astrid who nodded and smiled. He too let go. Régis had been staring at Karl; he now stared at her. She did not explain.

Thank you, Régis, she said, holding out her hand. It sounds very exciting. Keep in touch.

Régis gave his hand and let her shake it. She pointed her thumb in the direction of the reception. I'll just pick up my I.D. See you soon.

As she walked away, he called out,

Oh Astrid, I'll look into that window of opportunity thing and let you know.

Jerk, Astrid thought. She did not turn but raised her arm. She passed Karl without a look. The receptionist had resumed her position behind the desk. Astrid handed over her visitor's pass and took her *carte de séjour*. She spoke quietly, forcing the woman to lean forward.

A little advice. Don't judge on appearances. Aubry is a laboratory technician. I am a surgeon and that Arab you treated like a delinquent is a technical optometrist on a research grant from the University of Rabat.

There was a pause, then the woman gave her pleasant smile and answered simply,

I don't believe you.

When Astrid came out Karl was chatting with the old security guard while the young one hovered, drawing circles in the gravel path with his foot. The old man nodded at Karl and took discreet drags on what remained of the Gauloise he had managed to conceal throughout the whole scene in the cup of his right hand.

I could open the suckers fast, Karl was saying. But never as fast as old Yann.

At the sight of Astrid, Karl slapped the old man on the arm and backed away with a cheery wave.

They walked back across the lawn.

What are you doing here?

I forgot my stuff in your car. Just as well I found you. It's all my worldly goods.

Astrid walked so quickly he had to jog to keep up.

Slow down. What's the rush? When she did not answer: Do you work out? I bet you do. I bet you work out in one of those places where they have a fake beach and palm trees and real fruit juices made from real fruit.

They had reached the car. Astrid opened the boot and took out his bag. But he had climbed into the passenger seat. Astrid walked round to his door, dropped his bag at her feet and looked down at him.

Get out please.

Oh man.

Please.

Oh come on Astrid. My arm aches. I'm fucking exhausted from walking all that way in the heat. Just give me a lift some of the way.

A lift where?

Wherever you're going.

That's stupid.

Listen. It's simple. I'd like to go to Spain if that's where you're going. If you're not, I'm not interested in going there. I'd rather go to Marseille. So if you're going back to Paris that'll be fine too and I'll pick up the right motorway from there. He held out his hands. Wherever you're going is the right direction for me.

Astrid stared at him. Looking up at her made him wrinkle his brow. He reminded her of the young forward from the French football team who wept easily.

You look a bit like David Trézéguet, she told him.

He pointed at her.

It's true. You're not the first person's told me that. Do you watch football?

A little.

Do you support a team?

Reál.

He nodded at her and she saw kindness.

A good team, he said. Figo, Raúl . . .

And Hierro.

She felt tears well up inside her.

I'm supposed to support Atlético Bilbao. No Basque supports Reál Madrid. Initially I think it was just to irritate my father. But I love Reál. She rubbed her forehead and looked away. Especially Hierro.

Are you alright?

76

She was not. She did not know where to go. She did not want this boy in her car but she did not want him to leave. She knew she could not go south but she did not want to go back to Paris to her lonely flat, to the lab, to Chastel. Her conversation with Régis had brought home to her the fatuousness of her research. No one listened to her and no one cared about what she might have to say.

Lola, she thought. Lola where are you?

Do you want to go for a coffee or something? Kader was saying.

She nodded.

Do you want me to drive?

She must have acquiesced because he climbed out and picked up his bag and leant in front of her to throw it on the back seat. She watched him walk round to the driver's door and climb in. Lola should have called her by now, should have called her in. Chastel was right; without Lola's need, she was lost.

She watched a couple of oriental students, a boy and a girl, walking across the car park. The girl wore her hair in a high ponytail that swung as she walked. Astrid felt the tears rise again. She climbed into the passenger seat.

FOURTEEN

He was dressed in a black suit. At first glance Lola mistook him
for a priest. When she saw it was Txema she thought someone
must have died. But no, he was smiling broadly, hailing the barman, then cutting through the room. Still at fifty he had the poise
of a young man who has just come into possession of a grand
body. Lola watched him greet the three men at the bar, shaking
their hands warmly, turning his probing gaze on each one of
them in turn. All the while they watched his every move with a
kind of grudging fascination. He ordered a round of red for them
all and raised his glass to them. Lola was partially shielded from
him by the pinball machine but if he were to turn his head slightly to the left he would catch her in the mirror behind the bar. He
downed his wine. There, he had seen her. She could tell from his
reaction that he already knew of her presence in the village. He
said something to the four men that she did not catch. The barman laughed. Then the other three followed suit.

He was sitting down opposite her, stretching across the table,
taking both of her hands in his and squeezing hard. This was, she
realised, a much stronger gesture than a kiss. He took her in, as
though he was mapping every contour of her face.

You're still lovely, Lola.

This was not the language she was accustomed to hearing from
him.

Txema. How are you?

He nodded slowly.

You look a little tired, he said.

It's the journey.

He took away his hands and she found to her dismay that she
missed his grip. She sat back in her chair as though to protect herself from him.

You came from Paris. How is it there?

It's, you know. She felt herself blush. She could not find her
words. She was seventeen again. She looked down at her lap.

I don't, he said. I've never been there. You know me. I leave this place as little as possible.

She looked up.

I saw your assistant. Lorea Molina.

She's not my assistant. She deals with cultural affairs. She answers to the government, not me. It's better that way. You know the extent of my interest in culture.

Lola was baffled. Why was he speaking to her like this? He laid healing hands on the table.

Will you have something to drink?

They were not beautiful hands like Mikel's, but broad-palmed and short-fingered.

I'll have a beer, thank you.

He called out the order in a clear, expert voice. Until he moved back to the village and began his life as a public figure, Txema had been a waiter in Donostia.

He turned to Lola and looked at her. The expression in his eyes had always been one of enquiry, born not of self-doubt but of deep mistrust. He was an inquisitor.

I'm looking for Mikel, she said.

Txema looked at her, observing a cruel silence.

He leaned back to let the barman serve their beers. The evening sun shone through the plate glass, catching the golden liquid and making it glow. He took a sip. He was taking pleasure in making her wait for his answer. She saw then that he drank too much. The whites of his eyes were yellow and his cheeks were spattered with broken veins. From the indigo in his hair, she saw he dyed it. The shoulders of his suit were speckled with dandruff.

I remember teaching him to shoot, he went on. I've never seen hands so steady, he said, wiping froth from his lip. He put down his beer and looked at her. It made her feel unclean to hear him refer to the steadiness of Mikel's hands. She prayed that he did not know where Mikel was.

Do you have any idea where he might have gone?

Txema looked at his beer.

He called me this morning, from a phone box. He wanted a job . . .

He called you? What did he say?

He sounded tired, Lola. Very tired. You have to understand.

She could feel her face flush again. Her ears were burning.

79

Understand what?

He believes he has nothing to offer you.

I'm sorry?

He has nothing, Lola. He's been locked up for twenty years and he feels he has nothing to give anyone. He has to heal.

She could feel tears of rage rising in her.

I can heal him.

No one can heal him but himself, Lola.

Lola felt trapped. She picked up her beer and gulped. When she looked at Txema again, he was blurred by her tears.

You have to be strong for him, Lola. It is a woman's destiny to wait.

What bullshit you talk, Txema. And then she regretted it. She wanted to take back her words because she could see the inner shuffling, the mechanisms of calculation and revenge working inside him. With her hostility she had lost him for he knew now that she could give him nothing.

She rested her elbows on the table and covered her face with her hands. She hoped that he would get up and leave but he watched and waited. At last she felt his hand on her head.

Lola. Don't cry. He'll come to you.

She looked up.

Please, Txema. Tell me where he is.

He removed his hand.

I don't know where he is, Lola.

Oh Txema, please. I'm afraid he might kill himself or something.

He won't kill himself, Lola. Mikel does not have it in him.

How do you know? How could you possibly know?

Mikel is like a brother to me. I know him. We spent six weeks alone on a mountain together. There is nothing in a relationship between a man and a woman that comes close to that kind of intimacy. You don't know a man's soul until you have been close to death with him, Lola.

He picked up his beer and took a sip. Such cruelty was a rare thing. In a few minutes he had unravelled all her illusions and spread them out before her like her own guts. There was indeed something fascinating in the precision of such cruelty. Strange, though, how so many people mistook this gift for compassion.

When at last she spoke, her voice was a little slurred.

Tell me where he is, Txema.

I don't know where he is, Lola, and even if I did I would not tell you. For your sake. Wait for him. He'll come to you when he's ready.

Lola stared at Txema for what felt like a long time. He sustained her stare. At last she stood up. She edged past the pinball machine and walked a little unsteadily out of the café.

FIFTEEN

Kader watched Astrid sipping her coffee. They were seated at a small, square table, overlooking the motorway that ran underneath the restaurant like a deadly river. She was not speaking and Kader was becoming uneasy. His mind was on a useless loop. All he could think was: *This is you, Kader. This is you. This woman needs you.* Since her eyes had filled with tears, he had been aware that he had suddenly become someone to her. He knew that she expected something of him, knew that he was ready but he didn't know what for. He was charged with a grand energy. He felt like a warrior about to go into battle.

He had driven for two hours while she worked. He had listened to her speaking into a pocket-sized tape recorder. He thought she must be practising for some kind of a speech but when he had tried to ask, she had held up her hand and he had not pushed it because he was so happy there at the wheel of this tank with its V6 engine, her there beside him, doing her work. He could hardly contain his joy: he drove and she worked.

But she had not said a word and Kader could not for the life of him think of what to say to her. He wanted to ask why the thought of the Réal Madrid defender had suddenly made her so sad but he knew this was a stupid question.

He could feel something sticky under his elbows. He leaned back in his chair and folded his arms.

I hate that, he said. I worked in a McDonald's once and I always made sure my cloth was clean. He nodded at the table. My cloth for wiping the tables. It's a minimum.

Astrid put down her coffee cup. Her face was flushed and her eyes were shining. She seemed to be waiting for more.

When I was a kid, he said, I used to go to this motorway bridge with my mates. We'd hang our bare arses over the rail and try and make people crash.

Astrid stared at him as though from a long way off.

You look sick, he said. If you want to throw up, you should.

You'll feel better afterwards.

I'm fine. I'm fine.

You look terrible.

She seemed to be taking him in suddenly. He folded his arms in readiness.

Did you pay for the coffee? she asked him.

No, you did. She was withdrawing again: something happened around the eyes. Listen, Astrid, he said suddenly. My name's not Karl. It's Kader.

Why did you say it was Karl then?

He shrugged, then made a sweeping motion.

Karl, he said. I don't know. I just like it. Kaaaal, he said, dispelling all other names with the back of his hand. Don't you like it?

No.

What would you suggest? I want to change my name.

Carlos, she said.

Kader stared at her, then he looked down at the traffic disappearing beneath their feet. He let the idea settle on him.

No, he said, shaking his finger. It's no good. It's not serious. What will I do with a name like Carlos when I'm an old man? Be sensible.

Most of us outgrow our names, she said.

Karl's better, he said.

Karl's a Nazi name, she said.

That's why I like it. It feels like stealing something from an enemy, like a trophy.

Stick to Kader, she said. Think of your mother.

Astrid was amused to hear herself being drawn into this fatuous exchange.

Do you have kids? he asked her.

The question caught her off guard. She looked into her empty cup.

No.

Why not?

I've just never wanted them enough, I suppose.

You don't have to want them, he said. Plenty of people have kids without wanting them. You get attached to them once they're there.

You don't strike me as an unwanted child.

He looked pleased.

I'm my mum's prince, he said, slapping his chest with the gesture that was already familiar to her. I had a dog. His name was El Niño. It's Spanish.

I know.

It means the kid.

It also means the Christ child, baby Jesus.

No!

It's true.

Kader grinned.

Cool. A Muslim with a dog called Jesus.

She looked at her watch. It was ten past four. She saw Mikel standing beneath that ridiculous bandstand. She still saw his young man's face and his young man's body. Neither existed any longer.

She stood up.

Let's go, she said.

Where? he said, rising to his feet.

She faced him. For some reason he was clutching her handbag under his arm. She could not remember having given it to him. It occurred to her that to the outside world she could be his mother. She held out her hand for the bag. He gave it back to her.

Want me to drive?

She shook her head.

Oh come on.

Give me the keys, Kader.

He looked truly disappointed as he took the keys from the pocket of his tracksuit. He was a child.

Why do white girls go out with Arab boys?

I don't know.

To get their handbags back.

He raised his eyebrows at her, his face full of encouragement.

She began to smile but some demon stole it away.

She turned and walked back over the motorway to the doors of the restaurant, Kader loping beside her. He held the swing door for her.

Where are we going? he asked.

At the top of the stairs she stopped.

I'm going to Spain. I think you should go to Marseille. Have you got family there?

Nope.

No one?

No.

Then why Marseille?

I knew someone who went there to look for work and he never came back. He must have liked it there. It's full of Arabs, not just in the suburbs but in the centre of town. He paused looking about him as though for help. I don't know. The weather, the football, the beaches.

Astrid stared at him. His face stripped of mirth was entirely different. He stared back at her. She saw that his left eye was paler than the right. There was a pink scar across the bridge of his nose where she could still see the stitch marks and an older cut high up on his forehead.

Don't look at my scars, he said, covering his forehead with his hand.

How did you get them?

I box.

That's not a boxing scar. None of them are.

Just let me come with you, he said. They stepped out into the fading heat of the afternoon. Please. She looked at him. There it was, the child again. You can work while I drive, he said. His face was slowly lighting up.

Astrid began to walk faster, eager to hide her face from him. She did not want him to see that she had already given in.

Are you sure you've got a licence?

Fuck off. Course I have. Give us the keys.

The car park backed on to a field of rape in full bloom. The smell was sickeningly human and reminded her of early autopsies.

No, she said, turning her back on him as she opened the car door. Get in. I've got a long way to go and I don't like driving at night.

She could feel Kader's excitement as he turned and walked with his fake nonchalance round to the passenger door.

The traffic on the motorway had thinned. Kader sat beside her, tapping out a fast, elaborate rhythm on the dashboard. Astrid drove with her arm resting on the open window. She had decided not to question her need for his presence.

What made you leave home? she asked him. I presume you still live at home.

Kader turned away from her and stared out of his window. He sucked on his teeth by way of reply. The Arab women in prison had made the same sound when they were annoyed. It was the sound of their mouths holding back words of abuse they might regret.

You've got air conditioning, he said, facing her.

I know.

Why don't you use it then?

I don't like it.

Why not?

It dries up the mucus in my nose and throat.

That's disgusting.

Kader hawked, wound down his window and spat a neat glob of his mucus into the hard shoulder.

Why don't you let me drive? I know you'd rather work than make polite conversation with me. Anyway, I don't like polite conversation.

Astrid glanced at him. He was restless and his long body, folded into the seat, looked redundant.

The sun was beginning to burn her arm. She wound up the window. They were still half an hour from Tours and at least seven hours from the Spanish border. Even if she wanted to, it would be too late to meet Mikel now. He would soon settle into his despair.

Astrid indicated and pulled over onto the hard shoulder.

Kader opened the door before she had come to a halt. He glanced at her, then sprang out and jogged around the bonnet. She moved across to the passenger seat, pulling her dress over her knees, but Kader was not looking. He was adjusting the seat and the mirror, then gripping the wheel, his arms straight, like a child in a carousel waiting for motion.

Thanks, he said without looking at her.

She guessed how hard gratitude must be for him. She began to work, speaking into her tape recorder: *Since the late sixties death has been defined as the disappearance of brain function rather than as the cessation of heartbeat and respiration.*

She played back what she had recorded.

What are you grinning about? she asked him.

Your accent.

You should hear yours.

What are you talking about? I don't have an accent.

She turned on her recorder. *Until recently the greatest single source of heart-beating cadavers has been the car crash.*

You can't say that.

She stopped the tape recorder.

Why not?

'The greatest single source'.

Why not?

He lifted his hands from the steering wheel and dropped them again.

I don't know. It sounds bad.

She paused. He was working his jaw and she could see the muscles moving beneath the skin of his neck.

She held the recorder in front of her mouth. *Most brain deaths are today the result of brain haemorrhage, the increase of which has compensated for the reduction of road accidents.*

She clicked off the machine.

There.

You look a bit like my mum you know, he told her. There's something around the eyes, he said. He turned back to the road. Look in my Adidas bag. My wallet's in there. Get it out. There's a photo of her. He nodded at her. Go on. Have a look.

Astrid reached into the back and found his wallet. In the plastic window was a photograph of a woman in a sugar-pink headscarf. Out of the pale, fleshy face two black eyes shone infinite sadness and mercy. The picture reminded her of the lithograph of the Madonna that had hung above her and Lola's bed as children. The chest open like a cabinet to reveal the flaming heart had always scared her. Perhaps, she thought, this was the origin of her dislike of heart surgeons.

Isn't she beautiful? Kader was saying.

Astrid looked at him. She looked again at the photo. Under the flash of the photo booth the woman's moon face glowed with perspiration.

She looks even lovelier with her head uncovered, Kader

explained. She always wears the *hadjib* to go out. She's not a religious fanatic or anything, she just feels naked without it. Do you know the story of the headscarf? It's from the Koran. It's not about covering women up and shutting them away like French people say it is. I'll tell you. There was this young woman, very beautiful, out getting water or something, I can't remember exactly but anyway, she was raped. When she came home her father put a beautiful cloth over her head, to show that she was still a princess, that the rape could not take that away. It was a mark of respect. Do you see?

Astrid nodded. His innocence made her unable to object.

She folded the wallet and put it back into his bag. Then she turned on her tape recorder.

There is life so long as a circulation of oxygenated blood is maintained to live vital centres in the brainstem.

She turned off the recorder. They passed a vast, convex field of wheat, still uncut, the late sun setting alight the dust haze that floated above it. In the centre was a miniature wood, a small concession to wildlife. She suddenly longed to see the grand oak forests around her village.

I dream of a simple life with you, Astrid. I want to build you a house.

Kader was looking at her.

Are you OK?

She turned on the tape recorder and kept talking: *Departure of consciousness, however, may be said to be bilateral, irreversible damage to the paramedian tegmental areas of the mesencephalon and rostral pons.*

Then the phone rang. Her heart leapt. But it was not Lola.

Astrid.

Years of sorrow were contained in her name. She wanted to hang up but an old idea of sin stopped her. His voice was deeper than she remembered.

Lola's looking for you, she told him. She went to your mother's.

There was a long pause. She could hear him breathing. She closed her eyes, swallowed, opened her mouth to speak but could not make a sound.

Where are you, Astrid?

His voice was shaking.

Astrid clenched her teeth. Her fist ached from gripping the phone.

Astrid. Please come. I need you.

She could hear: the outside world was too big for him. He was terrified.

Please, he said.

Cool air seemed to be rushing through her head. She was calm.

I can't. Call Lola. I'm going to hang up.

No! His voice was hoarse.

She hung up.

SIXTEEN

Mikel Angel Otegui had no plan. He stood outside the call box, eavesdropping on the woman who had stepped in after him. She was discussing a trip to a DIY superstore called Conforama, planned for the next morning. She would pick up the dry cleaning and the mussels first. She did not want to barbecue the mussels, she wanted to cook them *à la marinière* and Mikel agreed with her. Her husband wanted sardines but she didn't because she said they stunk the place out. Not if he lights a barbecue, Mikel thought, and cleans it properly afterwards. And sardines were local. He thought the husband was right. The woman was now looking at him through the scratched glass of the phone box. Her face took on an indignant expression and she turned her back on him. Mikel moved on. The woman had an overshot upper lip which he found appealing and he imagined that it must have been this that had conquered her husband all those years ago.

Mikel walked across the square to the port and sat down, letting his legs dangle over the water. The light was dying but he could make out a shoal of dogfish, their noses nudging the slick dark surface. He watched the shapes they made, letting his mind empty. As the light faded and turned blue, a breeze rose and set the rigging slatting. He closed his eyes and raised his face to the breeze, laden with salt, and listened to the clatter of the rigging and the lapping of the water against the walls of the dock. A dog barked. There, he thought, was a plan. He would find a dog, then he would find a job that would be acceptable to the dog. If the job were tolerable to a dog, who did not like confinement, then it would be tolerable to him. Mikel's heart swelled and he smiled at the thought of this old dog that would be his companion. A moped without a silencer ripped through the scene and he opened his eyes.

He found that the world had turned in the interim. The light was no longer blue but grey. The clatter of the rigging was deafening to him now and the fish seemed to be fighting each other for an invisible prey. He thought of the noise of the canteen, the peculiar hostility in the air when the men were around food, how it had offended him, how he would take his tray to some empty corner in an attempt to find peace. But there was none.

Peace. He sought peace. His fellow prisoners soon understood this about him and distrusted him for it. To his former colleagues, it actually made him a dangerous man, to some a man who should be eliminated. Mikel knew that his pacifism had begun to roll off him like a bad smell in prison. He knew that everything about him – the way he walked, the way he ate, the way he spoke and the books that he read – was observed and noted by the organisation. At times the scrutiny had made him afraid. Even after he was moved and there was not a single *liberado* in his wing, he could feel them at his back and he had to summon all his strength to dissimulate his fear. Now he knew that the fear was part of a much deeper fear of the outside world. As time went by, the fear of his release grew. At night he would dream that he would be let out to discover that no one could see or hear him. He no longer existed.

His letters to Astrid were the means he had found to stave off this fear. He did not write them for her rare and hesitant replies. He did not depend on reciprocity. It was simply that her reading of his letters was proof that he existed. Without this idea, of her in the outside world, reading his letters, he could not be sure of anything.

Mikel stood up and shook out his legs. He was stiff these days, in the hips. The thought of his bodily disintegration made him smile. It was a kind of revenge. The organisation believed in eternal youth. The endless flow of young recruits encouraged this belief. The old did not die; they became Historics. Mikel could have acceded to this high honour. By rights he was an Historic. He had all the credentials; he had joined under Franco, in the days when every Basque had a place in their heart for ETA, he had assassinated state representatives, he had trained young commandos, been tortured by the Guardia Civil and spent twenty years in prison. But even when he had belonged, he had never been interested in any honours they might confer upon him, nor in holding any authority over his comrades. Now he wanted nothing to do with any of them. Inside he had been told that they had thought of him for the Refugee Committee. Quite apart from anything else, he no longer knew or cared who 'they' were. All the people he had joined up with were either dead or had settled comfortably into ordinary life after the amnesty. Some had taken up mainstream politics but only one, his old friend Txema, had any real power.

On the phone that morning Txema had told him that he would find him a job on the French side:

You'll be happier over there.

Mikel wondered how Txema would know that. He hadn't been to visit him for four and a half years.

I'll talk to people, he went on. We'll sort something out.

I just want a quiet life.

I know you do.

Without politics.

I know that. There was a moment's silence. You need a rest. Where are you?

Mikel hesitated.

Where exactly are you, Mikel?

He had heard the urgency in Txema's question.

Mikel. Are you there?

Yes.

Tell me where you are.

And Mikel had told him that he was on the French side.

Good. That's good. Where?

Someone wants to use the phone. I have to go. I'll call you back.

Mikel. Wait. I can find you a job. Where are you?

I'll find a job, Txema. Don't worry. I'll call you back. I have to go.

Mikel now walked past the bandstand. Planning, he thought, was indeed a futile business, either in prison or out. His plan, built in his mind over years, had collapsed when the first step had failed. When he had understood that she would not meet him here, that they would not catch the night train to Paris together, he had stood in the phone box that reeked of stale cigarette butts and cried like a child. When the woman had come to call her husband, he was hunched over, his hand covering his face. He had pushed past her on his way out in case she wanted to give him sympathy, but fortunately she was not the type. He had stood outside for a while, letting the self-loathing settle in and calm him down.

Mikel pushed the door to a café called L'Amiral and walked up to the bar. The place was busy and he had to raise his voice to be heard. He ordered a double whisky and paid for it with some of the money his probation officer had given him for his first month. The café did not sell tobacco so he asked his neighbour, a tiny little man with a face cut into sections by deep lines, for one of his Lucky Strikes. The man held out the open packet without a word and Mikel took one and nodded his thanks. He was grateful for the man's presence beside him as he drank. He liked the barman and the expertise in his every gesture and he liked the noise behind them and the silence between them.

SEVENTEEN

Kader was beside himself. He could feel this woman's unhappiness as if he were breathing it in. He wanted to help her but he could not speak. His heart was like a hot stone in his chest. All he could do was keep driving.

They had reached the outskirts of Bordeaux. The traffic on the ring road was moving very slowly. In the rear-view mirror he could see the remains of the setting sun, smudged on the horizon.

The traffic came to a halt. He turned and looked at her. He wanted to ask her . . . anything. Are you all right? Can I help? But he couldn't speak. He turned back to the road, sick with failure.

They were not moving. He checked his mirror. The sun had gone. Stuck there in the traffic, Kader felt anger rise in him.

I'm going to pull over, he said. He pulled into the slow lane. We're not moving anyway.

He stopped the car in the breakdown lane and turned off the engine.

Tell me about yourself, he said, leaning back into his window.

He felt like a fireman coaxing someone from the edge of a building. He would have been happy being a fireman but he had failed to get on to the course.

She was looking straight ahead. He looked at her hands, surgeon's hands that had rummaged in people's insides.

Tell me about your childhood, he said.

Astrid looked at him. She almost smiled. For a moment he thought she was pleased he had asked.

My childhood?

She faced forward again and shook her head.

Tell me. Why not? He folded his arms. Tell me a story, he said.

Astrid glanced at him.

All right. I'll tell you a story.

Something, as she shifted in her seat, indicated to him that she might lie.

My father's a lawyer, she said. Kader was thrilled by the sound of her accent. He suddenly thought of Amadou, wanted him to see her.

He works in San Sebastian – Donostia, the Basques call it. He defends members of the Basque terrorist group, ETA. His own father was a hero of Basque resistance against Franco.

Kader glanced at her. He did not know who Franco was but he did not want to interrupt.

Franco was a dictator, she said. He ruled Spain for nearly forty years. Under him the Basques were not allowed to speak their language or fly their flag. They were persecuted and imprisoned and killed just for being Basque.

Kader looked at her. He could see the shadow on her forehead again. He guessed that her story would set them further apart but he wanted to hear it.

When my grandfather died, Franco had been dead for seven years. There was a democratic government in Spain. He told my father that he should no longer defend people who killed. That there was no need for killing any more. But my father ignored him. He still defends the *liberados*, even today.

Who are they?

Liberados are members of ETA who carry out attacks. Commando members. She paused. I don't see my father any more. I hardly know him but what I know, I don't like. He claims to be a revolutionary and says that the members of the organisation he defends lead the lives they lead for metaphysical, not political reasons. He wears well-cut tweed suits, modelling himself on the English gentleman, and he stands very straight, always with one hand held behind his back.

She was settling into her story, staring off to the side, chasing her memories.

My mother is English. She came to San Sebastian to study art history at the university. She was rich and beautiful and romantic. She met my father in a bar in the old quarter and fell in love with him. I don't believe he ever loved her. For a time he coveted her.

Kader was not familiar with the word but he felt he understood enough.

We lived in a big house two doors down from one of General Franco's summer residences. Lola was born five years after me. She was my mother's attempt to bring my father closer to her but she drove him further away. He didn't like noise and Lola made a lot. My father began to hate my mother, the elegance that had drawn him, her beauty, her frailty and most of all, her wealth. He took a mistress, another lawyer who also defended the organisation. He stopped coming home. My mother began to drink. She would drink until she passed out. Sometimes, when I came home from school, I'd find her lying on the kitchen floor.

She stopped talking and began clicking her tape recorder on and off. Kader could not think of anything to say, so he waited.

I looked after Lola, she said. On my way to school, I dropped her off at the childminder and picked her up on my way back. I dressed her and fed her and taught her to speak. My mother sometimes tried to stop drinking, usually after her brother Angus had been to stay. He loved her very much and always made her feel stronger. Once, after one of his visits, she went to see my father at his office. She told him that she was going to move back to England. Very calmly he forbade her to take us out of the country. He told her that the organisation would make sure it never happened. I still don't know why. He has never shown any interest in us.

She paused and smoothed her face with her hands. She looked at him.

Keep talking. I like stories. My Mum only knew three, so she'd alternate. I had my favourite but I didn't tell her which one it was. I just waited for it to come round again.

Tell me, she said.

Kader shook his head.

Not now. Keep talking.

Astrid was staring at him but he faced forward.

Go on, he urged.

My father made my mother stay in the Basque Country. She decided to move out of town. She and her brother bought a beautiful old house in a village in the hills behind San Sebastian because it reminded her of the part of Scotland where she grew up. We moved there when I was eight. I loved it. My mother gave up drink. We spent three happy years there.

She stopped.

Then what?

Astrid looked at him.

He opened his hands.

That's not a story, he said. There's no ending.

You want an ending.

Do you want to get some air? he asked.

No.

Wrap it up, he said.

She took off her sandals, put her bare feet on the dashboard and hugged her knees.

The man who farmed my mother's land was called Josu. He was a big, quiet man in his fifties who had always been alone. Josu adored my mother. He came every day to bring her a present, something he'd found or made. I still don't know how it happened but after a year, Josu moved in with us. He and my mother slept in the same bed. Some people in the village were shocked but I didn't care. I liked him. He was shy and gentle and he made my mother happy. She began to cook and look after the house. With Josu's help she made a beautiful garden. She made a place, a kind of green alcove with a bench in it that had a view over the mountains. She and Josu would sit there in the evenings.

Astrid paused. Kader watched her, this time afraid she would stop. She let her hair out of its clasp. She put her feet down and put the clasp in the bag at her feet. He watched her look out at the world around them. He looked, too, at the traffic now moving slowly and the pine forest and the lake in the distance glowing orange and the birds flying across the sky in a formation that changed from a V to a U and then to the head of an axe.

Go on, he said. He cleared his throat. Astrid looked at him.

One Sunday my mother, Lola and I came back from mass.

Are you religious?

No. Everyone went to mass in those days. For some people it was just a way of seeing the whole village in one place, or it was a place to sing, or just be warm for an hour. I liked it because of the smell. It smelt of polished wood and damp stone. She paused. The women and men stood in separate parts of the church – the men in the wooden galleries high above us – and they sang at each other.

Kader thought of the mosque they had made in the basement of his tower block. He had always hated the place. It smelt of feet and the men and women couldn't see each other.

We came home from mass, Astrid went on. And my mother

went into the house to make lunch and Lola and I stayed in the garden. We had a bronze statue of a goat in the garden that Angus had brought my mother from his home in England. Lola loved it and I was lifting her onto its back when I saw my mother come out of the house and go down the stone steps to the wine cellar. She was carrying a red-and-white checked tea towel. I was holding Lola around the waist when I heard my mother's cry. It was more like a low moan. I let go of Lola, leaving her stuck on that goat, and ran to the steps. They were slippery from moss and rain. There was always this icy draught blowing up through the iron gate of the cellar. I didn't want to go down those steps, my heart was beating very fast. When I stepped into the cellar my mother grabbed hold of my arm, which made me bite down on my tongue. Josu was swinging from a rope. My mother was gripping my arm so tightly, it hurt. She was saying my name over and over again. I remember the sleeves of Josu's shirt were too short and his wrists were showing and his great big hands were dangling from his cuffs. She paused. Now whenever I taste blood I think of Josu hanging there in the light from that naked bulb.

Kader's own heart was racing. He had no wish to touch her now. Her sorrow was a wall, something insurmountable. He looked out at what he took to be the sun ahead of him but it was an orange moon.

Why did he do it? he asked.

I don't know. My mother said it was because he loved her too much. But she's mad. She lives in a fantasy world.

Kader was suddenly very tired.

What do you mean, mad?

She's not interested in reality any more. She lives in her memory, the bits of it that make her happy. Her childhood, moments with Josu. She forgets the rest.

So she's not crazy? Wild hair, shouting, drooling crazy.

He saw Astrid smile and he began to relax.

Shall we get out? he said. I need to move.

Astrid nodded.

I used to watch the sun come up with El Niño, he told her. It did us good. He climbed out of the car, walked round to her door and opened it for her. Look, he said, pointing at a freshly mown bank by the side of the road. It's perfect here.

Astrid sat for a moment, feeling the breeze on her face and breathing in the smell of cut grass. She watched him scramble up the slope and disappear over the top. She did not know why she had told him about Josu, except that the telling had led her there. She had shared more with this boy in the few hours she had known him than with anyone she had ever met. He knew more about her life than Chastel did. Perhaps because she knew she would not see him again, she had even been tempted to tell him about Mikel.

She got out of the car and slammed the door. As she climbed up the steep bank after him, she thought of Mikel's voice, laden with sorrow. It seemed to pluck at her from behind as she climbed. When she had been released from prison she had waited for a sensation of freedom but it had never come. She had just felt irrelevant. Now, as she crawled up the bank, she felt a lightness entirely unfamiliar to her.

At the top Kader was sitting on the flattened grass, one knee clasped to his chest, watching a large, yellow moon. Astrid sat down beside him.

El Niño didn't watch the sun, Kader told her. He wasn't interested in the sun. He'd watch me. He'd lie beside me with his tongue lolling, his mouth open, smiling. Kader turned to her. He was, he insisted.

I believe you.

He'd sort of turn his eyes up to me, then look away and start panting again, then back to me, then away. Back and forth, just checking that I was with him. Sometimes I'd smile back at him, sometimes not. He turned and looked at her. Lie down with me, he said, suddenly animated by the idea. Rest your head on my chest.

Astrid watched him lie back on the grassy slope. He blinked at her for a few moments, then at last closed his eyes in defeat. She lay down beside him and rested her head on his chest. She felt his breathing stop, then start again. After a short while he put his arms around her shoulder. They lay there in silence, Astrid listening to his heart beat.

I'm on my way to see my younger sister, she said. She's the only person in the world that I can't do without.

Kader laid one hand on her hair and began to sift strands of it through his fingers.

99

She's at home in the village trying to find her boyfriend who's been in prison for twenty years. He was a *liberado*. He got out yesterday.

And he doesn't want to see her, Kader suggested. Astrid heard his voice reverberating in his chest. He thinks he's going to be disappointed, Kader went on. And he's probably right. I was inside, he said. For eighteen months. Even eighteen months fucks with your head, believe me. Man, I thought about her so much – her name was Aurélie – when I saw her in the flesh, it just wasn't as good. She was hot but there was no way she could live up to how I'd thought about her when I was inside. No way.

Astrid realised that there was nothing that this boy could say that would make her judge him. He could not disappoint her, he was simply himself.

She took his hand from her hair and turned it over. She looked at the smooth, brown palm, the long fingers, the thin skin over the joints and the tiny purple veins running beneath. She held the fingers pressed between her two hands but they were slightly vaulted and would not lie flat.

She sat up and looked at the artificial lake, a bronze slick below them. On the horizon she could make out the glowing red sign of the Hotel Mercure against the night and in between lay the dark pine forest, slashed and bound in pale rows.

We should go, she said.

He caught her by the wrist as she moved to stand. She looked at him. His grip was firm but not commanding: she thought of a younger brother, stronger than her only in body. He held on stubbornly. In the moonlight she could see two scars glowing on the top of his scalp. He let her pull free her hand.

How did you get those scars? she asked him.

I don't know how to be with you, he said, looking at her, his face all open suddenly.

Astrid felt a rush of terror at her own sin. She had to be out of the way of his trust. She stood up, and with violent strokes, brushed the blades of grass from her skirt.

Let's go, she said.

Sure, Kader said, keeping his face from her as he rose to his feet, because he knew it was full of doubt.

EIGHTEEN

José Maria Egibar, alias Txema, sat in the orange glow from the dashboard of his Mercedes 4x4. He was waiting for Lorea Molina's banana-yellow Mégane to appear in his rear-view mirror. He examined his face and was as usual disappointed by the blemished skin, the broken veins, the sagging flesh on his neck. He disliked the expression in his eyes, tried as always when he looked in a mirror, to alter it. His eyes had once shone. Now they looked like two holes. The hollowness he knew, was the result of habitual fear. He was determined that he would not live in fear for very much longer.

On first meeting Lorea he had recoiled from the shrill timbre of her voice. Five years later he still recoiled. Even the organisation had sensed the instability in her, knew that it was not the kind they could use, and turned her down on three separate occasions. For this, Txema was grateful. He had seen her zeal, noted her disappointment and understood the opportunities the combination might offer him. Over the years he had fermented Lorea's resentments and carefully guided them towards the greatest danger to himself: Mikel Angel Otegui.

Lorea's car appeared on the bend. He watched her park, then check her make-up in the mirror. Lorea was incapable of ignoring a mirror and so she never lost track of her face. The first sight of that face without make-up had shocked him, not because he found it unattractive but because of the terrible vulnerability he had seen there. Blinking up at him in the harsh daylight coming through the hotel window, she had seemed pinioned. Her dark eyes no longer looked out but submitted to his scrutiny, full of shame. He had let her escape from under him to the safety of the looking glass in the bathroom.

He now watched her lock her car and walk towards him on her high heels. Txema prepared his countenance. He turned on the engine as she reached the passenger door. She climbed up and immediately pulled down the sun visor to reveal the vanity mirror, checked her teeth for lipstick, then reached over and kissed him on the mouth.

So, she said, leaning back against the window so that he could get a good look at her. Are you ready? Shall we do it?

Do what?

Let the cat out of the bag, she said smiling. Her lovely smile, that she could use to great effect, sometimes made him uneasy. Now, at night, in this enclosed space, with this ghoulish light, was such a time.

You're the cat, he said, driving off.

Stop, she said gleefully.

You're my Siamese cat, he said. Clever and elegant.

Oh Txema. He could feel her giving him a longing look. He kept his eyes forward. He had an urge to put an end to this mood.

Where are the letters, then? she asked shrilly.

They're in the glove compartment.

Lorea pulled out the green folder and hugged it. It was a precious package indeed, although it had been easily won. Until February of that year, when he had retired and moved to Baiona, Mikel's lawyer, Gomez Igari, had smuggled his client's letters out of prison for him. He had posted them all for Mikel but not without photocopying them first and giving the copies to Txema, who had convinced Gomez that it was for everyone's good to keep a record of Mikel's correspondence. Thanks to careful insinuation over the years, Gomez had come to believe, like Lorea, that his client was an informer. The letters in the green folder were all addressed to Astrid Arnaga.

Shall I visit Lola in the morning? Lorea asked.

No, he said dryly. We'll watch her first. And wait. He may contact her.

Lorea puffed out air and pulled down the mirror again.

Of course he won't, she said sulkily. He doesn't give a shit about her. I can't wait to wipe that smile off her dolly face, she said, keeping her eyes on her reflection. She now faced Txema. Honestly, what a sheltered life. They're both spoilt, that's their problem.

Txema found Lorea's jealousy of other women more and more distasteful.

I don't agree, he said. They've had hard lives.

But they don't believe in anything, she pleaded.

You don't know that, Lorea. Don't be so quick to judge. He felt her will slacken. We'll wait.

Lorea faced forward sulkily. Txema knew that she was going to bring up her brother again. As they drew near their spot he accelerated.

Are we going to our spot, she asked?

He nodded.

Oh Txema.

He kept his eyes on the road, keeping his pleasure from her. He looked at his watch.

I've got seven minutes, he said.

That's plenty.

As he came off the road he felt her watching him with admiration. He raced through the gap in the hedge, turned left along the dirt track and skidded to a halt beneath the chestnut tree.

He took off his shades.

Just one thing, she said.

Seven minutes, Lorea.

She smiled.

I know. Can't Anxton follow Lola Arnaga? He's good. He's had years of experience on a bike. He needs someone to trust him. He needs to prove himself.

I'll think about it. Then he reached behind her head and pulled her gently towards him. Come on you dirty girl, he said, and she gave a little moan. He saw her eyes close as she sank to his crotch.

This was their pact. This was what held them together. Neither of them liked taking off their clothes, nor were they particularly interested in penetrative sex. After that first night in the hotel there had been an unspoken agreement not to repeat the experience. They both preferred these fleeting encounters. Lorea, he soon discovered was perfectly frigid. Her pleasure seemed to be entirely in her head. She liked being dominated and told that she was filthy, which suited him fine.

Clasping a handful of her hair, he kept one eye on the dark road in his wing mirror because they could come for him at any time. His constant watchfulness did not interfere with his pleasure. He had the gift of being able to be on the outside and the inside at the same time.

Txema waited until the rear lights of Lorea's car had disappeared down the mountain, then he started up the engine and drove up the hill in the opposite direction. Ahead of him a large yellow moon hung oppressively in the sky. He drove past a cluster of modern houses, built in a geometric version of the vernacular that he himself had approved. As he went by, his car triggered the floodlight on the side of one of the houses. He turned into his mother's gravel drive and parked on the concrete ramp that led to the garage door. He turned off the ignition and sat for a moment with the window down. Behind the dusty smell of hydrangeas was a smell of sewage. It was coming from behind the neighbours' row of newly planted spruces. Txema climbed down from his car and stood looking up with hatred at the high wall of conifers. He knew that he could block the planning permission for their swimming pool, at least for a few summers, but this seemed thin compensation for the discomfort of their presence. They had bought the ruined farmhouse behind his mother's villa as well as three hectares of land and there had been nothing he could do about it. It was his great misfortune that the second wife of the Basque Minister of the Interior was from the village and had set her heart on a house here for their retirement. Now of course the minister came up from Vitoria almost every weekend with a brochette of bodyguards. It meant that at the weekends Txema could not risk coming to check on his money.

He walked up the steps and unlocked the front door. He hoped that his mother would be asleep. In his present mood he would not have been able to be kind to her. He stepped into the dark hall. His mother's light was on and the radio was blaring from her bedroom on the first floor. This did not necessarily mean she was awake. She was deaf in one ear and partially deaf in the other and the new quietness of the world frightened her. Even as she slept, either the TV or the radio was left on at full volume. He closed the door behind him and walked up the stairs.

His mother's door was ajar but he did not look in. He continued up the stairs to the attic. He had moved the last of the money here as soon as his mother had become bedridden and there was no chance that she might come upstairs. In prison he had lived in terror of it being found by the organisation or by the Guardia

Civil. Both sides were always roaming the hills in those days, training or scouting for caches. Now that the hills were no longer safe, the organisation hid its weapons in town and trained people in rented flats, which they made soundproof. After his release Txema had moved the money several times to various locations in the hills and each time had involved considerable risk. Today the hills were teeming with health fanatics. You could hide nothing there. Having it here meant that he could come and look at it whenever he liked. And since he had started visiting his invalid mother so regularly his popularity in the village had increased.

But it had been Lorea who had been his saving. When he met her it soon became clear that she would do anything for him. She understood that Txema Egibar was as close as she would ever get to the organisation.

When Txema had told her about the money, she had been overcome with love and gratitude. He had indicated, without ever saying as much, that he was holding it for the organisation. In January 1993 she had driven it all the way to Switzerland, except for a small portion of it which he had decided to keep with him to remind him of his good fortune. She had placed the money in an account in his name. The three days it had taken her to make the trip had been the beginning of Txema's addiction to tranquillisers. His libido had certainly taken a knock since then but he didn't care. The money was safe and not once had Lorea asked him where it came from.

Txema stepped into his mother's attic. It was filled with his father's possessions. She had moved all his stuff up here after his death in 1954 when Txema was ten. His father's guns were here and his clothes, his shoes and his fishing gear, every single magazine he had ever bought and his letters to and from his brother, Txema's Uncle Iñaki, who had been killed by a bull in Pamplona. Txema's mother had thrown nothing away but he knew that it was testimony not of her love but of her indifference that she had not sorted through any of her husband's possessions. Since Txema had started coming here to look at his money, he had developed a new attachment to the memory of his father. He fancied that this attic carried his father's smell, believed that up here he could remember him quite clearly.

What was left of the money was concealed in a trunk beneath

his father's civil war uniform. Txema loved this uniform, its smell of camphor, its weight, its lichen green. It carried a solemn magic for him. Indeed it was the symbol of his father's legitimacy and so of his own. It had guaranteed Txema a place in the world. He lifted it from the trunk, laid it reverently on the floor and pulled out his father's leather satchel. He did not open it straight away but clutched it to his chest and looked at the moon, now as it should be, filling the attic window.

Txema had always believed that he knew Mikel. He was one of those people who never did anything out of character and this, Txema felt, would ultimately be his downfall. He believed that if Mikel were to suspect him of having kept the money, he would not betray him but confront him. It was this confrontation that he had been dreading all these years. That Mikel should now hide from him, that he should elude him in this way, made Txema very uncomfortable. His heart filled with hatred at the memory of Mikel's friendship. He was aware that he hated Mikel the more for having lost him.

He opened the satchel and looked inside. The top notes were a little dirty. The notes beneath were clean and crisp. For Txema the satisfaction brought by these moments was dwindling. He had once felt entirely safe up here with his money, as safe as he had felt on the top shelf of the airing cupboard in his grandmother's house, where he would hide, burying his face in the lavender-scented linen, for hours on end. He would let Lorea go to Lola Arnaga. She had earned it. She could go in the morning while he was at his meeting with the blind man.

NINETEEN

It was past two a.m. and the barman of L'Amiral had locked the doors and stacked all the aluminium chairs and covered the bar with a powerful deterrent in the form of cleaning fluid, but the three men were still drinking. Mikel knew that the barman's name was Jean Louis but the little man to his right had not yet revealed his identity. It had occurred to Mikel more than once that he might be a cop. For some reason, he took the fact that he smoked Lucky Strike as an indication that he was not. At any rate, the man spoke little and Jean Louis did most of the talking while he replenished their glasses with Pastis 51. Jean Louis was having problems with a wife who was, he believed, too attractive for him. Cidalia, her name was and she was Portuguese. Mikel also knew that she had a tattoo of a dolphin on her hip. Jean Louis had pulled up his shirt and revealed a voluminous white belly in an attempt to show the exact spot. Mikel wanted to tell Jean Louis to stop believing the girl was his superior, that here lay the root of all his problems, but he was too drunk to find the words. By the time Jean Louis was ready to leave, Mikel was so far gone, he needed both men's help to walk.

They went out through the back door of the café. Outside in the street the smell of jasmine hung in the air and Mikel found him-self on the verge of tears again.

He tried to hold out his hand.

Mikel Angel Ortega. Pleased to meet you.

Jean Louis held on tightly.

You're all right, he said. I don't usually get on with Basques. They're too touchy. But you're all right.

Mikel tried to grab the little man's hand but he was too busy holding him up. In spite of the fact that he was half Jean Louis's size, he seemed to be carrying all the weight. Mikel could not seem to make use of his feet, which were trailing along behind him.

I'll call you Monsieur Lucky, if I may, he said. Monsieur Lucky or Monsieur Strike. Which do you prefer? You're very strong for a man of your stature. Here! he shouted suddenly. Leave me here. This is good.

He wanted to sleep on the bandstand.

But Monsieur Lucky was objecting.

I have to sleep here, friend, Mikel explained. Just leave me here.

The little man was holding out something in his hand but Mikel could not focus. He noticed that he smelt strongly of fish. He must, Mikel thought, be a fisherman. Then he sank to his knees.

When he woke up it was still dark and he was still drunk and there was a large ginger cat lying on his feet. He looked at the cat and the cat looked at him. Mikel did not want to move because the cat was keeping his feet warm.

I wanted a dog, he said out loud.

At this the cat got up, stretched itself and walked off.

No! Mikel tried to coax it back but the cat broke into a trot and disappeared into the night.

Mikel was more or less dead centre of the bandstand. His head was still spinning. He lay back and closed his eyes. The fantasy, to take Astrid into his arms on the night train to Paris, now seemed hollow. She had been to see him only once and they had not made love. He had run his hands over her body, compulsively, as though he were indulging in some complex scanning process for his memory. And indeed he had become dependent on that memory, her body under his hands, running beneath the sliding material of that green dress, and of her smell, that sometimes came to him at night, so powerfully that it woke him up. They had not made love during her visit, though the 'facility', as the authorities referred to the video-monitored coupling, was available to him. Mikel had wanted to wait until he was a free man. When she never returned he had cursed himself for having been so sentimental.

For some reason the sight of that ginger cat walking away had brought home to Mikel the fact that Astrid's visit had been an act of compassion directed not at him but at a human being deprived of his liberty. She was a woman of infinite compassion but she could no more love him than Jesus Christ could have loved Mary Magdalene.

TWENTY

Astrid looked at Kader's sleeping back. From the doorway she could see it rise and fall with his breath. She looked at the smooth, golden skin and the purple shadow made by the deep indentation of his spine. She looked at the back of his head. His face was turned to the window and she could see the hairline tapering into a V at the base of his neck. A brownish light from the lamps in the car park cast warmth over the dreary room with its white textured walls and its grey carpet that reeked of household insecticide. She hesitated at the open door, put down her bag, took out the disinfectant, four compresses and a roll of sticking plaster for his wound and set them on top of the TV at the end of the bed. Then, without looking back, she picked up her bag and left the room.

In the reception she pressed an electric bell that buzzed intermittently until the door behind the reception desk opened and a middle-aged man with an ashen face stood blinking sleepily at her while she explained that she wished to pay the bill for rooms 201 and 203. When she stepped out into the night, she found she was a little breathless. She stood for a moment facing the parked cars. The breeze was warm and smelt of lavender. Then she crossed the car park, grateful for the purposeful sound of her heels on the tarmac.

At the gate Astrid was forced to press the intercom and rouse the man a second time. He did not answer when she apologised but simply raised the barrier and hung up.

As she drove out through the gates she looked ahead at the sky turning pink on the rim and at the black lake set in its pale valley. She held her eyes wide open, letting them absorb the beauty of the world. The warmth spreading in her chest was gratitude. That boy had stepped into the stale room of her life and made her see its contours, shown her how ugly it was and how urgently she must leave it. She pulled out onto the motorway and accelerated hard.

The night before they had had dinner in the hotel dining room. He had told her, leaning forward confidingly, that he had never been anywhere this smart before and Astrid had let herself become infected with his delight, had felt laughter gathering inside her as she watched him tease the waiter, a pompous, jowly old man with dyed, auburn hair.

But then she had said joylessly:

We're not going to have sex, Kader.

And he had looked up at her and given her a dull, unseeing look and gone back to spearing his chips:

I can wait, he had told her.

After dinner they had gone upstairs and he had hovered beside her as she opened the door to her room.

Let me come in. I won't jump you, he had told her. Promise, he had said, lying his hand on his heart. And she had let him in because she found to her dismay that she did not want to be alone. He had sat on her bed watching loud TV while she changed into her nightdress in the bathroom. As she climbed into bed, he had averted his eyes.

She was on the dual carriageway that cut through the vast pine forest of Les Landes. She would have liked to show Kader the magnificent beach that swept unbroken from Bordeaux to Bayonne. He would have enjoyed the German bunkers dotted along the sand dunes. He would have marvelled at their indestructibility. She considered her meeting with Kader, saw how quickly and securely he had become woven into her life. In just twenty-four hours they seemed to have acquired a past. She remembered why she had for so long put up a wall between herself and other people.

Kader had asked her if he could hold her again and she had said, No. And he had not pushed it but nor had he moved from his place on the bed beside her.

She had told him that she wanted to work and he had immediately turned off the TV and lain there with his arms folded across his chest.

I'll watch over you, he had said.

And Astrid had not chased him away. Instead she had found herself working beside him, drafting a letter to the *Lancet* about the Council of Europe's recent stand on primate organ donors.

She had been improbably happy then, with Kader falling asleep fully clothed beside her.

He must have woken in the middle of the night and taken off his clothes and climbed into bed beside her. She had slept through it all. In the morning his skin gave off a warm, faintly rubbery smell. She knew that it was partly the act of tearing herself away from the pleasure of this presence beside her, the old habit of renunciation that had goaded her and filled her with this heady power. Now she drove fast. The accelerator was on the floor and the steering wheel was vibrating in her hands.

She pulled into a service station. As the attendant wiped clean her windscreen, she blocked her nose against the smell of petrol. Her father had driven an old, pale-blue Simca, which must have had a leaking petrol cap. No other smell, no other thought or sensation brought her father to mind like the smell of petrol.

The tables beside the coffee machines were at elbow height. She stood opposite two French truckies and drank scalding coffee from a plastic cup going soft under her fingers.

She plucked her ringing phone from her bag.

Yes?

Astrid?

It was Chastel.

Let's get out of here, the wiry man was saying to the tall truckie. If there's one thing I hate, it's listening to people talking on their fucking mobile phones.

She thought that he must be on speed. The tall truckie smiled apologetically at her, then followed the wiry man out of the shop.

I'm sorry, Jacques. I can't talk to you now. I've got to get on. Lola's waiting for me.

I'm calling to tell you about an offer of a posting in Kosovo, Chastel said. Jean thought of you. If you want it you just have to say the word. It occurred to me that I might be holding you back. That you might . . .

You're not holding me back and I have no desire to go to Kosovo.

Why not?

Because I hate those people.

Which people? The Albanians?

No. The Medecins sans Frontières people.

111

May I ask why?

I hate their self-righteousness. They're all overgrown adolescents trying to hide their disappointment. They depress me.

Surely all that is beside the point. They need surgeons.

Who needs surgeons? The refugees? They don't need surgeons. They need to go home.

Obviously, but . . .

It's as simple as that. The refugees need to go home and they're being held hostage by a group of self-righteous bourgeois intellectuals wanting to feel . . . human. The problem is that 'humanitarian' is not human.

Astrid, I think you're burnt out.

Of course I'm burnt out. Why? You don't think you're burnt out? I haven't seen the smallest spark of genuine enthusiasm in you for years. When I think about it, you were already burnt out when I met you. That's why you latched onto me. Because I was young and full of faith and enthusiasm.

Why are you so aggressive? Where's this coming from?

I *am* burnt out, Jacques but at least I know it. I've spent the past year and a half in an impasse. Not because of bad science but because I can't get the most rudimentary equipment. When it comes to my own research there's no money and no equipment. This I have learned.

Come on Astrid, you know I fight for your research.

You don't. You fight for me when I'm doing *your* research.

That's not fair.

I have spent nearly two years trying to build a machine that already exists on the market. Vincent and I have lost thousands of rats just because we can't get the pump to work properly. The blood levels fluctuate and the animal dies.

I did suggest you use bigger animals.

Like what?

I told you the people from the Natural History Museum would let you have some of their primates.

They're SIV-positive, for God's sake!

Not all of them.

Listen Jacques, I'm not asking for anything. I've accepted the idea that I'm basically a plumber. Transplantation is plumbing for me now. And I accept that. But don't ask me to play at science.

I won't research this conference for you. I don't subscribe to your ideas any more. I hardly believe in my own but I definitely don't believe in yours.

You're quite bitter. It's terrifying.

He sounded terrified.

Yes, she said softly. Because I think I've wasted my time.

Why? Why have you wasted your time? Without me . . .

Don't! she shouted. Don't even *try* to say that. It makes me sick. How dare you? I had a good head and boundless energy.

You did and we've done some remarkable things together . . .

We aborted a child.

She stopped, as appalled as he was.

She heard the silence and in the silence hung his hatred.

Today that's all I can remember, she went on.

But he had gone.

Astrid looked about her uneasily. But no one had appeared to notice her. The shop seemed unnaturally quiet. A woman sitting behind the till was peering at a large transparent egg filled with small, multicoloured eggs and trying to work out how to open it. A man in a tan leather jacket with epaulettes was hovering in the pornography section. Astrid swallowed. Her mouth was dry and she was perspiring. She wanted to leave but was not sure that she could reach the door. Walking had suddenly become unfeasible. She had evoked the child. For the first time she had thought, not of the act of abortion but of the child itself. Now it felt as though a great dam inside her was breaking. She did not know where to go. She had lied: Lola was not waiting for her. She had not called. Perhaps she had found Mikel. Astrid looked at the lino floor, glowing in the sunshine. She began to cross it, unsteadily, one foot in front of the other.

TWENTY-ONE

Painfully thin was an English expression that Lola knew from her mother who, whenever she used it, always wore a look of impatience rather than compassion. Painfully thin was what her mother had become and Lola found that she now felt the same exasperation. As she lifted the tray from her mother's lap, she inwardly recoiled from the thought of the birdlike legs beneath the covers, their swollen knees and their scaly skin.

You haven't eaten any of it, Mummy.

Lola looked down at the greenish soup she had made from a packet, at the plain yogurt and the glass of water, and saw how unappetising it was.

What would you like? Is there anything you really feel like?

There was always a delay in her mother's response these days, as if she had to drag herself away from a more alluring world.

Mummy?

At last her mother looked at her and gave her one of her closed-mouth smiles.What? Lola asked. Tell me.

But her eagerness triggered some alarm for her mother retreated to wherever it was that she went.

Lola put the tray down on the upholstered bench at the foot of the bed. Then she went and sat down beside her mother and gently held her forward with one hand, rearranging the pillows with the other. As she did so, she caught the sickly smell of her mother's body, like rancid butter. She helped her mother lie back against the big, square pillows.

Can I help you have a bath, Mummy?

Her mother began to smooth the bedclothes with her hands, meticulously taking out all the folds until her legs were encased in a perfect cloth sarcophagus. Lola took this as a sign of displeasure. She waited until her mother had finished, then picked up her hands and held them. She looked down at the purple veins that ran so close to the surface of the pearly skin.

Mummy?

114

But Margot Hamilton Arnaga was stubborn. If she wanted to answer, she would. Lola knew there was no point in goading her. She held her mother's hands and watched the pendulum of the carriage clock on the chest of drawers, swinging back and forth. Lola had always disliked her mother's things. Now that she had lost her mind, they seemed gloomier than ever.

The greatest shock to Lola this time had been the sight of her mother so physically diminished. Margot Hamilton had always been tall. She had towered over her husband and both her daughters. Lola saw her as a young woman again, during that interlude of happiness before Josu's death. She pictured her standing in the window of the dining room of this house, arranging purple flowers in a vase. It was early summer so they must have been lilacs. Her mother smoked cheroots in those days that Angus would have sent to her from somewhere exotic. They came in small boxes of blanched wood that she and Astrid would fight over. That vision of her mother silhouetted against the window, arranging the lilac branches, a cheroot between her teeth and smoke hanging about her head like a veil, had stayed with her ever since. She remembered standing in the doorway absorbing what she saw, overcome with joy at the idea that she too would be beautiful. In the end dancing had become her way of overcoming the shortfalls of her physique, an attempt to achieve in motion the grace that her mother achieved standing still.

What's the joke, Beatrice? her mother asked.

Lola had never recognised herself in her real name. Lola was the name Astrid had given her as soon as her mother had brought her back from the hospital. Everyone except her mother had always called her Lola.

Nothing, she said.

Where's Astrid? Margot asked suddenly.

She's in Paris. Working. She has an important conference to prepare . . .

Lovely girl, the old woman mused. Such difficult hair, though.

I was always jealous of it, Lola said.

I gave a lock of my hair to Josu before he left for Madagascar, Margot said. He insists on carrying it with him always.

Lola smiled.

You know, I do think I'll have a spot of smoked salmon.

Knowing that there was no smoked salmon in the house but relieved for the excuse to leave, Lola stood up.

I'll go and see if I can find you some.

Lola left her mother looking at a copy of *Paris Match*, dated April 1967. It was one of her favourites because of the photographs in it of Princess Grace of Monaco at the Cannes film festival wearing a black-and-white Dior dress. Lola wondered at the multiple faces of her mother's lunacy; a fascination for the Grimaldi family being the most recent.

Lola hated the kitchen of this house. It had been decorated by her mother in the early seventies and the driving principle at the time had been, in her mother's words, 'gay'. For Lola, the result was the opposite of gaiety, just as *The Sound of Music* was the opposite of gaiety. This kitchen with its varnished pine and its frilly red-and-white checked upholstery, from the small check of the 'Vichy' curtains to the large check of the gingham tablecloth, had for some reason always reminded her of Nazis. When she brought Mikel to live here, the first thing she would do would be to change the kitchen.

Lola looked in the fridge. The smell of rotting cheese wafted out. She registered the contents: a jar of pâté, three white eggs wrapped in a red-and-white checked tea towel, a piece of Brie congealed on a plate. What did that woman Gachucha do for two hours every day? Perhaps she could ask her to clean the fridge. Lola shut the door. She wished Astrid were there to fill the fridge with proper food and cook meals.

Lola sat down at the kitchen table and pressed the heels of her hands into her eye sockets. She tried to think of Mikel as he would look now, but could only see his face as it had been when he went to prison, without the deep vertical lines cut into his cheeks, the thin mouth, the dark shadows under his eyes. Last time she had seen him she reached out to run her fingers through his wiry hair and he had caught her gently by the wrist and smiled at her.

I'm an old man, he had said.

I like the grey.

Don't.

Don't what?

But he had let go of her hand and folded his arms and looked

116

at her as he sometimes did, with a benign detachment that made her want to cry. She knew better than to press him for an explanation.

Lola held her hands clamped to her eyes. She found herself inwardly calling for Astrid again, as if Astrid could help her this time.

She stood up suddenly to dispel her thoughts. She held her head straight, fixing her gaze on one of the tiles on the wall above the sink, red and white of course, with a cherry motif. She raised her arms, holding her elbows a little higher than her hands, letting her fingers curl and open, curl and open, with the slow movement of seaweed in the tide. And then she began to move from the waist down. Keeping her head and chest perfectly still, she moved, and the motion began with the gentle step and kick of her feet, flowed into the more complex roll of her knees and thighs and fed the ripple of her hips and back and arse.

While Lola danced she saw Astrid's face as she sat in the box listening to the verdict. Lola knew before the judge said it that Astrid was going to prison. Everyone in the courtroom seemed to know, not so much from a logical appraisal of the trial but from the expression on Astrid's face, which wore the resignation of a martyr. Lola had looked at her big sister, sitting about four paces away from her in the raised box. She looked at the pale cheeks, the calm black eyes, and the dark brows drawn on so beautifully that Lola would often run her fingers along them in wonderment. It was such a lovely face, but so intended for sadness that when the verdict came and Astrid was sentenced to five years in prison and through Lola's fault, it felt, in so many ways, right. As Astrid was led from the courtroom, she had looked back at Lola and her look had been one of anxiety, not for herself but for Lola, whom she was leaving behind. It was the same look Astrid would give her when she dropped her off at kindergarten. And Lola had cried, because the sight of Astrid's solicitude made her feel vulnerable and not because Astrid was going to prison instead of her.

Lola went on dancing until she could feel the sweat dripping between her breasts. The moment she stopped moving, all the grace vanished. She was human again, subject to the laws of gravity and decay. She went to the kitchen door, unlocked it and stepped out into the evening. She walked along the stone path that ran beside the old kitchen garden, past her mother's seat that overlooked the hills, now covered over with brambles. There was nothing left of the vegetable garden now but the ragged, knee-high box hedge that had framed it. The smell of it reminded her of Josu who had planted rows and rows of it around all her mother's flower beds. Lola hated Josu for what he had done. His death had ruined her mother and this place. She believed that only her own child could chase him away.

The latch on the gate had rusted and would not lift. Lola grazed her knuckles trying to force it. Clutching her bleeding hand, she gave up and walked round to the gap in the hydrangeas. Her mother had once sprinkled slate dust at their feet to turn them blue but they had reverted back to an ugly pink. As she stepped through, a bramble caught her on the thigh, tearing her skin.

Lola found Paco at the bar of Txema's café. She relaxed when she was sure that Txema would not appear.

He's in Donostia tonight, Paco said.

How do you know?

Everyone always knows what Txema is doing. Well, up to a point.

He raised his glass.

To your return. He took a sip, keeping his eyes on her. What will you have?

He ordered her a beer and they went to sit down.

The café was empty but for two young boys, playing pinball in the corner.

They're Txema's nephews, Paco told her. They're always in here. Pain in the arse, both of them.

Lola looked at the boys. Both had the same haircut: dark, shiny helmets. The younger must have been about ten. In the elder one's stoop, his dog eyes, was the shame of puberty. He slammed his groin angrily into the machine, then stepped aside to let his brother have his turn.

How did Txema afford to buy this place?

He exports Basque linen into Argentina, Paco said, raising his eyebrows.

Is that lucrative? Lola asked.

Must be. He has an expensive mistress and a four-wheel drive Mercedes.

What are you saying, Paco? Is he corrupt?

Paco raised his glass again.

Is Txema corrupt, Paco?

Paco leaned back in his chair.

Some people think he gets money from the organisation but I don't believe that for one minute. You know how badly they pay their people.

That way they know you aren't doing it for the money, Lola said.

Paco laid his big hands on the table.

Have you been running? Paco asked. Your cheeks are flushed.

Dancing, she said.

Lovely.

He peered into his beer, then took a gulp.

I can't stay long, she told him.

Of course not. His cheeks flushed.

It's because Mum's alone. I let Gachucha go early. Lola smoothed out the creases in her lap. I need your help, Paco. I asked Txema to help me find Mikel but he refused. He said he thought Mikel needed time. He said that he had nothing to give me. She paused. Paco kept a respectful silence. I think he might be in France. He wouldn't leave Euskadi. Do you know anyone he might go to for work?

Paco leaned back. The chair creaked under him. He looked towards the bar, caught the attention of the barman and pointed to his empty glass.

Another? he asked her.

Lola was sucking on her bleeding knuckles. She shook her head.

I'll ask a driver I know on the other side. He has a friend who used to help refugees find housing.

Oh, Paco. Thank you.

Don't look so sorry for me, Lola. Lola looked down. I'm your friend, he said.

I know you are, she said, looking up at him.

She sat with him while he drank his beer. She watched the big hand on the glass. He had the broad, sketchy hands of a simple man. She wished that she could have loved someone like Paco.

Don't you want to have kids, Paco?

119

Of course.

Maïté would have made a good mother.

No doubt.

His black eyes were shining. For the first time, Lola saw anger there. She knew not to apologise. She stood up.

I'll wait at Mum's.

I'll come after my shift. Around six.

Lola held out her hand. He pressed it to his lips, keeping his eyes on her.

I'm solid, Lola. Don't start being careful with me now.

Lola smiled.

Thank you, Paco.

As she walked out, the two boys burst into laughter. On the steps of the café she swept her hand over her arse. She had torn her dress in the hydrangeas and her knickers were showing.

TWENTY-TWO

Kader did not need to turn to look. He could feel her absence like a draught at his back. He sat up in bed, feeling the dark, empty room pressing up against him. He climbed out of bed and opened the curtains. The sun had already been doing its thing for some time and the blue sky was like an insult. He turned his back on the window and stood staring across the bed at the empty cupboard where she had hung her dress the night before. He suddenly disliked the feeling of the carpet against the soles of his feet so he went and sat down on the end of the bed facing the TV. He looked at the bandages she had left for him, reached out and picked up the bottle of pink disinfectant, then put it back. He sat there for a long time, picking his way aimlessly through his thoughts like the delinquent that he was. She had run away. She had a life; it was not her business that he didn't. He had tried to hijack her life and it had not worked. Now he was worse off than he had been before. He had thought that losing El Niño was the low point. It was nothing compared to this.

Kader turned on the TV and watched a Japanese cartoon about a teenage rock band that caught criminals. He then switched to MTV France. He sat there in his underpants, clutching his bandage, and watched three songs in a row. The last one was shot in a motorway tunnel filled with cars. Three black kids were climbing over the cars and singing US rap. Amadou could sing rap. His voice was soft and strong at the same time. He was as good as anyone Kader had ever heard. He had been in a band until Hocine, the only decent musician, had been sent down for car theft. Without Hocine Amadou had been unable to hold the other three together. Amadou was too gentle. They needed a thug like Hocine to make them get out of bed in the mornings.

Kader stood up and went to the telephone on the wall by the bed. He looked at it for a moment and picked it up. He dialled Amadou's number three times without success, then he saw the instructions on a card standing on the night table. Dial zero for outside calls. Amadou answered.

Kader, my old friend. It's you. I thought you'd died.

Kader smiled.

I did. I'm calling you from Heaven. It's called the Hotel Mercure.

No shit.

I spent the night with this woman. She's forty-two.

Amadou sucked air in through his teeth.

You want to explain?

I passed out by the side of the road. Fabien had a knife and I got cut. Not badly but I lost some blood. This woman picked me up in her Volvo. And now we have this. He hesitated. This relationship. I can't explain it, Amadou, but she is it. That's all I know.

There was no answer.

You still there Amadou?

Cool, Amadou said.

Yeah, but she left without me. I woke up and she was gone. Her, her doctor's bag and her Volvo.

You boned a doctor?

She's a surgeon. She's beautiful and I don't use that word lightly. She's Spanish. You've never breathed the same air as a woman like this, Amadou. I swear man.

But she's gone and you're left there like a wanker.

She's gone to see her sister whose boyfriend just got out of prison for murder.

Oh man, Amadou whined.

I'm gone, Amadou. You know what it's like.

Kader heard Amadou suck on his teeth.

Shit Kader. You found trouble.

This is no trouble, Amadou. This is the answer.

You have a plan?

I have a plan. I'm out of here as soon as I put down this phone. I'm going to find her.

You're going to find her.

Amadou liked to repeat what you said and then nod.

I want this woman, Amadou. We didn't fuck. And I swear I didn't care. I want to look after her.

I know how that feels.

I'm going to Spain.

You got no passport, man. You can't go to Spain.

Shit. Kader looked around the room. He did not have a solution to this particular problem but he knew he had to get out of this room. I'll think of something. I'll call you when I get to Spain. How's Aisha?

She's OK. She ate with your mum and dad last night. We had a chat outside the launderette. She told me to stop smoking. She put her hand on my cheek. I haven't touched a joint since.

Kader smiled.

You sucker.

Yeah.

I'll call you.

Yeah.

See you.

See you.

Kader put on a clean, white T-shirt under his tracksuit, put Amadou's Discman in his pocket and the earphones around his neck. He threw the stuff she had left for his arm into his Adidas bag, glanced once at the bed they had shared and closed the door behind him. In the corridor a woman was pushing a squeaking trolley full of cleaning equipment. Kader thought of his mum and smiled at her but the woman just gave him a mean look and walked on.

Old witch, Kader said.

The squeaking stopped but Kader kept walking and disappeared round the corner.

It was hot outside. The tarmac stuck to the soles of his trainers. He walked to the sound of Joey Star growling his anger into his ears:

Seine Saint Denis is down. Put on your bulletproof vests, he bellowed. But Kader looked at the smug blue sky and the motorway curling elegantly away in the distance and at the efficient traffic flowing one way and the other and all the chaos held so firmly at bay and he thought, Joey Star can growl all he likes, nothing is going to fall in this country: no Seine Saint Denis and no Bastille.

Kader had no watch but he had listened to one and a half CDs by the time he reached the Total petrol station. He had five hundred francs in his wallet and a bank card that would be able to access one thousand, seven hundred more as soon as Amadou had paid in his half of the money from the fake Chanel T-shirts they had sold to Khaled. The old man was pissed off because he couldn't shift them. They were still in cellophane in a sports bag under the bar of his stinking café. Kader knew when he had handed them over that the market for fake Chanel had come and gone. Girls wanted real brands now. Poor Khaled; his wife never got behind him on any of his deals. She never stops criticising me, he would say. Is that what a man needs from his wife? The woman did have insight, though. She would tell people: If Khaled had to buy a mule, he'd pick a donkey.

Kader bought himself a hot dog and a can of Coke and went and sat down on the steps of the garage shop. He watched the trucks coming in. He watched the truckies climb down from their stinking cabins with all their swinging toys, rub their big bellies and shake out their little legs. Some of them eyed him as they approached the shop, others ignored him. When he had finished his hot dog he went to have a piss and clean up. He brushed his teeth and washed his hands and face, then he set the disinfectant and the clean dressings beside the sink and carefully unpeeled his bandage. The wound was sealed with a ridge of blood and orange pus that looked like dried caramel. Kader stared at it. On either side of the ridge, the skin was purple but he thought it looked better. He dabbed the pink disinfectant on the wound, covered it with a square of gauze and then tried to reapply the bandage, but found he could not do it with one hand. He tried to hold the end of the bandage between his teeth but it was a mess.

Do us a favour, man. Hold this down for me, will you?

He was talking to a middle-aged man in a cherry-coloured blazer who was just putting his dick back into his trousers. The man looked up, startled.

I'm sorry?

The bandage. Can you hold it down for me?

The man smiled with relief. He had grey hair that stuck up in a brush on the top of his head and a pink, piggish face.

Do you speak French? Kader asked loudly.

Yes, he said. I am Polish but I speak. I am here with my mother. We are making a tour with camping car.

That's great. Could you just hold this here so I can make this bandage?

The man stepped forward and held out his hands as if for inspection.

I wash first. Yes?

Yes. Good idea.

The Pole did a fine job with the bandage and when they stepped out of the gents, Kader had a lift.

He bought some chocolate for the road and a copy of *France Football* that had a picture of Marcel Desailly standing beside one of those red telephone boxes they have in England. The inside of the Polish camper van was upholstered in brown carpet. It covered the walls and the floor and the roof. Kader sat on the bench seat between the Pole and his mother, Katya, who smiled and nodded at him as if his arrival had been preordained. Behind them in the living compartment was a small, dirty white poodle, who blinked patiently when it was knocked off its feet by the movement of the van.

Kader tried to read 'My Life in London' by Marcel Desailly, but the Pole was eager to talk.

My name is Piotr, he said. But you can call me Pierre.

Kader raised his head from the football magazine.

Great. He looked at the road ahead of them. The traffic was slow. How much further to the Spanish border, Pierre?

I must drop you before that. We will spend the night in the town of Bayonne. There is a festival there. My mother and I would like to see it. We would be happy if you will join us.

Thanks Pierre, but I can't hang around. I have to get to Spain.

You have family there?

No. No family. Kader watched the pine trees, flashing past in rows. A woman, he said.

Pierre glanced at him, then turned back to the road.

Good, he said. Excellent. Very good. Pierre was clearly over the moon. You're a romantic. This is fantastic. No? He turned to his mother. Mama, he said and then started gabbling at her in Polish. Katya just kept on nodding and smiling at Kader, as though whatever it was that her son was telling her, she already knew. By the end of his account, Pierre seemed to be weeping for joy. A romantic, he said wiping his eyes. Oh dear, that is excellent.

By now Kader was eager to get out of the Polish experience. It was only twenty kilometres to Bayonne.

I tell you what, Pierre. Leave us at the next service station, will you? It's easier to get a lift.

You don't want to come with us to Bayonne?

A service station's better for me. It's easier.

Whatever you wish.

Kader offered him some chocolate but he declined. Katya accepted and Pierre slipped into a sulk. He did not say a word until they reached a Shell garage just short of Bayonne.

Katya waved and smiled at Kader when it was time to say goodbye. As she was sitting right next to him, he found it hard to keep a straight face.

Bye then, Katya, he said, patting her on the arm. Then he climbed out of the van after Pierre. Pierre had taken off his red blazer. He was wearing a yellow, short-sleeved shirt. His arms were white as dough. Kader shook his hand, eager to get away. But Pierre gripped his hand, too tightly for Kader's taste, and then, to his horror, held on.

See you, Pierre. Thanks for the lift.

He patted Pierre on the arm but he still did not let go. He seemed to be trying to say something.

Let go, man, Kader said, trying to keep his tone light.

But Pierre gripped harder.

Shit. What are you on?

Kader yanked his hand free of the man's grasp and jumped back. Pierre swiped weakly at the air. Kader turned and sauntered towards the cafeteria. He did not look back until he was inside: there was Pierre standing in the same spot looking slack, as if someone had pulled out the iron rod that had held him straight. Kader could see his mother, a big, dark shape, waiting in the van.

Kader stepped through the sliding doors into the cafeteria. He knew he had not been at risk and yet he was shaken. He stood a moment by the doors and watched the van drive away.

Fuck me, he said aloud. What a weirdo.

Kader waited for the length of three CDs in the service station. He turned down three offers of a lift, all given by lone men. He did not want to get stuck with another desperate fucker. At two in the afternoon, a convoy of four circus trucks pulled into the parking lot. A group of about thirty people climbed out of the trucks and sauntered towards the cafeteria to have lunch. Kader was sitting at the table closest to the sliding doors, doing the football cross-word in his magazine. There was a plate in front of him. On it were the remains of the dish of the day: *osso bucco* and pasta shells. He watched the circus people queue for their food. They were noisy and, if he was not mistaken, Spanish. His attention was drawn to a couple standing quietly in the queue. He was very tall and his bare arms were covered down to the knuckles in elaborate, oriental patterns. She was small and slight. Her blonde hair was cut short and she was wearing a grey mackintosh. Kader thought she looked like a young boy except that she was wearing bright-red, high-heeled shoes. Although they didn't talk to each other, it was obvious from the way their bodies tilted very slight-ly towards each other that they were a couple. Kader waited for them to take their food to a table. When they had sat down he went over.

Do you speak French?

Both of them considered him for an uncomfortably long time before giving an answer. This was not a good start. At last the man answered while the girl went back to her food. They had both chosen the dish of the day, except, Kader noted jealously, they had chips instead of pasta.

We speak French, the man said.

Good. That's good. I was wondering if you could give me a lift to Spain.

Sure.

The man tucked into the food as though the matter were settled.

There's just a slight problem.

The man did not look up. He was now eating voraciously, they both were. The girl was tearing off lumps of bread, mopping up the sauce with them and stuffing them as fast as she could into her mouth.

I don't have a passport.

Do you have French I.D.? the man asked with his mouth full.

Yes.

Then you don't need a passport.

How come?

Kader was beginning to resent the fact that the man would not look at him.

Spain is in Europe, the man said.

Kader nodded, nonplussed. He pointed at his table.

I'll be over there, when you're ready.

Where in Spain do you want to go?

San something. He couldn't remember the name of the place.

San Sebastian.

Kader pointed at him.

That's it.

It's our next stop.

Kader waited a moment in case the man should decide to look up. He watched the gobbling couple a moment, then wandered back to his table. He dreaded to think how they fucked.

Kader ended up on his own with René, the man with the tattoos. The girl went in the truck behind. René was a knife-thrower and the girl was what he threw his knives at. He had a little dog who pulled the knives out of the board with his teeth. Its body was white and it had brown markings on its face like a mask. The dog growled at Kader as soon as he climbed into the truck. René kept the dog at his feet, just in front of the pedals.

All I ask, René told him, is that you don't catch his eye.

Kader glanced down at the dog.

Why?

Just don't or he'll attack.

Kader grinned.

You're kidding.

I'm not.

Cool.

Kader settled into his seat. He knew René was not going to hit on him and he was happy: soon he would be in Spain. Kader looked at the designs on René's arms, which seemed to depict trees with tits. He found them quite beautiful.

How did you get into knife throwing?

My uncle. He runs this circus. He taught me in secret. I've been doing it since I was a kid but always in secret because my mother was against it. When she died, I left my job and joined my uncle.

What was your job?

Security.

Where?

Bordeaux. Malls, mostly.

Shit job, Kader said. I've done it.

Not for nineteen years, you haven't.

No fucking way. I walked out after a week. I got a great job after that, opening oysters in a fancy restaurant in Paris. I worked with an old man from Brittany called Yann. He was a racist cunt but he loved me. He was sad to see me go.

Why did you go?

I got into a fight with a client.

René shook his head.

No. No, no. Kader held up his hand. Just listen. The man walks out of the restaurant with his wife. I swear his wife walks past me and gives me this look so full of sex it makes me blush to think of it. Frankly, it was indecent. Then this short-arse starts insulting me, using words of four syllables just to say: do us a favour, stop hitting on my woman. If he'd been polite I would have raised my hands above my head but he was a pain in the arse. Old Raoul down there reminds me of him a little bit, I have to say: short and touchy. Anyway I told him it wasn't my fault if his bitch was trouble and he called the manager. He was a regular, so that was that.

I avoid trouble, René said after a long silence. If I get into trouble, someone gets hurt.

Kader could tell this was no boast.

Have you ever stabbed the girl?

Carla? No. I caught the girl before her, just here. He pinched the flesh of his armpit.

Kader winced.

She was fine. But I had to let her go. When you've hit someone once, it's for a reason. It's too easy to do it again. Carla is unique. She has a technique when we're working that took me by surprise. When I first threw with her I could feel her wanting me to hit her, *willing* me. When you concentrate hard enough you can pick up on things like that.

She sick, or what?

No. Just a bit numb. René paused. She's had a hard time.

Raoul was growling again. Kader looked down and the dog showed its teeth.

She's all right now, René went on. She still tries to get me to hit her but that's the game. It's a battle of wills.

Are you two? A couple?

René looked at him.

A couple?

Yeah. You know. Do you love her?

We're not a couple. And I love her.

What does that mean?

Carla is alone, René said. She always has been. Any man who's been stupid enough to try and harness her to him in any way, got bitten – hard. Luckily I like her the way she is, so she lets me get close.

Man, you're surrounded by things that bite.

René smiled.

I am, he said.

Kader folded his arms and watched the road ahead of them. A road from this height was a beautiful thing, especially on a day like this. He liked this journey and he liked his goal. This new sense that he was in the right place and doing the right thing made him want to sing. So he sang. It was a song Khaled sang called 'Bakhta':

Bakhta is the light of Oran, he sang. *Her beauty burns me like the sun.*

His mother loved the song because it had an old-fashioned melody. He could tell from the way René was listening that he was enjoying it too.

Kader woke to find himself alone in the truck. He could tell from the light that it was late afternoon. The sound of people shouting came through the open window. His wounded arm was aching. He sat up and looked out. They were on a wide, flat piece of land about the size of a football stadium. On one side was a flyover thick with traffic, and on the other was a railway line. The circus people were grouped together about fifty metres away. It felt like a fight. Kader climbed out and began to walk towards them. He could see René towering above everyone. He was shouting in

Spanish. On the breeze he could smell something sickly like rotting vegetables. He looked about him and saw a mountain of multicoloured rubbish beneath the flyover straight ahead of him. As he drew near the group, Kader stopped. Two men in uniform were facing the group. They were wearing strange-looking uniforms with red berets tilted at a stupid angle on their heads and white holsters for their weapons. They may have looked like toy soldiers but there was no doubt they were cops and whatever the discussion, their answer was No. Kader decided it would be better for him not to get involved. He turned and walked idly back to the truck. Within seconds Kader heard the dog's strangely womanish growl. He spun round to kick out but it was too late. The dog's teeth clamped down on his heel. A fierce pain shot up his leg. He felt his balls contract and for a moment he was completely blind. He heard himself cry out. The smell of refuse was making him feel sick. His sight returned as René was prising open Raoul's jaws. Kader thought he saw the dog resisting, saw its bared incisors, saw the blood seeping through his white sock.

I didn't look at him, he moaned. I didn't even look at the bastard.

TWENTY-THREE

Mikel stood in the entrance, half in and half out of the shop. The shop smelt strongly of bait. Monsieur Lucky was serving a fat man with a dagger dripping blood tattooed on his fleshy arm. The man was wearing a short-sleeved shirt with a Hawaiian pattern on it. His dark hair was shoulder-length and greasy. He bought a reel of nylon thread and a box of hooks. Monsieur Lucky had seen Mikel but gave no sign of recognition. Mikel watched the two men shake hands, then stood aside to let the fat man pass. The man cast his sleepy eyes down at Mikel. He had an imperviousness about him and a docility that reminded Mikel of the dog that he planned to own.

When he had gone Mikel hovered a moment in the doorway.

Come in, Monsieur Lucky said. His name, as Mikel had learned from his card, was Pierre Etcheberry. They shook hands. Etcheberry picked up his Lucky Strikes from the counter and held out the packet to Mikel. He took one.

Thanks.

You found my card, Etcheberry said.

Mikel nodded, patting his pocket.

Thanks.

Etcheberry drew on his cigarette and started looking for something behind the counter.

He put a black notebook on the counter.

You mentioned you were looking for a job.

So I did talk then.

A little. Etcheberry went back to the book. I have a friend. He has vans that sell stuff. He needs someone to cover the markets.

Which side?

I'm sorry?

Here in France?

Yes. Is that a problem?

No, no. A van that sells stuff. That sounds good. What does it sell?

Some of them sell underwear and some sell brooms.

Mikel laughed too loudly, then he couldn't stop. The little shop was filled with his stupid laughter. Etcheberry looked on, a little embarrassed, waiting for him to finish.

I'm sorry, Mikel said, wiping his eyes. Oh dear.

Go and see him. His name's Lamarck. We were in the merchant navy together. Etcheberry wrote down the number and handed it to Mikel. He's a loudmouth but he's OK.

He had written the number on another of his cards. Mikel thanked him and put it in his pocket with the other one.

I'm grateful, he said.

Etcheberry looked at him and Mikel saw that the man ran on alcohol. His eyes were pale blue and set in cloudy yellow.

You'd do the same for me, he said.

Mikel shook his hand and turned to go. He was eager to get the dog before he met Lamarck. In the doorway he turned back.

Can I ask you one more thing?

Etcheberry opened his hands.

There is someone I'm trying to get in touch with. May I give her your number? Until I get one of my own.

Of course.

Thank you.

What's her name?

Mikel considered.

Carmen. Her name's Carmen.

Lovely.

If she calls . . . Mikel stopped himself from giving more information.

I'll let you know, Etcheberry said.

Mikel stood in the doorway, wishing he could take back his request. But it was too late. Etcheberry was looking at him expectantly, in readiness to give more.

Can I buy you a drink later on? Mikel asked him.

I can't, I'm afraid. I'm going fishing tonight. You're welcome to come if you like. Philippe, the big bloke who was just in, has a boat. We meet up with a group from the other side, from Hondarribbia. We see who can take the biggest catch. The losing boat has to shout the winners a meal at a place called Chez André in Biarritz. He planted a kiss on his fingertips.

133

Suddenly Mikel did not trust him.

Maybe another time. He held up the card. Thanks again for this.

Etcheberry shook his head.

No problem. If you need a place to stay I know a woman who takes in lodgers. Here in Saint Jean but it's cheap.

Mikel wanted to be out of reach of the man's kindness.

Thank you. You've done too much already, he said.

Tuya, the woman's name is. Hortense Tuya. Say I sent you. She's in the book!

But Mikel had left the shop.

He walked along the port to the same call box where he had called Astrid. He was angry that he had been unable to trust Etcheberry. In prison, knowing as he did how the environment could erode faith, he had forced himself to trust people and it had paid off. He would never anticipate betrayal. On the few occasions that it had come, he dealt with it according to the nature of the betrayer. Mateo Cruz he beat because there was no alternative and the Fuentes kid he ignored. Both had tried to make amends. Now that he was free, he felt himself closing up, turning inwards. The man was offering friendship. He had been out for forty-eight hours and he already had a worthy friend. But he did not want a friend. The only relationship he could contemplate now was with a dog.

There was no phone book in the call box so he went to L'Amiral and asked the barman if he could look at his Yellow Pages. He found a vet that caught his eye on the Rue Garispe called Pascal Pasqua. He drank a beer and smoked a roll-up and walked with his new stiff walk, past the beautiful church where a great French king had married a Spanish princess in an attempt to stop the bloodshed, past the shops selling berets and sheepskins and fudge and local textiles, past the tall, narrow houses which inclined a little towards him and were now inhabited only by people who could afford to live somewhere else.

Pascal Pasqua's surgery was down an alley that smelt of human urine and air freshener. Above the frosted glass door was an illuminated sign with blue letters saying *Vétérinaire*. Mikel rang the bell and the door clicked open. He entered a waiting area with a red lino floor and pale-green walls covered in soft-focus posters of cats and dogs. An old man was waiting with an old labrador. Mikel nodded at him and sat down two seats away from him, but even this was not far enough to elude the smell of the labrador.

Soon the old man and his dog were summoned by Pascal Pasqua whose tanned face appeared around the door. Mikel sat reading a leaflet about animal vaccines and rabies and wondered at the new physical affliction, which had set in as soon as he had stepped out through the prison gates and which he had attributed to the sudden change in his circumstances: a strange numbness in his legs that made him want to kick out or run. As he had no desire to run, he decided that his legs or perhaps his nervous system must have an albeit rudimentary mind of their own. He must remember to ask Astrid about it. Astrid.

He could see her face, captured by the TV camera during the press conference that was held when she was let out of prison. He had guessed that it had been because of that face that Euskal TV had taken an interest in her case in the first place and followed the campaign for her release. She had become the picture of innocence, the symbol of wrongful punishment. He had sat and watched the report for the local news, faintly irritated by the sound of inmates playing ping-pong in the background. Even as he contemplated the cynicism of the press, he too had been beguiled by that face. He had seen the pallor, put there by prison life, and the shadows under her eyes and the little gold hoops, glinting against her dark hair, a tiny vanity, and he had believed that behind the beauty he could see all her strength and patience and compassion. He had believed then that if Astrid could love him, he might have a chance, and he had begun to write to her.

Mikel watched Pascal Pasqua escort the old man and his dog to the door. The dog was now limping and the old man looked cowed. It seemed like the vet's affability was too much for him and he left with his head low.

We're on, Pasqua said with an encouraging nod, and Mikel followed him into his surgery, which smelt of the same air freshener as the alley. The walls in here were covered with posters relating to golf: a golfer in full swing, an impressionistic drawing of a golfer and the sea and a watercolour of a woman in twenties clothes leaning on a golf club.

In the centre of the room, beneath a neon strip light, was a Formica table on which Mikel thought the animals must struggle and slide beneath the vet's grasp. Pasqua leaned against the table, his legs crossed at the ankles, arms folded.

How can I help you?

I'm looking for a dog. Mikel hesitated. To adopt.

Pasqua looked at his shoes. Through the thin, blond hair Mikel could see a bald patch the size of a communion wafer on the crown of his head. Mikel looked down. The man's shoes were long and tapering with leather tassels on them. At the sight of them, he felt he had come to the wrong place.

There is a dog, Pasqua said, looking up. He's quite old though. His owner's been hospitalised and can't keep him. I've been treating him for an infected paw. The dog, I mean. My wife's treating the man. He smiled. She's a nurse.

Mikel arrived at the animal shelter late in the afternoon. It was outside a village in the hills behind Biarritz. It had taken him three hours on foot. If the dog were badly injured he would have to hitch back. As he walked up the dusty drive the chorus of barking grew more and more frantic. Some dogs threw themselves at the chicken wire, others barked from a safe distance. Mikel watched them fondly, his ears ringing.

A young woman in dungarees made her way through the crowd towards him. The dogs clamoured around her, hindering her progress as if she were their guru. The girl stood on the other side of the gate and asked him sourly what he wanted.

I've come to see about a dog called Castro.

No one told me anything. Who sent you?

Pascal Pasqua, the vet.

The girl looked him up and down. She had a ring in her eyebrow and a silver stud in her nose and her dark hair was cropped short.

I need I.D. and proof of residency.

Mikel fished in his pocket.

He held up his frayed I.D. card. She peered at it through the chicken wire. The photo was over twenty years old.

A German shepherd jumped up at her.

Down Toto, she said softly, scratching him behind his ears.

You're Spanish, she said curtly. We don't send dogs to Spain if we can help it.

I live here.

I need to see a bill or something.

I've just moved here. I live in Saint Jean. I'm lodging with a Madame Tuya. She's in the book.

The girl scowled at him.

Castro's injured.

I know.

He needs to be given medication. Antibiotic cream. Every day.

Mikel's heart was pounding in his chest.

That's fine, he said, watching her unlock the gate.

TWENTY-FOUR

Astrid hugged Lola for too long. Lola pulled away and studied her face.

What is it? You look upset.

They were in the hall. The grandfather clock was ticking imperiously in the corner. Astrid had always hated that clock, the way it would strike just as you were walking past it. Lola laid her hand on Astrid's cheek.

Tell me, she urged. What is it?

Lola had her head tilted attentively to one side. She was still in her nightdress.

I had a row with Jacques, Astrid said.

She watched the pleasure settle in Lola's eyes.

What about?

We talked about my abortion.

Lola made her small mouth.

What did he say?

He hung up.

Lola raised her arms and dropped them in an overblown gesture of exasperation. Of course he did, she said, turning and stalking off towards the kitchen.

Astrid looked up the heavy oak staircase towards her mother's room. She had forgotten how much she disliked this house.

I should go and see Mummy, she said.

Afterwards. Come and have a cup of coffee first.

Astrid followed Lola along the dark hall to the kitchen.

Are you smoking? Astrid asked.

Yes. Do you want one? Lola seemed excited at the idea of sharing a vice with her sister. I have so much to talk to you about. I'm so glad you're here. God, I can't believe Chastel.

Astrid sat down at the table with her back to the glass door. Lola began to make coffee. She seemed to stretch for everything. It was the way she moved. Astrid watched her, feeling the sun heating her back.

We've never talked about it, she said. Not once.

Lola spun round.

You can't be serious.

When I found out I was pregnant he was leaving for Gabon to visit a new lab. I had the abortion and went out to join him. It was clear as soon as I got off the plane that he didn't want to talk about it. I got an infection out there and put myself on erythromycin. My womb is a sieve now but we've never talked about it.

Lola was staring at her. She seemed not to have heard. For an irrational moment, Astrid thought that she had been discovered and her heart stopped.

What is it?

I have to tell you something, Lola said, reaching out and touching her lightly on the arm. I woke up this morning and I knew that he'd come to me. It might take a while but he'll come. I had a dream last night. You and I were on a high wall. You were ahead of me and the wall was getting narrower and narrower. Then it was only a thin line and you were balancing but I knew I was going to fall, it was only a matter of time. You kept on encouraging me, saying it's alright, Lola, I'm here but I couldn't go on and my legs began to shake and I knew I was going to fall. And then I did fall and I fell a long way but then I found that if I kicked my legs I could stay up, I could fly and then I was flying and dancing and it was a circus and Mikel was there, sitting in the audience and you were beside him and you were both clapping.

Lola performed a pirouette, then flicked her wrists, flamenco style. Astrid smiled, drawn in.

Today I have hope, Lola said, pulling a stool close to Astrid and sitting down. It may be gone tomorrow but I'm going to enjoy it while it's here. Then she remembered her solicitude and she looked tenderly at her sister. But I want to hear about you.

Astrid passed her hand over her face.

Can I have a cigarette?

Lola sprang to her feet.

I've only got strong ones, she said, picking up the packet from the draining board. She seemed to have forgotten the coffee. Paco gave them to me, she said.

Is he still in love with you?

No. She handed Astrid a packet of Ducados. Yes.

Astrid lit a cigarette and inhaled deeply.

Lola found a silver ashtray in the cupboard under the sink. It had their mother's crest on it. She put it in front of Astrid and sat down. For a few moments she watched Astrid smoke. At last she said,

I've been thinking a lot since I got here. She paused, her eyes full of compassion. Was prison terrible, Astrid?

Astrid shook her head, holding in the smoke then exhaling. No, it wasn't. Boarding school was worse. I was less bored in prison than I was at school and less unhappy.

I thought you *liked* school.

I hated it. I hated those English girls. They were insipid and cruel at the same time.

God, I wanted to be like them, Lola said. I wanted to love ponies and be good at tennis. Then she stopped. Why didn't you ever tell me, Astrid?

I don't know. You didn't ask.

Lola looked down at the checked tablecloth.

There's so much about you that I don't know.

Astrid put out the cigarette.

I should look in on Mummy.

They left the kitchen and went upstairs to their mother's bedroom. Outside the door Lola rested her hand on Astrid's cheek.

I don't know how I would have got through this life without you, she said.

Astrid took Lola's hand from her face and held it tightly. She looked at Lola's smooth forehead and at the deep blue eyes with their golden flecks: five in the right eye and six in the left, like shards of light. The love she felt for this face came from a deep knowledge. She had been reading it since Lola was a baby and knew it better than she ever would her own. As a child she had watched Lola's eyes flicker and close for sleep. She had seen the way they rolled as her lids opened. Now she felt ashamed of this knowledge, as though she were watching her sister live her life from behind a one-way mirror.

She found nothing to say.

Lola squeezed her hand.

Let's go, and they stepped into the ornate bedroom.

Astrid, Margot observed calmly. You're wearing your hair down.

Astrid clasped her mother's frail body to her. There was that barely perceptible resistance, that inner shrinking she had always felt from her mother whenever she sought physical contact. She now believed it to be something older than experience, something inscribed in her like genetic material. Astrid pulled back and looked into her face: nothing new; the grey eyes, under scrutiny, had always flicked away like that. Her mother patted her hand. Had she been able, Astrid knew she would have drifted away to occupy herself with something else. She had always eluded intimacy, Astrid thought. Even when she drank, she would always be doing something, generally sorting, until she passed out. She had a great many possessions and beyond what she had inherited, had accumulated so many objects throughout her life, that there was invariably something to sort through. Since she no longer had the strength for this, she sorted and resorted her ramshackle mind instead. Astrid smoothed back her mother's hair. It was soft as cotton wool.

Are you eating, Mummy?

Of course I'm eating.

Properly?

We had some lovely quails' eggs, didn't we, Beatrice?

Lola nodded. There had been no quails' eggs but she did not say so. She noticed how her mother became less composed in Astrid's presence. She seemed hunted.

Are you taking the pills I sent you? Astrid asked.

No, dear. They make my mouth dry and they give me a fiendish headache.

How are you sleeping?

I'm an owl. I nap in the day but I'm as bright as a button at night. Aren't I Beatrice?

Lola nodded again.

As soon as I can make these stupid legs work properly I'm going to get up and do some work.

What sort of work? Astrid asked.

Margot's eyes flicked mistrustfully over her eldest daughter.

Angus can't do everything himself, can he?

Angus is dead, Mummy. Remember? It's just Mary now. And the trustees take care of things for her, and for you.

Lola watched Astrid. She was always calm and unrelenting with their mother. She never let her settle into delusion. Lola could see Astrid's gentleness but knew there was something cold and hard lying there at the core of her feelings for their mother. Ever since she was a child, Lola had seen flashes of it. Suddenly she wanted to leave the room.

I'll go and see about lunch.

Astrid looked up.

I'll make it. What is there?

There's pâté and some smoked salmon that Gachucha brought this morning, Lola said.

Mummy, you can't live off this deli food. It isn't good for you.

No, quite right. Margot gave a long sigh. When Josu gets back we can all start eating properly again. He'll go up and shoot us some *palomas*.

I'll make something, she said, heading for the door. I'll bring it up.

And she quickly left the room, closing the door.

In the kitchen she reached into her bag and found her phone: one missed call. As she waited for the message, she watched the door, ready to hang up if Lola should appear. She had learnt to practise deceit with the same ease and detachment she used for vivisection.

Mikel did not use her name. His voice had none of the assurance of his letters.

I have a number. You can call it if you want to see me. Tell the man who answers that your name is Carmen. He will tell you where I am.

Then he gave the number twice.

Astrid hovered between the two digits for save and delete. She pressed three for save. Then she turned off her phone and returned it to her bag. She went to the larder and found potatoes, tomatoes, eggs and onions to make a salad. She stood over the sink and peeled the potatoes under the cold tap. Her hands were soon red and smarting from the cold but she did not allow herself to remove them. She was thinking of his first letter to her:

142

You have moved to Paris. I have never been there, nor anywhere in fact. I have never left Euzkadi or Spain, the land of my oppressors, because it seemed a sin to see the world until my homeland was free.

She remembered how appalled she had been by what she recognised as the dead language of liberation movements. But very soon the letters had lost their ideological veneer and Mikel began to use the mystical language of the unrequited lover:

Astrid,

I have a view. I can hardly believe it. For the first time since I was incarcerated I can see earth and sky. Today the sky is filled with big clouds racing past. I can see the shadows they make on the plain. I believe this is a sign that I will soon be free. I am filled with panic at the thought of freedom. This view opens up my mind to hope. I have begun to hope again and with hope comes fear, a feeling that fills my chest and makes me weak. My love for you fills my days and my nights. Sometimes it suffocates me. But I believe it is my destiny, that without it I am nothing at all.

Her memory had kept this letter. Her phenomenal memory, that had carried her effortlessly through her exams, that had charmed Chastel and so enslaved him to its infallibility that he was losing his own through disuse. She hated it.

She drove the point of the knife into the potato and gouged out the grey eye. Do not manufacture belief out of me, she thought.

TWENTY-FIVE

Kader sat on a bench on the promenade in San Sebastian. He lifted his face to the sun and closed his eyes. The episode with Raoul had depressed him. He believed he had a way with dogs. But that treacherous cunt was no dog.

I didn't look him in the eye, he murmured. He had not looked the mongrel bastard in the eye.

René had been mortified.

Don't worry about it, Kader said, patting René on the arm. Raoul's a racist, that's all.

That's what I'm afraid of, René said, looking sadly at his dog who was chained to the back door of the truck, his head between his paws, sleeping unashamedly.

René had driven him into town in his uncle's Jeep. As they were driving along the river, René had said,

I'll give you my mobile number, kid. In case you ever need anything while you're down here.

Fine. Just try not to call me kid. OK? Kader had answered.

But René was all right.

The sea had been as Kader had expected: no more, no less. The sight of it had made him grin stupidly. He had stood staring at it, watching it move in and out. He had stared for so long, he felt himself being gathered up by it, as though the turquoise sea were breathing his soul, in and out. He forgot the pain in his heel and the older pain in his shoulder. He forgot where he was and who he was.

Kader now stood up from the bench and limped back to the ocean. A few people were swimming in the shallow water, splashing in the waves. He wanted to get into the sea too, immerse his aching body, but he wanted to find Astrid's father first.

He turned his back on the ocean and walked towards the Hotel Londres. He was not sure what he was going to do but a fancy hotel was a good place to start. Kader limped across the wide esplanade towards the hotel. He liked the way this town made

144

him feel. He liked the smell of the air and the light from the sun, which seemed to make everything sparkle. He looked at the people on the esplanade; three old men conferring in the shade of those graceful trees; two girls, walking fast towards him, arms linked, talking furiously in their language, eyes and mouths serious. He stopped to watch them pass, enrapt. This was a grand and beautiful city but unlike Paris it seemed not to shun him.

He passed the entrance to the hotel bar and walked round the side to the main doors at the back. He did not acknowledge the poor man in livery standing at the foot of the steps. He pushed the revolving door and walked into the lobby as if the whole place were waiting for him and only him.

Kader had never been inside a place like this. It was a palace. Beside this, the Mercure was a dump. But he did not betray his awe. He walked up to the desk and stood in front of an old queen in a grey uniform and waited patiently for him to look up from the checking-in book. Soon Kader knew that to wait any longer would ruin any chance of being taken seriously.

Do you speak French?

The man raised his head and just closed his eyes for a Yes.

I have an appointment with a lawyer called Arnaga. But I'm very late. I got held up. Did he leave a message? The name is Benmassoud.

The man sniffed once, then turned to look in the pigeonhole marked B.

Kader found he was actually irritated when the man informed him that there was no message.

Shit, he said, tapping the desk. Then he looked about him, just to make sure. Do you mind if I check in the bar?

The man opened his hand and motioned towards the bar.

By all means.

Kader made to leave, then turned back and tapped the desk again.

I suppose I'll have to stay the night. You'd better book me a room.

I'm afraid we're fully booked, sir.

Kader was truly vexed. He swung his head from side to side, then faced the man with a look that could indicate he was ready to throw a punch. The queen wavered.

145

You're going to have to help me, Kader told him. I need to find this lawyer. And I need a room. A decent one. I've had a long journey. Do you understand?

The man looked at him with a pinched mouth. Kader held his gaze, knowing that this was the moment: the queen either caved in or called the cops. At last he gave a little sigh and Kader knew he had won.

What's the name? Arnaga, you say?

That's it, Kader said. Arnaga.

The man disappeared behind a tapestry curtain and came back with a phone book. He set it down in front of Kader.

I hope you have the first name, he warned. There are a lot of them.

Kader picked up the phone book and went and sat down in an armchair behind a pillar and out of the man's sight.

Kader sat there scanning the Arnaga pages. He noticed that they all had two surnames. The inside of his head began to heat up, as it had at school when he had a test. He tore out the three pages with Arnagas on them, folded them into his pocket and felt better. He took the book back to the desk, patting it gratefully.

You've been very helpful, he told the man. Then he turned and limped away.

In the network of avenues behind the hotel, Kader found a bar called El Bikini with a nice swirling neon sign. He would love to have a bar. But a bar with live music. He would bring Rai, the music of pleasure, to the sexually impoverished and ignorant. He walked into El Bikini and took a seat in one of the booths. The place was pleasantly lit with little lamps on each table. Mick Jagger was crooning 'Angie' in the background. Kader had taken the piss out of Amadou for listening to the song. He was overjoyed now to hear it. The smell of chips warmed his heart. On the menu were photos of what he could order. He pointed to number seventeen, a shot of lamb chops, chips and two fried eggs, with tomato, onion and lettuce on the side. He looked up. To his delight, the girl who had come to take his order was wearing a sky-blue bikini.

She had a stud in her tongue, which flashed when she opened her mouth. She did not speak French but she was friendly and she smiled a lot. She repeated what he had ordered in a hoarse voice.

Then she pinched her throat and smiled apologetically to say she was sorry but she was losing her voice. Kader watched her boy's arse as she walked away. She was thin and muscular and tanned with a frosting of blonde hair all over her body. Behind the bar a kid of about his age with a large tattoo of a sun on his breastbone was cleaning glasses. Kader noticed that he too was wearing a bikini and his was pink.

Kader sat in the bar and looked through the Arnaga pages and underlined two lawyers. When he had finished, the bikini couple handed him a spliff. They slid into the booth opposite him and began to make conversation. They did well considering they had no common language. The boy was called Chech or Ketch or something and the girl was called Natalia. Kader gathered after some lame miming from Ketch that they both liked surfing. Kader managed to take the piss out of them a little, to tell them about the death of his dog and about his run-in with Raoul. After a few joints, the three of them were weak with laughter.

TWENTY-SIX

Castro was a sleek, honey-coloured mongrel with a dark-brown muzzle and carefully drawn eyebrows. He wore a dirty sock, once white, on his front right paw. Castro's previous owner was a busker called André who was HIV-positive. André was taken into Bayonne hospital for pneumonia. He had no family or friends who could take Castro in, so he asked his nurse, before she put him on the respirator, to make sure his dog found a good home. She had told him her husband was a vet.

No fascists, André had told her. I beg you. Castro's a political animal. I don't want him with a fascist.

Mikel was drawn to Castro because he was so obviously not political.

Sit, boy, Mikel said.

Castro sat, then lay on the pavement outside the newsagent.

Mikel emerged from the tabac with a small packet of tobacco and a copy of yesterday's *El País*. He was looking forward to reading the news and smoking a cigarette on the bench outside the graveyard. An old yew hung over the wall above the bench, giving shade from the sun and shelter from the wind. He had a few minutes before he had to start opening up the van for the market.

Mikel sat on the bench and looked down at his new companion panting at his feet. It seemed to him that the dog knew he was looking at him but did not turn his head.

Let's see that paw, Mikel said, laying down his paper.

Castro turned and sat. Mikel held out his hand for his paw. Castro looked about him, tongue lolling, while Mikel examined it.

Beneath the sock was a dressing. Mikel checked to see if there was any pus seeping through but the lint was clean. Two weeks ago Pascal Pasqua had removed a snapped syringe needle from the abscess between the dog's pads.

We'll be able to take that stupid sock off soon, Mikel told him.

He picked up his paper and turned to the sports pages. Astrid's team, Reál, was top of the league. Atlético Bilbao was fifth.

The room in Biarritz had turned out to be unsuitable for Castro. The landlady, Hortense Tuya, had stood in the hall, her face glowing with night cream, and told him kindly that she loved dogs but not in the house, which was full of highly varnished wood and bibelots. She did not mind making a bed for Castro in the garage. Mikel had decided that he would look for a room somewhere in the country, preferably on a farm. Until then, he and Castro would sleep in the van.

Mikel looked at the patch of dark fur between Castro's ears and felt a wave of gratitude. He had slept the night on his side with the dog curled up against his body. He had found that there was no need to train Castro. He was, Mikel felt, obedient because he chose to be.

I dream of a simple life with you.

The dog turned and looked at his master.

Time to go? Mikel asked.

Castro stood up and wagged his tail.

Mikel dropped his cigarette, rolled up his paper and shoved it into the back pocket of his jeans.

When they got back to the van, a fishmonger was pouring ground ice into polystyrene trays two slots down from him. She was a big woman dressed in a blue-and-white checked apron. Her face and hands were red-raw. He opened up the side of the van and pulled up the orange awning, transforming it into a stall. When he had finished arranging the goods, he sat down on the back step and smoked another cigarette. Castro lay at his feet and rested his head between his paws.

As he smoked, Mikel watched the dawn sky above the tall, square steeple change colour. He tried to see the change, tried to trace the colour gathering depth and intensity. He decided that not being able to see the change was a miracle. He had once written a letter to Astrid with the word phantasmagoria in it. The word had come into his mind a few days earlier and he had been waiting to use it. It had occurred quite naturally as the letter unfolded:

My daily life seems to be made up of phantasmagoria. You are the only thing that is real to me.

Mikel had always thought there seemed to be more space and light on the French side of the border. He looked at the clean, white church with its stone windows, its pure lines and the grand proportions of the oak portal. Basque villages on the Spanish side seemed huddled and defensive by contrast. One thing he had been right about was his suspicion that this side would never be dragged into open conflict. They had been pacified centuries ago. You could feel it in the sleepy air.

Delbos, the baker, arrived in a beige van with gothic lettering on it. Mikel dropped his cigarette and climbed into the van to await his first customers. In French his stall was a *quincaillerie*, a word he particularly liked. Sadly, though, his was not a real iron-monger's because he sold only cleaning utensils. It was no surprise to him to learn from Etcheberry that this arm of Lamarck's business thrived. He had always known that the women of his country were obsessed with order and cleanliness. It would appear that women on this side were the same. He sold everything they would need to preserve their illusions: brooms, mops, buckets (with or without sieves, in galvanised iron or plastic), sponges (organic and synthetic, abrasive or otherwise), sponge-brooms (with or without a squeezing lever), J-cloths, tea towels, packing-cloths and chamois.

He now smiled at his first customer, a chubby teenage mother with gold earrings that quivered on the end of her earlobes. Her baby was asleep in a buggy with a torn back. The baby looked like it was about to slip through the tear in the fabric but the young mother did not seem worried. Even when she was still, Mikel noticed, the earrings quivered. They reminded him of the earrings Astrid had worn at the press conference. The mother bought a packet of abrasive sponges and moved on.

Mikel could see that the world had shifted slightly in his absence but he could not identify the change. Like the sky, he knew it had happened but he could not say how. This must explain his feeling that everyone he met was involved in a game that he did not know how to play any more. He felt content in his van. He liked the pleasure he could see a woman got from buying a new sponge and he liked his dog.

TWENTY-SEVEN

Kader wandered the streets for hours in search of the first Arnaga. The office was on a street called Loyola but no one seemed to understand his pronunciation. In the end, he showed the address to a young cop who took a map from his breast pocket and puzzled over it for a long time. Kader could see that he was a simple and conscientious man and he suddenly felt sorry for all the shit his cop's life would inevitably deal him. In the end the cop indicated that he would escort Kader to the address. Kader limped beside him through the streets until they reached a building that looked like a bank, with broad steps leading up to carved wooden doors.

Kader shook the cop's hand and limped up the steps and into the big marble hall. White marble steps curved on either side of him to the first floor. He heard heels clicking along the balcony above him. The clicking stopped and a door opened and then closed. On the wall to his left were black plaques with gold lettering. He gathered that the place was filled with lawyers: *abogados*. He read, Elisegui, Lopez, Lopez; Fernandez, García, Sepel; Abberribat, Garcón, Ortega; Borges, Arnaga, Fando. It was on the first floor.

He stared at the opaque glass doors to Arnaga's office and waited for his heel to cool down from the walk upstairs. He took a deep breath and blew air slowly out from his lungs as his karate teacher had taught him, then he knocked firmly. There was a buzzing sound and the door clicked open. A very pale young woman with steel-rimmed glasses and dark hair pulled back into a ponytail looked up at him. She did not smile, or speak, she just looked at him and waited.

I've come to see Monsieur Arnaga, he said in French.

He's abroad, she answered. He could not believe how cool she was. He thought she might even be cooler than his sister, Aisha.

Maybe you can help me, he said.

Maybe.

Kader smiled stupidly.

I'm looking for a lawyer called Arnaga who defends a terrorist group. I've forgotten the name. They're Basques.

The woman did not answer but went on staring at him. Her eyes behind her glasses were small and very blue. She seemed to be trying to hold perfectly still.

I guess I've got the wrong Arnaga, he said at last. I should go.

Why are you looking for this person?

He knows someone I'm looking for. A friend. It's personal, he added.

The woman stared at him again as though she could learn more from what he did not say than what he did.

Kader let her stare. He was getting used to it.

If you can't give me this man's address then maybe you can tell me where I can find a doctor. I got bitten by a dog this morning and it's fucking painful.

Let me see.

Kader walked over to the woman's desk. She stood up and smoothed the creases from her skirt. She was wearing a brown suit of the kind that he would like Aisha to wear. Kader tried to get a look at her legs but he was too close. She smelt of lemons.

Show me, she said.

Kader turned round and pulled up the leg of his tracksuit. The bite was red and angry and swollen.

The woman sucked air in through her teeth.

You go and see a doctor right away. Before you do anything. Then you go and find your lawyer.

She stood up and walked back to her desk and sat down. She opened a drawer and pulled out a sheet of plain white paper.

Kader watched.

You write fast, he said, watching her.

She looked up and almost smiled. Almost. She folded the paper and handed it to him.

The first address is the doctor and the second is the lawyer.

Kader put the paper in his pocket. Then he considered the woman a moment and decided that it could do no harm. He reached out and kissed her hand.

Thank you, he said, letting go.

You're welcome, she answered, as if from far, far away.

*

Kader went to the second address first. He wished he hadn't because the avenue was steep and miles long. A bus rushed past him. He watched it pull into the next lay-by, its lights flashing. Kader broke into a hobbled run, slowed down as it pulled away. His throat was dry and his body ached. He sat down on the pavement and smoked a cigarette. As he smoked he tried to remember the woman he was doing all this for. He closed his eyes and tried to see her face but he could not. All he could see were horizontal red bars.

When he reached the address the sun was setting. A black Mercedes was parked on the pavement in front of the house. A big man with a shaven head was sitting behind the wheel. He had the windows up and the engine running but Kader could hear the thumping bass line of some dance track coming from inside the car. He stood at the bottom of the steps staring at the number on the house: 1277. It was a big house made of yellowish stone with a flag sticking out from the balcony above the front door, as if it were some kind of embassy. The flag was red, green and white. It was not a flag he recognised from any World Cup so he thought it must be Basque.

He walked up the steps and rang the doorbell. A bronze plaque beside the door, engraved with curving letters, read: Eugenio Riano Arnaga. A woman opened the door. She had short dark hair and shadows under her eyes like bruises.

She spoke in Spanish. Her voice was soft and weary.

I'm looking for Monsieur Arnaga, Kader told her in French. The woman held the door just wide enough for her tired face to poke through. I am a friend of his daughter's. She stared at him. Astrid Arnaga.

She opened the door and let him in.

You can sit here, she said in French. She was pointing to a low, squat armchair. Kader knew that if he sat down, it would be hard to get out of it.

I'll stand, he said.

She left him, disappearing through a set of double doors at the end of the hall. The hall was covered in portraits of old men, some of them with wigs, some without. The most modern was a painting of a man wearing a tweed suit and a pair of square, black-rimmed glasses of the sort that white DJs often wore. He was holding a book. The background struck Kader as botched.

The woman was coming back.

It's not finished, he said, pointing to the painting.

She glanced at it, then seemed to decide not to reply.

He will see you.

Is it safe to leave this here? he asked, pointing to his bag.

Of course.

He followed her through the double doors into a large, bright room with grubby mirrors on every wall and a chandelier hanging from the ceiling. A little old man in a maroon three-piece suit was sitting behind a large, white desk with gold trimmings on it. The man, he thought, must be loaded. He held out his hand.

Kader Benmassoud. Pleased to meet you.

Astrid's old man had a face like a mask that was too big for him. His skin was yellowish and he looked sick. Ignoring Kader, Arnaga spoke in Spanish to the woman. He had a voice like a loud whisper. Kader watched her leave the room, then turned back to the old man.

I won't take up your time, he said. I just want to ask you something.

Even if you want to ask me what my favourite colour is, Arnaga said in perfect French, you have to make an appointment.

Kader nodded, unsure whether or not to smile at this. Without a tone in his voice, it was hard to gauge the man. Kader looked at the wet, black eyes, at the sagging cheeks, the thin, slack mouth. There was no trace of Astrid anywhere.

It's a question about your daughter, he said.

Arnaga sat back in his chair.

Which daughter?

Astrid.

What about her?

Kader cast about him.

Can I sit down?

Please.

There were two chairs opposite Arnaga's desk. Arnaga looked at the one to Kader's left. Kader sat down in it.

She's in danger, Kader said.

Arnaga did not answer for what felt like a long time. Kader was not relaxed. At last the old man said,

Would you mind telling me who you are?

Kader Benmassoud, a friend of Astrid's. She operated on me . . . on my liver. We became friends. She called me two nights ago saying she had to leave Paris. She said she had received threats over the phone.

What kind of threats?

Kader had not rehearsed this. The old man's scrutiny was making him uncomfortable.

She told me she was taking her sister and going home. Then she hung up. I rang straight back but it was engaged. I rang the next day. Still engaged. The operator said the phone was off the hook. I got on the train and here I am. I knew she was in the Basque Country but I didn't know where.

Arnaga leaned forward and folded his hands on the desk.

What do you want?

It occurred to Kader that the old man had gone soft in the head.

I need the name of the village.

Why?

So I can go to her and make sure she's OK.

I don't know you.

I'm her friend. I know all about her. I know she had a stone goat in the garden. I know her mother drank . . .

I have no interest in knowing the level of your intimacy with my daughter, Arnaga croaked. Who she chooses to tell her life story to is none of my business.

Kader stared. Something about this man intimidated the shit out of him.

Listen, he said. Let's keep it simple. Just tell me where I can find her.

There is no need for you to find her. I know where they are. If they were in any danger I would know about it and would do what was necessary to protect them.

Then he looked down and opened a large red folder on his desk and began to look through some papers.

Kader was staring again. He felt like a kid.

Just give me the number.

No, Arnaga said without looking up. Now please go. I have work to do.

He sounded out of breath.

Kader's ears were red-hot. He stood up. As he left the room, he felt as though he were watching himself. It was a sorry sight.

In the hall he looked at his Adidas bag and stopped. For some reason the thought of Amadou made him bold. He sat down in the squat armchair.

I'm going to wait, he told the woman. She was opening the front door.

You can't, she said. You'd better go.

I can, Kader said. I'm going to sit here for as long as it takes.

The woman sighed and shut the front door, then she went into one of the rooms off the hall. Soon he could hear the pitter-patter of her typing fingers.

He tilted his head back and closed his eyes. Suddenly it came to him: Aisha Benmassoud, you have to break free. She had to free herself from all of them: himself included. Amadou might be the one to help her and he might not. Kader told himself that the next time his sister saw him, she would not know him. She would love him and respect him.

Kader woke up to find the big chauffeur striding towards him across the hall. He was wearing a ridiculous navy-blue blazer. Kader did not have time to react. He could only prepare himself improperly for the collision. The big man plucked him from the chair by his tracksuit. Kader registered the look of alarm in the sad, tired eyes of Arnaga's secretary as he floated past her in the hall. He was being borne aloft by the ogre who had foul-smelling breath and he knew seconds beforehand what was coming to him. He saw the front door wide open and he could feel in the man the purpose and concentration of the discus thrower. And when the big man let go of him Kader felt his bowels contract. It felt as if all his internal organs were shrinking back in preparation for the impact, which was long in coming. He had time to smell traffic dust in the warm air, register the darkness, see the white steps below him, the tree tops all lit up by the floodlight of a small football stadium and the exhaust from the Mercedes curling into this same beautiful light, and then, only then, did he hit the pavement.

Kader had no sense of how long it was before his Adidas bag came flying after him. He was lying on his side, half in the road and half on the pavement. His head was in the exhaust fumes of the Mercedes but he could not move. He was thinking about his father, Adel Benmassoud. He could not remember a time when the very sight of his father had not annoyed him. Everything about him, his face but in particular his eyes, which were so sad, made Kader want to scream: Shit, man, how do you ever expect anyone to give you a decent job with eyes like that? You make a man want to weep. And yet Adel had the same eyes as his father who had been a successful horse dealer in Oran. But that was because sad eyes in a horse dealer were a good thing, like long arms in a boxer. No, not like that. Kader heard himself moan as the Mercedes pulled away. It was the idea that he might be bleeding again. He could not face losing any more of his blood. He imagined he could feel the stuff pouring out of him into the gutter, down the hill and through the sewage grill.

Kader woke up to pain. There was pain everywhere. It had got inside him, like cold. He looked up at the sky. It was still dark but he could already smell day. The birds were singing. He turned and saw that his Adidas bag had gone and Amadou's Discman with it. He could still feel his wallet in his back pocket; they had not turned him over. He closed his eyes. There was no blood.

When he woke again the pain was no longer tolerable. It made him curse and grimace like a street crazy. It was all in one place now, in his left hip. Kader tried to stand but could not. His left leg would not move and the pain was draining all his upper-body strength. He ran his hand over his hip and felt something hard that he knew was his bone, poking up under the skin. He cried out. Waves of nausea swept over the pain and he passed out.

When he came to he was surrounded by faces all speaking at him in Spanish.

French, he said.

A red-headed woman with freckles all over her face, even on her lips, barked orders at two men who were lifting him onto a stretcher. Kader saw they had cut a hole in his tracksuit.

Fuckers, he groaned.

They must have given him something because the pain had gone and he was grinning from ear to ear. He could not help it. Straight away he could smell it: hospital.

157

Bliss, he murmured.

The blue day floated behind the window.

A nurse came in making that swishing noise that he loved so much. He kept his eyes closed, listening to her move about the room: swish swish, swish swish.

Later a doctor in a white coat stood over him with his head tilted sympathetically on one side. Half-moon glasses were perched stupidly on his forehead.

I am Dr Ribeiro, he said, holding out his hand.

Kader was scared. He did not move. It was like waiting for your sentence.

You dislocated your hip, the doctor said. His accent was thick. It's usually straightforward, you just push it back in. He made a fist with one hand and punched his other palm. Easy. But they didn't get to you until a few hours later so there was severe bruising and inflammation. We had to put you to sleep.

Kader's eyes filled with tears.

Will I be able to walk again?

The doctor smiled. Kader shouted at him:

Don't laugh, you cunt!

The doctor's smile vanished.

I'm sorry, he said. You're fine. You'll need crutches for a few weeks until the bruising heals. Keep your weight off it. You're fine. He hugged his clipboard.

Kader grinned and held out his hand.

Thank you, doctor.

But the doctor had lost his enthusiasm.

Just drop by the reception on the ground floor and they'll give you your bill.

Kader nodded slowly. Fuck that, he thought. In France hospital was free.

Doctor. Do you know a surgeon from round here called Astrid Arnaga?

By name, why?

I'm looking for her.

I believe she's in Paris.

She's not. She's on holiday. I just need to know the name of her village.

I'm sorry. I wouldn't know. I'm quite new here.

158

Who isn't?

I'm sorry?

The man was an idiot.

Who isn't new? Who would know Astrid Arnaga?

The doctor raised his chin in order to think and his glasses dropped onto his nose.

Ask the sister, he said. She might know.

The sister?

The woman in the office at the end of the corridor. He nodded, then quickly left the room.

Kader put his hand under the covers and felt his hip. The bone had gone. He pulled back the covers. He was wearing a white dress. They had taken off his tracksuit and his underpants. He kept his finger on the bell until an enormous woman with a chin that waved from side to side, came marching into his room.

I don't speak Spanish, he said.

But she did not care. She just went on talking at him in a voice like a drag queen.

I want my clothes. My wallet? My fucking tracksuit with a hole in it.

Kader tried to get out of bed. The woman kept talking.

Look, shut up. Shut up!

She stopped talking, her mouth tight shut now.

Please, Kader said, holding up his hand. And he began to mime.

They made peace. The big woman helped him dress. He asked her about Astrid Arnaga, said her name several times but she looked blank, then shook her head. She helped him like a mother and did not say a word. He listened to the air whistling through her nostrils and smelt the delicious smell of talcum powder on her skin. She went to fetch him a pair of crutches and then helped him learn to use them in the corridor. She walked him to the lift and Kader kissed her soft cheek.

He took a taxi to Arnaga 's office. He had no plan as he paid the man and watched him drive away. He hobbled up the steps, suddenly filled with anger at the loss of Amadou's Discman.

He held down the bell until the tired woman came to the door. He grinned at her.

No està, she said.

But he pushed past her on his crutches. He went straight to Arnaga's office and opened the door. Arnaga was behind his desk. He had a nail file in his hands. The discus thrower was nowhere to be seen.

Kader sat down in the same chair. He brandished the crutches then let them clatter to the floor.

Look what you've done to me!

Arnaga opened his mouth to speak.

No! Kader shouted. He was charged with an energy that he knew was fake. He was play-acting. If you weren't Astrid's father, he said, I'd beat the shit out of you.

I do not give in to threats, Arnaga whispered. I never have and I'm not going to start now. I've been in situations a great deal more threatening than this one, believe me.

Listen, I'm not threatening you. I said, If you weren't Astrid's father and you are. But what I will do is sit here, day and night until you tell me where she is. You can get the big man in the little blazer to throw me out but I'll keep coming up those steps. I've got nothing else to do.

You can sit then, Arnaga said. It'll do you good.

Fine, Kader said. But in the mean time I'll tell you a story. Once upon a time there was a brilliant young lawyer. He was clever, passed all his exams, straight off. Kader used his hands to help him along.

The man was elegant, Kader said. And witty. He was short but he didn't care because women wanted to fuck him anyway because they knew he'd go far. One day he met a beautiful woman. He knew right away that she was the real thing. Kader held up his index finger. Unlike him, he insisted. *She* was the real thing. This woman was a princess. All she wanted from life was to give the lawyer children and make him happy. Kader paused, putting his hands together in prayer. He felt exalted. Now he was a black preacher. But this man had a flaw. He had no love. All he had was ambition. Because he had no love, everything that loved him got destroyed. He couldn't help it. In the end he had to move away from anything that loved him. Kader paused. But Arnaga's little black eyes were hard to read. All he could see in them was his struggle with the sickness. Soon the lawyer became very ill,

160

Kader said. It was inevitable. Now the man is going to die and he knows that he's lived his whole life without love. He's lucky because his daughters are not like him. Kader bent to pick up his crutches. Your daughter Astrid can do miracles, he told the old man. She can make criminals repent. She can make a man walk across the world for her.

Kader was overwhelmed by his own performance. He felt like crying. Arnaga was looking at his empty desk. His face seemed to have slipped a little further. Kader knew that it was important not to speak now. It could go either way.

Get out! Arnaga shouted as best he could but his voice was trapped in his throat. The old man seemed to be shaking. Kader stood up and hovered a moment trying to think of something to say. Leave! Arnaga croaked.

Kader turned and left the room.

In the hall he met the woman. She looked at him and appeared wearier than ever. It occurred to him, as she walked back to her office, that she must have overheard them. Kader decided to sit for a moment on the steps to collect his thoughts. Outside the sky was heavy with rain. He had no decent clothes, hardly any money and no way of tracing Astrid. Not only had he failed but he felt bad about the things he had said in there. Even if he was a cunt, Arnaga was old and Kader believed his mother when she said you have to respect old people.

The door opened behind him and he felt a jab on his shoulder. The woman was thrusting a piece of paper at him.

What's this?

Go, she said, nudging his shoulder again with the hand that held the paper.

What is this? he said, taking it from her. Is it the number?

Yes. Now go and don't come back.

Kader stood up.

Thank you, he said.

But she did not smile back. She turned and slammed the door behind her.

TWENTY-EIGHT

The sun was setting as Mikel drove his van past the golf course at Saint Jean de Luz and across the bridge over the Nivelle. The river was high and fast here. A group of children carrying a kayak were making their way up the bank, their skinny legs poking out from beneath the boat. A childless man, he was. He considered this and felt no regret. With the life he had led, he could not bring up a child. They would want to know who he had been and he could not tell them. He could not say: this is the life I've led, this is who I am. Only now did he feel that his life resembled him. And it had been only three days since his release. He patted Castro who was lying beside him on the bench seat, his muzzle resting on the open window.

We're lucky, Mikel told him. Good old Monsieur Lucky.

Castro moved his ears.

Lola, he remembered, had expressed a love of bench seats.

Prison had not just frozen his own life. Nothing had changed for any of them in twenty years. Mikel believed that his love for Astrid had been there all along, waiting to declare itself. He loved Astrid and Lola was his girl. She would be thirty-seven now, hardly a girl. To have wasted so much of her time was his sin.

It was dark when he drove into the village. He averted his eyes from all that was familiar and drove slowly up the hill towards the Arnaga house. As he climbed out of the van he felt no dread, only peace brought by the smell of the fig tree in their garden. This was happiness: not hope, but memory.

At first the house looked dark, then he saw the light from one of the sitting-room windows projected onto the patch of lawn at the side. As he reached out and pushed open the gate, Castro whined. What is it, boy? The dog hung back. I just want to have a look. But Castro backed away, whimpering. Mikel dropped to his knees and held out his hand. The dog came forward and licked it. You don't want to go in there? He stroked his dog's head.

Someone died in there. Is that it? Castro half closed his eyes as Mikel scratched between his ears. You stay here. I'll be a few minutes. Castro watched him push the gate and walk along the path and around the side of the house.

The house was more deeply shrouded in vegetation than he had remembered. He stepped up to the sitting-room window and held aside the trailing ivy to look. Lola was standing in the middle of the room performing some kind of mime to an unseen audience. Her hair had grown and she looked more beautiful than he could ever remember. Perhaps he had been too close to see it but her radiance struck him now as proof that he was right: she would be happy without him. The window recess was too deep for him to see who she was performing to but it was clear that this was the game she had played at boarding school in England. The game, which involved miming a book, film or play to be guessed by your teammates, had bored him. As a young man he had been incapable of humouring her. He smiled now at the sight of her childish enthusiasm, her magnificent body moving in that red spotted dress she had always loved and he had always found a little too skimpy. Now she clapped her hands in delight and disappeared from view and Mikel was looking at Astrid, standing there in her place.

Astrid stood still a while, her hands pressed together in prayer held to her lips. Then something Lola must have said made her laugh and she slumped forward like a puppet making its bow. Mikel smiled as he watched her straighten up, run her hands over her face as if to wipe away the mirth and then make the sign denoting a film.

Film, he murmured. She held up one finger. One word. Then she sat down on the floor and began to row with invisible oars. Rowing, he muttered. She clasped her wrists and ankles. Galley slave, he said. She jerked forward, her face twisted in pain. She was being beaten. Spartacus! He watched the rest of the performance, knowing that he was right. He watched her mime the three syllables with expert precision but her audience could not guess it. Spartacus, he murmured. And he cast one more look at her. Still, he thought, she was not quite of this world. There was something in her face and her demeanour that set her apart. Like the engravings of the saints he had seen in his father's book, *The*

163

Lives of the Saints. There had been one, Santa Barbara, whom he would linger over as a child. The account of her life was brief but her picture and her story had mesmerised him. She had had unruly hair like Astrid's. Her father had kept her locked away to preserve her beauty and her virginity. As a boy Mikel had been fascinated by the cruelty of the father. He had had his daughter tortured for her beliefs and then he had beheaded her with his own sword. As a boy, Mikel had wondered in his bed at night, what did torture mean?

He turned away from the window and walked back along the path towards his dog, who sat panting on the other side of the gate. Astrid had looked happy, so had Lola. He had no place in their lives.

TWENTY-NINE

Astrid was in the kitchen making breakfast for Lola and her mother. She had been thinking about Mikel and had prayed that he would choose to disappear. In her old room it was easy to pray. Lying in her old bed, the familiar smell of dust on her counterpane and the same shapes reflected by the moonlight on the wall, she could pray to her childhood memory of God. She had thought of Kader, had smiled in the dark at his peculiar energy and she had prayed for his success.

Lola stood in the doorway in her shell-pink nightie, dripping with sleep.

I was going to bring it up to you, Astrid told her.

OK, I'll go back to bed then.

Lola turned and Astrid listened to her stamp unsteadily along the hall.

While she was filling the tray, Paco knocked at the kitchen door. She smiled and waved at him through the glass. He stepped into the kitchen and hugged her closely.

Astrid, he said. She smelt his sweat when he pulled away. It's good to see you, he said, looking around the kitchen. I like this family. It makes me happy to have you living in this house.

I'm not staying, Paco. I don't think Lola is, either.

Paco smiled.

We'll see.

Do you want some breakfast? I'll make you some eggs.

I've eaten, thanks. He looked at the trays. Is one of those for Lola?

Yes.

Can I take it up to her?

Astrid hesitated but Paco picked up the tray.

I know the way, he said.

Astrid watched him leave the room. There was something disconcertingly gentle about Paco. It was as though his strength were shameful to him. She remembered him in the playground,

165

this big child, built like an ox but pigeon-toed, his hands in his pockets, ashamed even then. Paco had been in her *cuadrilla*. There had been six of them, sworn friends for life. All of them except for Paco and herself had joined the organisation. The gentlest of them all, Paxti, had been the last to join and had become one of its most remorseless and unrepentant members. He had been shot dead by the Guardia Civil on his arrest in 1981. His best friend, Kepa, who was with him at the time, had been shot in the knee and sent to prison. The other two, twin sisters, she believed had moved to Venezuela.

She picked up her mother's tray and went upstairs. As she passed Lola's room she heard Paco's deep voice and then Lola's laughter. It occurred to her, and not for the first time, that Lola had a chance of being happy with Paco.

Her mother was sitting up in bed, her head against the pillow, apparently fast asleep. Astrid knew she was pretending because of the flickering around her eyes. She stood over her mother, wondering at their lifelong estrangement. She believed that her mother had always thought that Astrid could do without her love. She looked at the eggs getting cold, then set the tray down on Margot's side table and left the room.

Lola burst into the corridor as she was going downstairs.

Astrid!

Astrid turned and looked up at Lola. She had egg on her nightdress.

What?

There's a man in Bayonne. Paco says if anyone can tell me where he is, it's him. He's got a button shop in the old quarter called Le Bouton d'Or.

Great.

Will you come with me?

Now?

Yes.

Astrid hesitated.

What about Mummy?

Gachucha's coming at twelve.

Astrid's heart was beating faster.

I'll meet you downstairs in half an hour.

Lola . . .

But she had gone. The door of her room slammed. Astrid imagined her stripping off in front of poor Paco and pulling on her clothes.

When Lorea Molina, the woman from Cultural Affairs, knocked at the kitchen door, Lola was washing up her breakfast things at the sink. No one tried the front door any more. From the great crack in the stone steps and the moss that grew on them, it was so obviously condemned. Lola wiped her hands on a cherry tea towel and wished that Astrid were down here in her place. She would have preferred bathing her mother to talking to this woman. She decided not to smile back at Lorea Molina. Instead she nodded.

Come in.

Thank you. What an exquisite house.

Lorea Molina was clasping one of those small leather briefcases without a handle. She wore a red dress with dice on it. She matched the Nazi kitchen.

It needs redecorating, Lola said.

Lorea bobbed her head equivocally from side to side.

It has a lot of charm.

Would you like some coffee?

No thank you. I don't drink coffee.

Tea?

Thank you. Yes.

Lola began looking for tea.

Please, she said. Sit down.

When Lola turned her back on her, she felt in danger, as if the woman were an attack dog at ease.

You're not from here, she said, turning round. Your accent. Is it Catalan?

Lorea Molina smiled, but to herself. She unzipped the briefcase, pulled out a thin, green folder and laid it on the table. Lola did not have time to see what was written on it before she turned it over.

I was born in Valencia but brought up here. No one has ever accused me of being Catalan.

I didn't mean it to sound like an accusation, Lola said, smiling. She set the mug of tea down on the table. Milk? Sugar?

Nothing, thank you. She took a sip. My mother was Basque, she said in a tone that told Lola the subject was closed.

Lola poured herself some cold coffee and stood leaning against the sink.

Lorea Molina rested her palms on the green folder.

I want to talk to you about Mikel, she said.

Lola did not trust her voice so she simply nodded.

I understand you're looking for him.

Lola kept silent.

What I am about to tell you will shock you. I'm prepared for the fact that you will not believe me. Everything in you will rebel against this knowledge. You will refuse it. And yet I have the proof.

Lola shook her head. The woman was performing. She would not be drawn in. She put her coffee cup down on the draining board.

You sound very dramatic, she said. But her voice failed her, betraying her fear. She felt sick.

We think that Mikel was turned around in prison.

Lola felt anger rush through her body. It rescued her.

We? she said, her face burning. Who's we?

A letter that he wrote to you was intercepted.

What letter? What did it say?

Lorea Molina opened the green file, pulled out a piece of paper and held it out to Lola. It was a faded photocopy of a letter that Lola knew well. She could see the dark shadows marking the folds on the original, for Mikel folded his letters into twelve so that they would be easily smuggled out of prison in his lawyer's pocket. Lola read it again:

I cannot say how I will be when I get out. You are right. I have changed, Lolita. I am not the man you fell in love with. I no longer like myself, for one. Your hero has lost the self-love that made him a hero. Perhaps this is what was meant by the word honour. It is an old-fashioned word but that is what I had and have lost. I believe it is something that cannot be retrieved.

She looked triumphantly at Lorea Molina.

That says absolutely nothing.

Lorea Molina held out her hand for the letter. Lola folded it into four and put it into the back pocket of her jeans.

It was written to me, she said.

Lorea Molina smiled again.

We would like you to let us know if and when he gets in touch with you.

Oh certainly, Lola said. She could still feel the anger humming inside her but it was growing toxic. She wanted this woman out of her house.

You owe it to the movement.

What? Lola spoke quietly. I'm sorry?

The refugee committee paid for all your trips to visit him over the years. You had funds. You didn't have to take their offer.

So I have to pay for that by betraying him. You're crazy, she said, tapping her temple with her finger.

If I'm crazy, Lola, then Mikel is crazy too. He's one of us.

You just said he'd turned grass. Your logic is at fault somewhere.

Lorea Molina's smile lost its veneer. Her neat mouth slackened and the keen intent went from her eyes. Lola saw Lorea Molina's complex laid bare. She was not clever. It had been the bane of her life. She had sought to dissimulate her stupidity with political engagement. Lola felt it was important to keep talking to cover her knowledge. She sat down opposite Lorea at the table.

There is no way Mikel would have turned grass, she said. After his arrest, he was tortured by the Guardia Civil for four days. And he didn't talk.

Opinion is divided on that matter.

Did any commandos fall in the wake of his arrest? Lola asked her. Was anyone arrested?

Well, there was Txema Egibar, she said.

Mikel didn't give Txema away. Txema knows that.

And there was your sister.

Lola shook her head.

That was different. That was my fault. It had nothing to do with Mikel.

That surprises me. She was staring at Lola with glassy eyes, a faint smile on her lips. Lola thought she looked stoned.

Why does that surprise you?

It surprises me in view of his subsequent relationship with your sister.

169

What relationship?

Lorea Molina turned over the folder.

Lola read: Mikel Angel Otegui / Astrid Hamilton Arnaga.

Lola reached out and touched the folder with her fingertips. She looked at Lorea Molina who seemed to be studying her through the bars of an invisible cage.

What is this?

Open it, she said gently. Read.

Lola picked up the folder and opened it. She recognised Mikel's close, furious handwriting slanting across the page. *Astrid* . . . Her chest, her arms and her hands had gone numb and she had a constricted feeling in her throat. She looked at Lorea again.

Read, Lorea said again.

I can't. She was feeling faint. Get out, she said. Her voice was weak. She folded her hands on the table and rested her forehead on them. Get out, she said again. She sounded drunk.

You can keep those, she heard Lorea say. We have copies.

At the sound of Lola's cry Astrid dropped the sponge she was using to wash her mother's back. She jumped to her feet, leaving her mother in the cooling bath, her hands over her ears in terror. Astrid ran down the stairs:

No. Please God, no.

When she ran into the kitchen Lola was kneeling on the floor, the letters all around her.

Astrid stood there staring at his madman's writing. She knew she could not go near Lola and kept back, close to the door.

Suddenly Lola looked up and shrieked her name. Astrid could see Lola's face, distorted with rage. She knew Lola was screaming at her but she could not hear what she was saying. Her whole body was shaking and the room was falling silently around her like red-and-white snow.

Astrid is sitting on the sofa in the sitting room. It is a hot summer after-noon and all the windows are open. The windows, set deep in the thick, stone walls, frame a green landscape and a blue sky. Although it is warm, Astrid is wrapped in a blanket. She has a high fever. Her mother, who is dressed in an orange, silk kimono with emerald-green birds of

paradise embroidered on it, is sitting beside her stroking her hand.
Margot Hamilton Arnaga does not know what is wrong with her
daughters but she believes it has something to do with Eugenio. He does
not try to hide his preference for their younger daughter. Beatrice has
shut herself in her bedroom and won't come out. Astrid is crying and her
teeth are chattering.

There there, she says. Mummy's here.

Astrid covered her mother with the blanket and lifted her frail
legs onto the sofa so that she could sleep comfortably. Getting out
of the bath by herself and walking downstairs had exhausted her.
Astrid crept from the room. She stood in the hall, trying to pull
the shards from her memory but the complete picture was irre-
trievable: she saw herself running down the stairs and she saw
Lola sitting on the kitchen floor surrounded by Mikel's letters; the
rest was missing.

She climbed the stairs, walked along the corridor and stopped
at Lola's bedroom. She leant against the door and listened. She
could hear only the sound of the pages. Lola would be reading
the letters one by one; every letter sent over five years. She would
see his obsession, how it was born, how it had grown into the
monster it had become. Did she have her letters to him too? She
had not seen her own handwriting in the mess of paper on the
floor.

Lola?

She rested her forehead on the door.

Please, Lola. Let me in.

The door opened. Lola's face was distorted from crying.

I dream of a simple life with you, Lola quoted. I want to build
you a house.

Suddenly her expression softened and she put out her hand
and laid it on Astrid's cheek. It's so sad. Our lives have been wasted, she said, taking Astrid into her arms. All our lives.

As Lola held her, Astrid felt as though all the shame and fear
that had accumulated over the years was draining from her. They
clung to each other for a long time. But when Lola pulled back
and Astrid saw her face, it was as if they had been set down on
opposite sides of a rapid stream. She knew she had lost her.

She found as she watched Lola move away that she no longer

felt any pain, only a fascination for everything that her sister did. She watched Lola carefully; watched the movement of her skirt as she bent to gather up the letters from the floor; watched her put them neatly into the folder; straighten up and walk to her bed, turn and face her.

He wants to have children with you.

I can't have children, Astrid answered.

You tell yourself that. You don't know.

I know.

Lola set the folder down on her bedside table. She seemed to be looking at her as though she might find something in her face that she had missed, some detail that could have warned her. Astrid felt that Lola had a new authority. She wanted to know but she was afraid to ask. She looked down.

Who gave them to you? she asked.

That's not important, Lola said.

Was it Txema?

No it wasn't. Why didn't you tell me, Astrid? Her voice was light. It sounded like curiosity.

Astrid shook her head.

Why didn't you?

I tried.

No you didn't.

Astrid was now simply a child trying to reclaim something she had lost.

I was afraid of losing you, she said.

You've lost me by not telling me.

I know.

Will you leave me alone now?

Astrid went to the door and stood on the threshold. She was suddenly convinced that if Lola closed the door behind her, she would never see her again.

Did you visit him?

Astrid stared at her sister.

Lola shrieked,

Answer me!

Yes.

When?

Once. I went once.

When?

In the summer. Four years ago.

Lola slammed the door in her face.

Astrid stood staring at a knot in the wood. Something prevented her from moving, an old sense that she would be punished if she did. She held still as the door opened again. Lola's face was distorted with an emotion that Astrid had never seen there before. She tried to look beyond it to a face she knew.

I remember, Lola was saying. You lied to me! You told me you were going to Morocco, didn't you? For a conference with Chastel. Was it then? Astrid looked at the vein sticking up on Lola's forehead. Was it? Lola shouted again.

Astrid nodded.

He was in an open prison. You made love.

Astrid could not find her voice. She swallowed and looked down. Lola's voice was flat now.

I hate you. You've stolen my life. Get out of this house.

But Astrid could not move.

We didn't make love, she said. I didn't go back.

You should have. You're a monster. You should have made love to the poor man.

Astrid looked at her sister and for a moment believed that there might be a way back to her. But then it became clear that Lola had made a decision.

Leave this house, she said gently. Go to Mikel, or don't go to him.

I won't, Astrid said.

I don't care what you do. I just don't want to see you again.

This time she closed the door carefully, letting the latch slip home.

THIRTY

Astrid had walked out through the gate and down the hill to the pelota court before becoming aware of her surroundings. The day unfolding around her was grandiose. She walked shabbily through it all like a stagehand – the joy cries of children, the mountain sunlight, the cool breeze. She was ridiculous; for once truly punished. Her parched throat waited for tears.

None came; she was calm. After all the torment, after the rebellion of her mind and body in anticipation of this moment, she was calm. Pain, she knew, would come, when the longing to be re-attached set in. Now she floated, in between two states of anguish.

Then she saw Txema. He was crossing the road ahead of her. She halted. Fear filled her upper body. He had seen her. He came towards her, striding, looking about him like certain prison guards she had known who needed to make a great show of their strength. His mouth hung open; he was smiling at her. Close up she saw the alcohol in his eyes and had the presence of mind to think that she would not take his liver if his next of kin begged her.

She greeted him in Basque.

Astrid. What a pleasure to see you.

Next of kin, she thought:

How is your mother?

Thank you. She's eighty-seven, he said, blinking slowly, as though this were information enough.

Is she well?

She is. She sleeps a lot. But she's in good health.

And you?

He smiled.

I'm fine so long as I stay away from doctors.

It works for some people. But you should look after yourself. You look tired. It's nice to see you, Txema.

She stepped back, trying to get away.

174

I don't sleep much, I never have. He looked about him. I saw your lovely sister, he said. We had a drink together. She was worried about Mikel. He hadn't called her. I told her she must try and be patient, Txema said, closing his eyes. Astrid remembered his sanctimonious manner from his days on the Executive Committee.

Has he called you? she asked.

Txema hesitated.

He has. He watched the effect this might have on her. She stared back at him, her gaze level. Will you have coffee with me? he asked.

The will to know, to be in possession of the elements, her old demon, drove her up the steps behind him.

He gestured for her to precede him through the door of his café. Txema cultivated the gallantry of an old commando member.

She went to sit down while he went to greet the barman. She watched him slap the man's hand, then grip warmly. He leaned right over the bar to talk to him. Astrid saw the admiration in the barman's face, his quickness to laugh. Txema Egibar was a local hero. To most people he still had the freedom fighter's aura. Knowing him made them feel virtuous. He was an historic member of the armed struggle, they thought. Although everyone knew that the armed struggle was no longer entirely glorious, no one would condemn it, not in this village.

Txema sat down opposite her. She could tell from the way he shifted uncomfortably in his seat that he did not like to have his back to the entrance but she did not offer to change places.

Lola *is* patient, she told him. She's the most patient person I know. Twenty years is a long time to wait for someone.

I suppose it depends on what you mean by wait, he said.

She looked into his lustreless, black eyes.

What do you mean by that? she said, keeping her tone light.

Oh come on, Astrid. Lola's had boyfriends. Plenty of them, as far as I can gather.

That's none of anyone's business, Txema. Except for Lola and Mikel's.

And yours.

Astrid flushed. She opened her mouth to speak but he interrupted her.

What will you have?

Coffee.

Shaken, she watched him raise his arm and summon the barman. She watched him order but realised that she had not heard a word that had been said. When the barman had gone, he faced her again with perfect composure.

Again she wanted to leave.

Txema rested his hands on the table. She saw that they were spattered with pigmentation.

I think he's terrified, Txema was saying.

Of what?

Of the outside world. He leant back again. It happens.

Astrid leaned forward, speaking quietly. She felt trapped and knew that he wished her harm.

How do you know? she asked him. You were only inside for nine months.

Txema looked up at the barman who was now at their table. He watched intently as the man put down her coffee and his lager. Astrid could see he was grateful for the interruption. He waited for the barman to leave before taking a sip. When he looked up at her again, his lips were wet. It was disgust that made her go on.

You must have been distraught when they refused an amnesty for Mikel.

Have I missed something? he asked. Do you actually *know* Mikel?

He went out with my sister for four years before he went to jail.

Txema smiled. His teeth were grey.

Of course he did.

Once again she could feel the blush spreading from her neck up. She swallowed. He wished her harm and he knew about the letters. Unable to look at him, she took a sip of coffee. What could she fear now? She had lost what she cared about. She put down her cup and looked him straight in the eye.

I'll be frank with you, Txema. I've never liked you, but more importantly, I don't trust you. And I don't think Mikel should, either.

The lids of Txema's eyes seemed to sink a little, giving him a weary look.

You've always been clever, Astrid, but never politic.

He took another sip of lager.

Again, the sight of his wet mouth filled her with a repulsion that spurred her on.

Do you know so little about me that you don't know how much I hate politics?

I know more about you than you think, he said, setting his glass down.

What are you talking about?

All knowledge has a price, Astrid.

Astrid huffed out a laugh. She knocked back her coffee and stood up. Thank you for the coffee, Txema.

She pushed back her chair. Txema did not raise his head. He was moving his glass in circular motions, widening the ring of moisture left on the table. She watched, alert, ready for a fight. Dandruff speckled his shoulders. The sight of him sitting there in the café he owned in the village he ran filled her with indignation. Why had *he* eluded punishment?

She sat down again.

I've often meant to ask you, she said. What happened on the night you were arrested?

Which night? I've been arrested more than once.

With Mikel, she said.

She watched him carefully, measuring his reaction. She saw a tightening around his mouth.

What about it?

She allowed a pause. Her heart was beating fast but she felt invigorated, not afraid.

You were arrested by the French, weren't you? How come you weren't together?

Txema's eyes seemed to turn a deeper black. It occurred to her that this was the veil that had enabled him to carry out acts of violence.

I went one way, he said, parting his hands. And Mikel went the other.

Astrid nodded.

You must have felt terrible. Mikel must have been tortured in custody, she went on. Don't you think?

Txema looked down at his glass.

I would be careful about discussing matters like these. You

177

haven't been back for a long time, Astrid. You're no longer familiar with the lie of the land.

She leant towards him, full of rage.

Even I was made to sit naked on a chair for a night in the basement of the Guardia Civil and I was only being charged with logistical support. Txema had a vacant look, even unashamedly bored, but she pressed on. That was the longest night of my life, she said. I was too afraid to sleep. Every time I heard footsteps come near the door, I thought it was my turn. I was shivering and I couldn't stop. Every muscle in my body ached. Then I think I started to hallucinate. I saw this woman in khaki uniform spraying blood off the tiled walls with a hose and I thought the blood was mine. When they came for me the next morning, I passed out. They hadn't laid a finger on me but the fear was enough, Txema. I can't imagine what Mikel must have gone through. What about you?

Txema did not answer. He was drawing patterns in the beer with his finger. The gesture was disconcerting. He looked up and smiled at her. Suddenly he had become dangerous. He sat with his finger poised in the spilled beer, as though some scruple was preventing him from speaking his mind.

I should go, she said.

He did not move.

You, of course, have nothing to hide, he said.

I suppose we all have something, she said.

She stood up and held out her hand. Txema looked at it.

We don't shake hands with women here, he said, rising to his feet. He gripped her shoulders hard and kissed her on each cheek. She could smell his rancid scalp.

Outside in the fresh air Astrid felt unclean. She had been drawn back to her old ways and had been humiliated. Her only desire now was to escape from the beautiful day. She needed a bath and a dark room. She walked back up the hill towards her car.

The man at the reception of the Hotel Lagunekin thankfully did not recognise her. He was Gachucha's nephew and he had been a child the last time he had seen her, a child playing marbles on the steps to their cellar. She asked him for a quiet room and he gave her the key to room nineteen. She walked up the back stairs to the first floor, along a windowless corridor with a stained burgundy carpet, past a wall light with a flickering bulb, to a room squeezed behind a partition wall. The room had twin beds, a cot, a sink and mirror and a window that gave on to a concrete courtyard, just big enough for a municipal dustbin and a car covered with an electric-blue tarpaulin. On the wall above the beds was a poster of a bowl of fruit and a pitcher with a droplet of wine hanging from its lip, executed with obscene realism. Astrid opened the window and let in the smell of fried food but no children's cries. She pulled the curtains, which had a motif of flying ducks and were lined with plastic for opacity, and went and lay down on the bed nearest the door.

She folded her hands on her stomach, crossed her ankles and closed her eyes. Txema knew about Mikel's letters to her. But how did he know and why had he made it his business to know? She believed that Txema's ascension to power would never have happened if Mikel had not been behind bars. Mikel had always overshadowed him. He was his moral superior and he had always showed Txema up, both inside the organisation and out of it. She was sure Txema had betrayed Mikel, she just didn't know how.

She lay on her back, eyes wide open. She could hear her own pulse in her ears, like the sound of footsteps on gravel. It drowned out the sound of the extractor fan below her window. I must not seek to know, she told herself. She thought of Kader, of his innocence. This was where peace could be found, in a nature like his. She must keep out of other people's lives. She could seek understanding only in her field.

As she waited for sleep, she tried to recall her first procurement. It had been more than fifteen years ago, a woman weighing over a hundred kilos. Astrid had been struck by the brightness of the colours on the inside of this body. She had seen the gaudiness of autumn: the orange of the fat, the rich brown of the intestines and the red of course, the cardinal red. This was a multi-organ harvest for heart, liver and kidneys but still she had not been prepared for the crowd: twelve of them, like the disciples, leaning over the woman's beating carcass. In the complex staging of the operation she had been criticised for speaking her part too softly, for speaking too quietly behind her surgical mask. And there was her accent too, making it hard for the surgical nurse to recognise the terms and respond quickly. The quantity of fat had made Astrid nervous and it had taken her nearly three hours to harvest the woman's liver. The kidney surgeons, waiting for their turn, had hardly been able to conceal their impatience. But Astrid was Chastel's protégé so they stitched and cut in tense silence.

That first time had seen the birth of her mistrust of cardiac surgeons. She remembered hearing the heart surgeon's booming tenor next door in the antechamber. He was pacing in wait for the fresh organ and showing off to the nurses. She had never met a cardiac surgeon who did not have a great, booming voice and an operatic demeanour. Even at four a.m. in a hospital corridor when they were clearly exhausted, they still performed. And they seemed to follow their grand destinies, unhampered by scruples of any kind. What was it about the heart, she wondered, that drew these vainglorious people? Did they really believe the heart was the seat of the soul? It was just a pump. The liver was a far more intelligent organ. It had over seven thousand functions, most of which were only partially understood. If the brain was an electrical circuit, the liver was an infinitely complex factory. And she was more drawn to factories than to computers.

Still it was undeniable that the moment the heart was stopped, flushed through with cooling fluid; when it was lifted from its pearly cavity and put in the plastic jar with a screw-top lid and then into a plastic bag, tied in a bow with a green ribbon; as soon as the heart team left the room with their prize, there was a drop in intensity. She remembered being struck by the fact that they had called out:

Bye!

And the others had called back without looking up from their work:

Thanks!

Even now, there was always a sense, to the others left behind to harvest the remaining organs, that when the heart team left, the glamour went, as it does when the most interesting or desirable member of a dinner party goes home.

She had worked on for another hour beside the kidney team while her assistant, a young Vietnamese intern, held back the

180

intestines with swathes of muslin, dyed pink with blood. Never since had the strangeness of this world she had chosen to inhabit been so vivid to her: the sweet smell of cauterised flesh, the disinfectants that hung in the throat, the respirator, like the sound of someone doing breaststroke in the blue light of that underground room, and the shrill metronome of the electroencephalogram. Then the depth of the silence after the respirator had been switched off and the anaesthetists, like three sulking puppeteers behind their green curtain, had taken the probes off the cadaver and the screens had gone dark.

THIRTY-ONE

Txema walked quickly past Lorea's open door but her voice clawed at him from behind. He hurried on along the corridor and shut himself into his office. By the time he got to his desk she was knocking.

No! he shouted. Not now!

There was a pause.

Is everything all right?

Fine. I need some peace.

He sat down in his chair and watched the door slowly open.

What is it? she asked.

She was wearing her dress with the dice motif. He had once made the mistake of telling her he liked it and now when she wore it, her self-satisfaction galled him.

Nothing, he said. I have to make a call.

She stepped into the room.

You look pale. Are you all right?

Her head was tilted slightly to one side and her straight black hair obscured her face a little.

Txema's shoulders fell forward in defeat. He glanced at the engraving of the whaling scene hanging on the wall opposite his desk. The shafts penetrated the whale's body from every angle while the boat balanced on the crest of a great curling wave. In the next instant all the men would be drowned.

I met Astrid Arnaga just now, he said.

Here, in the village?

We had a drink.

What did she say? she asked, taking another step into the room. Her eagerness deterred him. He sat back in his chair.

I want you to have Anxton follow her, he said.

Now? Today?

Yes.

Good.

Lorea smiled. She did have a lovely smile.

Off you go, he said, putting his hand on the phone. I have to make this call.

Lorea made a balletic turn, causing her dress to swing outwards and revealing, for an instant, the backs of her thighs, then stalked out of the room, closing the door behind her.

Txema sat for a long while with his hand on the phone, his mind free of intent. He stared, unseeing, the sounds of children playing on a hot day coming through an open window. Suddenly there was an explosion and glass shattered all around him. Txema leapt from his chair and dived under the desk. He sat there, his heart pounding, watching the pelota ball roll along the parquet towards him. Txema crawled out from beneath the desk and picked up the ball from among the shards of broken glass. He walked over to the shattered pane, and hurled the ball, with the full force of his anger, into the group of children gathered beneath the window. He could feel the blood pumping in his temple. One of his well-kept secrets was that anger had always affected his vision. He looked down, as though through a tunnel, at the gaping children gathering around the comrade who had been wounded by the returned missile. Txema realised that his hands were shaking when he picked up his car keys from the desk. He drove both hands into his pockets and walked out of the room.

Txema pulled into the car park of the beach that the French called the 'Chamber of Love'. He had spotted Gomez's battered Renault 12 parked close to the steps that led down to the beach. He was ten minutes late. He walked past a family of four in bathing suits, hobbling barefoot on the burning concrete. He was too hot in his dark suit and he regretted his choice of a meeting place.

The blind man was in the passenger seat, his window down. Txema did not look inside so he did not see Gomez. He stood beside the car, facing a showy sea. On the horizon clouds were gathering. The bathers were cramped in a corridor of about ten metres wide marked out by two red flags and under the watchful eyes of a handful of lifeguards slouching on their look-out platform. Obedience was indeed a miraculous thing.

Itxua's voice was rasping.

What can I do for you?

He had prepared his opening line and he would not change it now.

I have some good news about the retirement home, he said, keeping his eyes on the sea.

This was not strictly true. On paper there was no room in the new retirement complex that was being built at the entrance to the village but Txema was confident that for the right price, someone would give up their place.

That's good. It's time for me to come home, Itxua said.

It is, Txema told him. It is. Then he added, You know Mikel's out.

Of course, Itxua said.

He's disappeared.

What do you mean by that?

Txema paused.

He called on the day of his release and then nothing.

How long ago was that?

Three days ago.

You can't say a man's disappeared after three days.

Perhaps you're right. I'm just wondering why he should be hiding from us.

What makes you think that he is?

This is hard for me to say. He paused. He could hear Itxua breathing noisily. I was the first to defend him when people started saying he'd been turned around.

What are you saying? he barked.

Old and maimed, Itxua was still a formidable man. When Franco was alive he had jumped from a five-storey building in Bilbao to avoid arrest. His fall had been broken by a web of washing lines and he had got away with two broken legs. They had still arrested him and, it was alleged, tortured him for ten days. It was said that he had woken from a coma in prison hospital angrier than ever. Txema was sure Itxua still had close ties to the organisation. He pushed on.

The only reason I can find for him not getting in touch is that he's turned grass.

I can think of other reasons, the blind man said.

Txema knew Itxua disliked him. Ever since the seventies, in the days when the military wing took orders from the political wing,

Itxua had considered Txema soft. While Txema was on the Executive Committee discussing Marxist method and setting targets accordingly, Itxua was making bombs and training commandos. Txema knew he thought him impure but in those days Itxua had to keep his mouth shut. After the schism the military apparatus started making all the decisions. If Itxua had not been blinded by a letter bomb he would probably have become head and Txema's life might have been in danger. Calling him in now might well be like calling for fire on his own position.

If Mikel was turned around in prison, Itxua said at last, I'll know just by talking to him.

I dread to think of the damage he could do, Txema said, looking out at the corralled swimmers hurling themselves at the waves.

He could do very little, Itxua said coldly. He's had no contact with anyone since he went inside. But that's not the point. As you know there is a policy.

Txema smiled then feared the blind man had sensed his pleasure. He opened his mouth wide and clicked his jaw. He ground his teeth at night and the constant friction sometimes made his muscles go into spasm. On some days he sat in his office, unable to close his mouth.

Policy, he repeated. Yes.

Policy was, death to informers. It was as simple as that.

Why did you contact me, Txema? Itxua said.

Txema hesitated, sensing a trap.

I thought, if anyone can find him, you can.

There was a pause. Txema listened to the blind man's wheezing. He regretted his attempt at flattery.

Looks like rain, the blind man said.

Then he must have made some signal to old Gomez because the engine started before Txema could reply. He stood facing the sea until the sound of their car had died away. Then he turned and walked, this time without shame, back to his Mercedes.

THIRTY-TWO

Paco parked beside Bayonne cathedral. Lola had always found it inelegant and sombre. The stone was darkish pink. People pissed in the recesses of its walls. She walked along the town battlements towards the river. They had left the village under leaden sunshine. On this side, the sky was filled with churning cloud that looked like brown smoke. In the distance rain hatched the surface of the river. She could smell the dusty plane trees above her waiting for the rain, feel them straining towards it. As she walked into the narrow, pedestrian streets of the old town, the rain broke over her. It fell hard, drumming the stone pavements. It poured through her hair, blinding her. Soon her clothes were soaked and her feet were slipping in her sandals.

She stepped into the cluttered shop behind a middle-aged woman with highly colourful make-up and an auburn crew cut. The woman was looking for flesh-coloured elastic. Lola waited while she dithered over elastic of various widths. The man who served the woman seemed to be involved in her dilemma. Indeed he seemed in no hurry for her to make a decision. Each time she came close to choosing a calibre, he would throw in a further consideration to make her change her mind.

It all depends on how often you're going to wash the garment, he told her. This elastic holds up well in the wash.

It's not as attractive, mused the woman.

The man clearly loved his shop, loved opening the little drawers, and loved pushing aside display racks to get into nooks and crannies that might conceal more flesh-coloured elastic. At last the woman settled on 1.5 centimetres.

If you're sure, the man said. You can always come back and change it, Madame. You know that.

When the woman left the shop, he set about restoring it to the same disorder it was in before his search for the elastic began. Lola watched him, wondering what could possibly explain this man's link to the organisation. He was very small and thin.

Indeed, he must have had difficulty finding the grey work coat he wore, unless perhaps it had been made for school children. His wiry, sandy hair was clearly a toupee of some man-made fibre. Lola saw that his little hands were covered in eczema.

How can I help you, Madame?

I'm looking for someone. She had the photo that she kept in her wallet. She held it out. The man blinked at the photo with piggy eyes, then looked at her and shook his head.

Sorry.

Look again. Lola could hear the desperation in her voice and she could see that the little man already wanted her out of his shop. It was taken twenty years ago, she urged. You have to imagine this face, but older.

The man gave a cursory glance at the photo but his mind was already made up.

No. As I say, I'm sorry.

The little man stood there with his wounded hands clasped in front of him, looking at her patiently, a beacon of non-commitment.

Lola left the shop. She walked slowly through the empty streets letting the rain soak her again. She climbed into Paco's car and shut the door. She sat in silence beside him until the glass had steamed up and they could no longer see out.

THIRTY-THREE

Kader had never seen a place so green, sunshine so golden, rivers so clear. It was like a video game he had once played. He and Amadou had played it for twenty-four hours, stopping only briefly to eat, piss or shit. They had not slept. When they had finally got to the end they had both felt depressed to be out of the game's magical landscapes. He remembered sitting in silence in Amadou's room, smoking good pollen in order to soften their return to the real world.

Kader had a grin on his face as he walked on his crutches up the main street of Astrid's village. There was a space like a gigantic playground surrounded by trees. A group of old men in berets, each with a walking stick, sat on the low wall watching the children play. Kader felt an overwhelming sense of goodwill towards the old men and the kids. It was as if he had a new heart.

He wanted to stop and sit down on the wall to savour this feeling but the urge to see Astrid's face again was too strong and he walked on. She had not exactly sounded enthusiastic when he had called her but she had given him her address and directions to the bus station in San Sebastian and Kader thought she might be one of those rare women who, like his mother, did not like the phone.

When he had stepped off the bus he had been given directions to her house by the first passer-by he had asked, a woman with long, grey hair held back with a pink hairband. She had a wispy beard and moustache that had made Kader smile. She had smiled with him and pointed up the hill.

La última, she had said.

Kader decided that he would go and get her and they would come and sit on the wall together, their backs to the sunshine. When he came in sight of the last house the dog bite on his heel was throbbing, his hip ached and the knife wound on his shoulder itched beneath the dirty bandage. In spite of the pain, he was overjoyed. He stood in awe, looking up at the grand stone façade, with all its big windows and its dark blue shutters and the roses growing all over it. He looked down the street. A woman carrying a baby on her hip was crossing the road. He heard the bell sound as she opened the door of the bakery. Then he looked the other way at the cobbled street running into a path that disappeared into a wood. He pushed open the iron gate and limped up the path to the front door.

THIRTY-FOUR

Lola wanted Paco out of her room. She was in bed and he was sitting naked on the edge of the bed with his back to her. The sight of his great shoulders hunched forward irritated her. He turned.

Why did that happen?

It was my fault, she said.

Paco turned his head as if he had received a blow, then turned back.

What do you mean, your *fault*?

I needed to be held.

I could have held you, Lola. Why didn't you ask me just to hold you? he pleaded.

I can't explain, Paco. I'm probably not who you think I am.

He shook his head.

I don't judge you, Lola. I want to understand.

Lola tried to keep the anger out of her voice.

I needed to anaesthetise myself. I'm in pain.

About Mikel?

About my life.

He just needs time, Lola.

That's what Txema said.

Paco turned his back on her. His weight was pulling the bed-clothes taut, trapping her legs.

I'm going now.

Lola watched him stand. She watched this poor, naked giant stoop to gather up his clothes with the gestures of a maiden.

I'll come back tomorrow after my shift, he said.

She nodded, unable to meet his eye. His slowness and gentleness made her want to hit him.

She glanced up and smiled at him, keeping her mouth closed.

When he had shut the door behind him, she stared towards the open window at the blue sky. Paco was still seeping out of her and she could smell his spit on her face. She was growing cold but she could not move. A solitary phrase turned in her mind: *I*

190

am Lola and I have a cunt. She pulled the sheet up over her shoulders.

The sound of the doorbell woke her. Her head had been lolling at an uncomfortable angle and her neck was aching. She did not move. Someone who did not know them was ringing at the main door. The bell rang again, more insistently this time. Knowing that the portico concealed visitors from her view, she went next door to Astrid's room and looked out. A boy on crutches was making his way down the stone steps.

What do you want? she called out in Spanish.

The boy looked up at her, head thrown back.

I don't speak Spanish, he called in French. He grinned at her. You must be Lola.

Who are you?

Carlos, he said. I'm a friend of your sister's.

She's not here.

Where is she?

Gone. I don't know. And she closed the window.

He leaned on the bell.

When she opened the front door Kader was unprepared for what he saw. She was wearing nothing but a silky pink nightdress with her nipples showing through. Her blonde hair was a tangled mess and her eye make-up was smudged. She stood and scowled at him, one fist on her hip. He thought there was something of old Arnaga in the way she held her head, stiff and proud.

Who the fuck are you?

Kader. I'm a friend of Astrid's.

I thought you said Carlos.

You can call me Carlos if you prefer.

She stared at him as though trying to work something out, then she shook her head and closed the door.

Kader used the rubber stopper on his crutch as a knocker.

He banged firmly until she opened up again.

What do you want?

I've come a long way. Can I come in for a coffee or something?

Lola turned and walked away, leaving the door open. Kader hobbled after her into a dark hall with antlers on the walls. The place smelt of dust and made him want to sneeze. He followed her past a wide, wooden staircase and into a brightly lit kitchen.

191

Lola padded over to the sink, her bare feet making a sticking sound on the linoleum. He watched her arse as she filled a saucepan and put it on the gas.

He pulled a stool from under the table and sat down. Then he began to prise the old bandage from his congealed knife wound.

So you're Lola, he said.

She faced him.

Who are you? Where are you from?

I'm from Nanterre. Outside Paris. But I was born in Trappes, like Anelka. Do you watch football?

No, she said. How do you know Astrid?

She gave me a lift. He held out his arm. She treated this wound. But I didn't change the bandage so it's going septic.

You came to have your bandage changed.

But she was not smiling.

Kader went on peeling off the bandage. Lola stepped forward.

It's not septic, she said, looking at the wound.

She smelt of sex.

Are you a doctor? he asked.

No I'm a dancer. I teach salsa.

I've got a friend, Kader said. A black kid called Adel. He loves that Latino shit. Goes to all the clubs in Paris. He started because he liked to hit on the white women who go to those classes, but then he got into it for the dancing. He knows all the moves.

She looked at him with new curiosity.

Adel who?

I don't know his surname. He's from Mauritania.

Adel Kamara, she said. He's a pain in the arse. He tries to put African rhythms into every *passe*. Calls me a fascist because I stick to Cuban salsa. I like him, though. He makes me smile.

She had not smiled yet.

It's healed, she told him, pulling back. The movement revived the smell. You'll have a neat scar to remind you of the event. Is it a knife wound?

No, he said.

She picked up the bandage from the table and walked away, winding it into a ball. She opened a cupboard under the sink and threw it into the bin. Then she took the boiling water from the stove and made two cups of tea using tea bags. She put his cup

192

down on the table and wrapped her hands around her own. Kader averted his eyes from the stains on her nightdress.

You should go back to Trappes, she said. If you've come on a love quest for Astrid, you'll hit the wall. She's not capable of love.

Nanterre, he corrected her.

She can't love because she has to be in control.

Can you tell me where I can find her?

No I can't, she said. Then she stood up and swept out of the room.

When she had gone, he went to the cupboard under the sink. He opened the bin, pulled out the dirty bandage, the only souvenir he had, and put it into the pocket of his ruined tracksuit. He poured the tea down the sink, stood for a moment, looking about him, then picked up his crutches and went out through the back door.

Upstairs Lola got down on her knees and reached for the wooden box under her bed. It had a transfer of an Old English sheepdog on the lid. She sat with the box in her lap and began to look through the memorabilia she had stored there as if in readiness for this moment. Here was understanding.

A school photo. Black and white. Summer term, 1971. She was nine. Astrid was fourteen. She peered at herself, looking carefully. Straight back. Open smile. A few teeth missing. A little girl standing beside her best friend, Angela Sharpe. She tried to remember. She had loved Angela, her freckles and her lisp and her fluffy pink dressing gown. She and Angela had made perfume together out of squashed petals, then they had smoked together on the roofs, then they had gone looking for boys in the village near the school. Lola liked knowing that Angela was in a ditch close by. She could sometimes hear Angela's giggle resounding in the dappled wood. Astrid thought that Angela was simple. I like Georgina Fiennes better, she would say. She's interesting.

Lola looked for Georgina Fiennes. She found her in the back row: a tall girl with flaxen hair parted in the middle and falling like austere curtains on either side of her face. Astrid was right. Georgina was more interesting than Angela. At thirteen she drew anti-nuclear symbols in felt tip on her jeans and had read Plato's

Republic. Angela had gone into decline when Lola left her for Georgina. She gave up boys and spent all her time in the pottery room. She grew chubby and plain and could not meet your eye. Lola ran the tip of her finger over Angela's beaming moon face.

Astrid was in the same row as Lola at the far end. There was the same sad look in her eye.

She pulled out one of the press cuttings about the campaign for Astrid's release. There was a photo of Astrid taken at the press conference. She was sitting behind a microphone, looking dazed. She scrunched up the cutting in her fist and threw it across the room. She had paid too dearly for Astrid's sacrifice. She had believed all this time that this was what it had been. But now it was no longer clear. Astrid had been to prison instead of her; this she knew. At the age of seventeen, Lola had borrowed Astrid's ID card to get into an X-rated film. Absurdly, she had forgotten which film it was. When the police had searched Mikel's apartment after the Donosti commando fell, they had found the card and Astrid had been arrested and charged with logistical support. Astrid and their father had both insisted that they say nothing about Lola having borrowed it. Lola was to be protected at all costs. To this day, she didn't know why.

She pulled out the only photo they had of herself and Astrid with their father. She knew that her mother must have taken it with her Hasselblad because the image was square. It was a winter's day in their garden in Donostia. She recognised the brutally pruned plane trees in the background. There was frost on the ground. Her father was wearing his stiff camel-hair coat. He had a hat with a narrow brim and a scarf crossed between his lapels. Lola remembered that Eugenio had chosen the lawyer who was to defend Astrid. The choice had been a bad one. Astrid had been accused of logistical support but there was no proof of this, other than her I.D. card among Mikel's things. Instead of debunking the charges, the lawyer had built a complex ideological argument around the idea that Astrid was being persecuted simply because she was from a politically engaged family. Nothing, of course, could have been more maddening to the judge than the accusation that he was biased, and Astrid was sentenced to five years.

Lola looked at the photo again. She was still a baby, trussed up in a tartan coat lodged stiffly in her father's arms. Astrid was also wearing a tartan coat that looked too short for her and tights, baggy at the knees. There was a gap between her and Eugenio and it looked as though his hand was fishing for her to come closer. The distance upset the composition of the photo. Unlike Lola and Eugenio, Astrid was not looking at their mother but straight at the camera. It seemed clear to Lola that the clue to her sister's betrayal was there in that photo.

Lola was Astrid's link to the outside world. This was clear. Astrid had never had any connection to either her mother or her father. She had come into the world and found it hostile and had set about trying to protect her little sister from it. The path Lola took had been marked out for her by Astrid. Whenever she had tried to step off the path, Astrid had coaxed her back. Mikel had been the only real threat to Astrid's guidance. Lola leaned her head against the bed. She felt a new pity for her sister. Sacrifice came naturally to Astrid; she was afraid of life.

THIRTY-FIVE

Txema sat high in his Mercedes, facing the newly cut field of wheat, and waited for Lorea. The sun was a huge red ball in his wing mirror and the field was alight with it. Lorea had always thought she wanted to be married to him but he knew better. When the subject came up he liked to tell her that she would be a puma in a cage if she married him. This usually softened the blow.

When she arrived, Txema watched her pick her way through the stubble. There was no doubt: this woman made him feel powerful. He hoped he was not about to throw that away.

She opened the door and climbed in and leaned across to kiss him as she always did. Then she sat back and flipped open the sun visor, looked at her reflection in the mirror and faced him with her smile.

Txema turned on the engine.

I thought we were staying here. The disappointment he heard in her voice thrilled him. Where are we going?

We're going for a drive.

What for?

Txema did not answer. He drove out through the gap in the hedge and took the road that led into the mountains.

Lorea crossed her legs and began to sulk.

I have something to tell you, he said.

She uncrossed her legs.

What?

He glanced at her. She was wearing a pale-blue sundress with thin straps over her narrow shoulders. Her hair was tied back in a ponytail. He wanted to touch her long neck.

Did you go to San Sebastian today?

Of course. It's Friday.

Lorea went into town every Friday for a facial.

Did you swim? he asked.

Yes.

He smiled at her.

What is it, Txema? You're being strange.

I'm about to put my life into your hands, Lorea. I want to make sure I know you.

What are you talking about?

But he did not reply.

He drove through the last hamlet before the border and stopped in a lay-by beside a stream. The sound of rushing water came through the open window.

Where are we? she asked.

We're near a farm that used to belong to a man called Joakin, Txema told her. He hid Mikel and me for a night before we tried to cross the border.

Lorea always paid particular attention when he spoke of Mikel. Mikel to Lorea was an object worthy of hatred. He had been an historic member of the organisation and he had become a grass. She had never doubted this fact, probably because her imagination was more susceptible to tales of betrayal than to accounts of heroism.

Neither of us slept, Txema went on. We smoked and talked all night. The next evening Joakin took us in his truck to the café in the village and we met the two *mugas* who were to take us across the border.

Lorea shifted uneasily in her seat.

You don't have to tell me if you don't want to, Txema.

He leaned back into his door to get a better look at her. He had no choice. This woman was the only person in the world who could deliver him from his fear. He had stolen a large sum of money from the organisation. It had been collected from Basque companies, a month's worth of revolutionary tax. Every single day Txema saw himself being killed. He saw himself being shot expertly in the back of the head with a silenced Browning. They could get him anywhere: in his bed, in his car, in his office. Someone with a black balaclava over their face would come up to him and ask him, Are you Txema Egibar? And he would nod or shake his head and whatever his reaction, however cowering or dignified, they would pull their weapon and shoot him in the head and the heart. Lorea loved him. Lorea was a fierce animal. If anyone tried to hurt him, she would attack, no thought for herself.

197

I want you to be my wife, he said.

She was looking at him now, her hand over her mouth.

I want to marry you, he said.

Txema reached out and took her hand. She was shaking. She never cried. She watched her hand in his, unable to look him in the eye, aware of how much harm he could do her. He pressed his lips to her hand to still it.

I brought you up here to tell you everything, he said.

Txema . . .

He kissed her hand again.

The money you took to Switzerland belongs to the organisation. It was revolutionary tax.

Lorea pulled her hand from his grasp. She looked at him now, her eyes wide with fear.

When the Donosti commando fell Mikel and I were both identified and we received orders to disappear. Months later, we were told to cross over to France and to take the money with us to give to somebody, living in Biarritz, who went by the name of 'The Belgian'. When we began the journey, I was carrying the bag. We left with Joakin in his truck. When we got to the village it was ten-thirty on a Friday night. I didn't know either of the *mugas* who were taking us across. They were brothers. Mikel had met one of them at a rally in Guernica. Txema nodded at a narrow wooden bridge that crossed the stream. We started walking from there, he said. It's a public footpath now but it was barely a track then. That bridge wasn't there. We jumped across. The money weighed a ton. Apart from the password, no words had been exchanged between us since the meeting. It was a clear, cold night in October. We could see our breath in the moonlight. We walked up a steep path through this old oak wood I've known since I was a kid. The trunks were all twisted and covered in moss and lichen. It's supposed to be haunted. The ground was damp from recent rain so the climb was hard. The eldest brother led the way, then Mikel, then me, then the youngest brother. All of us were armed.

Lorea had stopped shaking. Her face wore an expression he had never seen before. She was listening wholly to him. Every part of her was attentive; all vanity, for the moment, had disappeared.

We were on a thinly wooded plateau, only minutes away from this pile of rocks where we were supposed to meet the other two refugees who were coming back the opposite way. They were to be escorted by our *mugas* to Joakin's. At first, I thought it was a wild boar running through the undergrowth. The others scattered and I stood there, frozen. There he was, a man, four paces away, pointing an automatic weapon at me. He was in combat gear and his face was blacked out. His eyes were very white. A shot rang out. In that instant, the man's attention wavered and I ran at him. He should have shot me but he didn't. As I threw my weight at him, I remember thinking that he must be very young. He fell back like he was made of sticks. His head hit a rock. I didn't think of the money then. I thought of Mikel.

He looked at Lorea, at her eyes, full of fear and pity, and he knew that she would never again look this beautiful to him.

I heard two more shots behind me as I ran towards the border. There were about five hundred metres of open country to cross, with only the occasional tree, too thin to hide behind. The place was flooded with moonlight. As I ran I was anticipating the shot so strongly that the back of my head ached. I went on running downhill. I kept running until I reached a pine forest growing on a steep slope. I dived into it. As I lay panting beside a tree, I thought of the money. It gave me a new energy. It made me brave. It took me hours to dig the hole with a piece of rock. There were roots everywhere. When I had finished my fingers were bleeding. I buried the bag under that tree and carried a rock from the plateau to mark the spot. When I left it was dawn. The money was mine. He squeezed Lorea's hand. Now it is ours, he said.

She looked down at her lap. And Txema knew that he would stay with her simply for what he felt for her at this moment.

I want to feel safe now, Lorea, he told her. After the money disappeared, the organisation carried out an investigation. The two *mugas* were shot by the Guardia Civil up there on the mountain, so all they had were Mikel's account of his arrest and my own testimony to the French gendarmerie. Still to this day, I don't know what Mikel thinks. No one ever managed to get hold of a copy of his *cantada* as far as I know. When I was questioned in France by Iñaki, the man who trained me, and Koldo whom I trained, I told them that one of the *mugas* was carrying the bag. I said that the

Guardia Civil must have taken the money. I don't know what Mikel told them.

Why didn't you ask him?

He wasn't listening. He was looking out at the narrow bridge. One thing I do know, Astrid Arnaga will lead us to Mikel.

Lorea's eyes had lost all trace of tenderness. She was herself again.

Anxton is on her, she said. She's at the Hotel Lagunekin. She hasn't moved all day. She smiled at him. He has the bike. I'll do the rest.

Txema was suddenly helpless with desire. He reached over and caught her behind the neck.

THIRTY-SIX

After only two nights, Mikel was growing attached to the smell in his van. Castro's fur gave off a scent like burnt sugar and his warm breath, which enveloped them both at night, made human breath offensive to him in its blandness. The blind man's breath was making him lean back a little now as they sat together at the bar in a café in the village of Ascain where he had been working at the market. Castro seemed like a model of good digestion in comparison to this creature.

You don't listen, Mikel. Do you?

Mikel gave the old man a light slap on the shoulder.

I'm afraid I may have lost the knack of human intercourse.

Don't touch me.

Forgive me . . .

It's something I have been unable to tolerate since I lost my sight.

I understand.

You don't!

Castro jumped to his feet and snarled, baring his teeth, neck outstretched, eyes savage.

Easy boy, Mikel soothed.

Castro lay down again, keeping the man with the stick always in his sights.

Mikel faced Itxua with new attention.

What can I do for you, old friend?

Nothing. Absolutely nothing. I'm here to find out what I might do for you.

Castro growled.

I'm doing as well as I could have imagined. Mikel reached down to scratch his dog between the ears. I have a job I enjoy and an honest companion. He sat up and looked at the blind man who was listening carefully, his head jutting forward. Mikel could see the faces of all the Basque prisoners reflected in the old man's glasses. The faces came from the poster on the wall behind him.

Thank you for asking, he said.

Itxua leaned forward and the faces of the prisoners disappeared.

I offer my help, Mikel, because you are a superior man . . .

Mikel shook his head. An unpleasant taste had settled in his throat.

You are a man of great integrity. I've always known this and I'm not alone. Your life should have been different. You were made for leadership. I have often puzzled over the circumstances that led you to lead the wrong life.

Mikel shook his head again and looked away. He caught the barman's eye and nodded at him. He was hungry now and wanted his supper. Itxua was an unwelcome intrusion from the past. He should have known as soon as the old man walked up to his van and invited him for a drink. But he was so changed, so diminished, Mikel had taken pity on him, had imagined that the venom had gone from him.

The old man took a packet of cigarettes from his pocket. Gently Mikel took the packet, lit one for him and put it between his lips. Itxua drew deeply on the cigarette.

I'm here to talk to you about Txema Egibar.

What about him?

I'm here to warn you that he is no friend to you.

Mikel smiled.

You're probably right.

He is a disgrace!

Itxua spat these words. Here was real bitterness, Mikel thought. He looked down at Castro and saw that he too wanted his supper.

I must tell you something about myself, he said. I've been in prison for most of my life. And I *have* learned something. Probably only one thing. The importance of leading a simple life.

Itxua turned his head away in disgust.

A simple life. What is that? How is it possible to lead a simple life in a complex universe, unless you are either mad or a simpleton? He stubbed out his cigarette in a tin ashtray on the bar.

I may well be mad. I cannot rule that out.

The old man made a guttural noise that set Castro growling again.

That dog is a liability, he said.

Mikel let his hand dangle so that Castro could lick it. He wanted the old man to leave now. He could feel anger gathering and he knew that anger had put the sour taste in his throat. Castro stopped licking his hand and lay down.

What exactly do you want? Mikel asked, his voice cold.

Itxua leaned towards him so that Mikel found himself enshrouded in his foul breath again.

I want to help you. You should know that Txema would like you dead.

Mikel closed his eyes.

I don't want to hear this, Itxua. And he stood up. This is shit, he said.

This, this, this. This is your life, Mikel. Your duty, your heritage.

Fuck my heritage. I'm a free man.

Itxua smiled.

Have you have forgotten that there's no such thing as a free man?

Well what on earth are you all fighting for then?

We're fighting for our dignity.

I'm afraid I don't know what that means. But I think that whatever it is, I'm not interested in it. It's certainly not worth killing or dying for.

You're not mad, Mikel. You're a simpleton.

Mikel slammed his hand down on the bar catching the edge of the tin ashtray which clattered to the floor. Castro jumped up.

Itxua stepped back. Mikel reached out to support him.

Don't touch me! Keep your dog away from me.

Mikel clicked his fingers and Castro came to heel.

The old man seemed to be quivering with rage. Mikel watched. He was dimly aware that the longer he stayed in his company, the more he would pay.

Listen to me, Mikel, Itxua said, trying to soften. I am your friend. I have known you since you were a child. I want to help you. But the anger was still there in his mouth, in his purple gills. Txema has what does not belong to him, he went on. You must get it back.

Get it back? And give it to whom?

Don't, Itxua began. Then he stopped. Don't, he said again, shaking his head.

You know, for years I wondered if Txema had that money, Mikel said. I wondered in prison for a long time and then I stopped wondering. I realised that I didn't care whether he did or not. I thought, if he does, I feel sorry for him. He can't spend it and he's living in fear, which is a worse prison than the one I've known.

That money doesn't belong to him.

Who does it belong to? He waited, but Itxua said nothing. Mikel saw that he had retrenched. It belongs to the Basques who earned it . . .

Who earned it through collaboration with the occupying forces and exploitation of their people, Itxua said. I personally have never doubted his guilt, he went on. But proof is of course needed. There have always been a few who thought it was you. But they tended to be Txema's lieutenants. I knew when I saw you in that van of yours and I caught the stench that you live in that it couldn't possibly have been you.

Mikel longed to leave but knew it was important to hear the end.

Txema has been careful, the old man went on. He's a disciplined man, I'll say that for him. Setting up an import-export company covered the purchase of the café, the villa his mother lives in and that ridiculous car he drives. All those purchases were investigated by people who know about fraud and nothing was found. We believe that he gets advice from someone who once advised us and who is now living in Venezuela.

Ah, there it was, the 'We' Mikel could no longer abide.

The man's alias is 'The Belgian', Itxua said.

I'm afraid I can't listen to this, Mikel interrupted. I wish no disrespect to you. But I must go.

You will go when I have finished.

I'm sorry, Mikel said.

We have a copy of your *cantada*, Mikel.

I don't give a shit.

It is in safe hands. We know you did no wrong.

Itxua. You can tell 'We', they can do what they like with my *cantada*.

Itxua grabbed his wrist and clamped against the bar.

If you don't testify against Txema, Mikel, then you'll put yourself in danger.

Mikel looked at the hand gripping his.

Let go of me.

Castro was snarling. Itxua let go. He was making a kind of smile that looked like a gash in his face.

You can go, he said, relenting suddenly. Of course you wouldn't betray Txema. You're one of us.

Mikel hesitated, suspicious of the change of tone.

Just then Castro trotted out through the open door of the café. He thinks I should leave him the last word, Mikel thought. And he's right.

Mikel followed his dog back to the van and began counting the takings for that morning. The unpleasant taste still hung in his throat, though he chain-smoked to try and cover it. Castro slept fitfully in the back. Occasionally he would puff air out through his flews, his flank would quiver and his paws would twitch. Mikel looked up to see Itxua walking across the deserted square to a beige Renault 12 parked next to the church. A street lamp jutting out from the church wall lit the scene. He watched the driver climb out and help Itxua into the passenger seat and he recognised his former lawyer, Gomez Igari. He saw them drive slowly away. How could a couple of old men still have so much harm in them? He turned back to the hardbound notebook his employer had given him. He tried to put Itxua out of his mind. He enjoyed writing in neat capitals between the columns: article, quantity, cost. It was simple, sane work.

Castro was panting. The sock was slowing him down. As he ran, he tried to shake it off. Every time his bad paw struck the pavement his left eye twitched with the pain. He was running through a town that smelt of fish. The salt in the air made him thirstier still. His tongue lolled as he ran. He came to an overturned dustbin. Rotting fruit. He plunged his nose into the refuse and jumped back, yelping in pain. The bee in its death throes clung to his nose. He shook his head wildly, spraying saliva. There was no food and no master. He found himself on the beach where he had trodden on the deadly metal thorn. He walked, head hanging, to

the sea and dipped his throbbing nose in the water. He lapped
twice then lay down in the sea and let the water wash over him.
As he lay there he saw a man walking towards him across the
sand, his dark figure distorted by the heat. When he drew close
Castro saw it was the man with the black glasses and the stick.
Again, he bared his teeth, but the man called him and spoke to
him of food in a good man's voice. And Castro followed him
along the beach, keeping his distance until they reached the park
where the children play with the ball and it was night and the
place was lit up with lights that blinded him. He blinked, trying
to avoid the light, but wherever he turned it shone into his eyes.
All the time the man talked to him in his good man's voice and
Castro kept blinking against the light, waiting for the food that he
could smell now, and he whined for joy. Then the lights went out.
At first there were spots in his eyes and he could not see. Then he
saw: his master, lying on the hard ground, his body open. The
man with the black glasses was standing behind his master's
body, calling him forward. Eat, said the bad man, and Castro saw
butcher's bones lying in his master's body, big bones with flesh
on them. But his master was alive and calling him: Good boy,
Castro. Eat. And Castro began to yelp and cry. Then something
gripped his throat and he snapped his jaws shut.

It's all right, boy. Mikel soothed. You're alright. He could see fear
in the dog's eyes. He put his hand on Castro's chest. His heart
was racing. You're alright, boy. Come on, let's walk.
    He locked the van and they walked through the empty market
place, Mikel waiting for Castro while he sniffed at the debris and
then took the path, scattered with boulders, that led through the
chestnut grove. A harvest moon hung low in the sky and Mikel
tried to enjoy the night breeze and the smell of freshly cut hay. He
hummed 'Desperado', a song that he had always loved, but he
could not escape the sensation that Itxua, his voice, his rationale,
was polluting his mind.
    He stopped humming and talked to Castro:
    What exactly do they want? They want the money back, right?
Castro shot off through a gap in the beech hedge.
    No doubt, Mikel thought, making him denounce Txema was
simply a way of putting pressure on him to give up the money in

exchange for his life. Then they would kill Txema afterwards. And probably me as well, he said aloud. Castro was at his side again, trotting unevenly. What do you think, boy? Will they kill me too?

Itxua had wanted him for a leadership position; something in the public eye like the refugee committee. Mikel gave a short laugh at the idea.

Whatever it was that had been holding his anger at bay then gave way. Mikel made a fist and punched hard at a tree trunk. He felt nothing for several seconds, then smiled at the pain and the sight of the blood blooming on his knuckles.

THIRTY-SEVEN

Kader looked through the passenger window into the Volvo and smiled. He would have sung for joy if he had been alone but people were watching him. He supposed that in a place like this, a face like his would not go unnoticed for long. Let's not even think about *your* mug, Amadou, he thought. He looked for any trace of his presence in her impeccable car and found none.

He walked into the hotel reception wishing that he was not on crutches. Yes, he wanted to say to the man behind the counter, an Arab *and* a cripple. But the man was friendly and spoke to him in English.

Do you speak French? Kader asked him.

Yes. How can I help you?

The man had a pale face and eyebrows that were blacker and covered more of his forehead than most humans. Kader sensed the eyebrows had been a problem in his life.

Is Astrid Arnaga staying here?

She is. I'll just ring up to her room. What is your name?

Kader hesitated.

Kader, he said.

The man picked up the receiver and pressed a button on his antiquated switchboard. Pressed was hardly the word: it was more like a push that engaged the full motion of his right arm. The number nineteen lit up orange.

He spoke to Astrid in Spanish but Kader knew that the conversation was not going the way he would have liked. He pretended that he had not understood and wedged his crutches snugly in his armpits, ready to proceed.

She says that she does not want to be disturbed.

I'll come back later, then.

She says that she doesn't want to see you. That you should go.

His manner was patient but suddenly Bushy had become more like a wolf than a squirrel. Kader scanned the premises. There was no lift and on crutches he doubted that he could outrun him. He decided to retreat.

He went to the café next door and bought himself a bottle of beer and a sandwich with an omelette in it, and returned to the big square up the hill. A few remaining children were playing football under the floodlights. Kader sat and drank his beer and ate the sandwich, which was not nearly as bad as he had anticipated. He wished he could have played with the kids. Instead he shouted instructions:

Spread out! he yelled. Don't all chase the ball, you fucking halfwits!

They ran about, craning their necks, trying to understand.

When he had finished eating, he returned to the hotel. He walked through the lobby without greeting Bushy, who was watching a football match on a TV screen so far above his head that he had to tilt back his chair.

As he reached the stairs, he heard Bushy's chair clatter to the floor and a muffled shout. He hobbled as fast as he could up the stairs, trying to keep his hip still, but each step produced red-hot pain. Bushy overtook him in the narrow corridor and stood before him, out of breath. His eyebrows had taken on a life of their own.

You have to leave. You can't be up here.

Kader cast a glance to either side of him. Room number thirteen to his right, fifteen to his left. He was not far but there was no getting past Bushy who, from his calm expression, seemed to bear him no hard feelings. He just stood there, waiting for Kader to draw back.

Kader thought of the karate master back home. The man's quiet voice, his long blond hair and his headband had annoyed the shit out of him. It is all a matter of approach, he would say. You must pass *through* your adversary. Think of rushing water. This way your hand can slice through it. This way you will be swept away.

Bullshit, Kader thought, and he gave Bushy a firm push with both palms that sent him reeling backwards onto his arse. As he lunged towards Astrid's door, Bushy's fist grabbed his bad ankle and he cried out in pain. Bushy gave a sharp tug and pulled him to the floor.

Astrid's door opened.

It's all right, she said wearily. He can stay.

Bushy looked down at Kader, as though deciding whether or not to give him a kick, then turned and walked back along the corridor.

Kader stepped after her into the room. He could see nothing but red spots in the darkness. Then he saw her, sitting on the edge of the bed, her head bowed.

Why did you come? Her voice was so sad, for a moment Kader couldn't answer.

Can I turn a light on?

No.

He hovered a moment, then sat down on the edge of the other bed and faced her, making sure his knees didn't touch hers.

What are you doing here? Why aren't you with your sister?

Astrid looked up and he strained to see her expression but could only see her outline.

I'm going back to Paris, she said.

Why? You just got here.

He could tell from the set of her shoulders that she was in despair. He sat facing her, so close that he could feel the warmth of her body. He had no desire to touch her. It felt to him that all the desire and rage that had driven him here had vanished and he was a kid again, but not the kid he had been, the one he was meant to have been.

He took her hand.

To Astrid, all movement had started to feel slow and laborious. She looked at her hand being held but could not hold his in return.

He let go and laid the crutches on the floor, then he knelt in the gap between the two beds and put his arms around her. He clasped her for some time and she listened to his breathing. Suddenly he pulled her hand from her lap and wrapped her arm around him.

Hold me, he said.

So she held him.

The more she clung to him, the more separate she felt.

Kader, she said. She held him closer, trying to annihilate his

210

pain with the strength of her embrace. She could feel the discomfort of a new kind of deceit settling into her heart. She pulled away.

What have you done to yourself? she asked.

My hip came out of its socket. He took her hand again. You have no idea, Astrid.

She covered his hand with hers.

I'm the one who's going to look after you, he told her. Do you understand?

She recognised that remoteness and clarity that came over her when she was operating.

I got thrown from the top step of your father's office, he went on. He was smiling and she remembered how beguiling his joy had been only four days before. Now she looked at him with detached curiosity.

You met my father, she said.

I did. What a sad old bastard he is.

He told you where to find me.

No. Kader paused. Let me turn a light on. I want to see you.

Astrid let him stand. He hobbled, without the crutches, over to the sink and turned on the light above it. The yellow tube gave off a warm light that filled the room with shadows.

I love this place, he said, returning to the bed. This village is the most beautiful place I've ever seen. I mean it.

I hate it, she said.

You hate it now . . .

Who told you where to find me? she interrupted.

His secretary told me. She looks like she hasn't slept for about ten years.

That's not his secretary. That's his mistress. She's a lawyer too.

Well she took pity on me. Look at me, he said. This time his smile reached her.

I have to sleep, Kader. Will you let me sleep and then we'll go?

Go where?

Back to Paris.

He lay down on the bed.

Sleep here, he said, opening his arms. Sleep in my arms.

Astrid shook her head.

I can't sleep in someone's arms.

Well it's time you learned. Come on.

His innocence made her resistance seem petty. She lay down with him.

You had a row with your sister, he said.

She found out.

Found out what?

His voice had a softness. Astrid could not see him, she could only hear his breath and feel his voice vibrating in his chest.

What did she find out? he urged.

Astrid closed her eyes and was in the confessional again.

What I've been trying to hide for so long, she said. That I lied to her. That the man she's been waiting for all her life is in love with me, that I let him love me.

And what about you? Do you love him?

She opened her eyes.

I don't love anybody, she said.

You love your sister.

I don't know.

Kader reached out and gathered an edge of the dusty counterpane and wrapped it around her, holding her more tightly.

I met her, he said. She's like you and the opposite of you. She looked . . . He hesitated. She looked like she'd just been fucking.

She often looks like that.

He squeezed her.

You do love her, he said.

Astrid closed her eyes. She dreaded emerging from this embrace when she would see once again how separate they were.

Do you love him? he asked her for the second time.

No.

Are you sure?

I hate him. When I went to prison I made Lola promise to stop seeing him.

Kader lifted his head.

What do you mean, prison? Have you been inside?

For two years.

Fuck, Astrid. What for?

Logistical support of a terrorist organisation.

Fuck me, he said, lying back.

Astrid hoped he wouldn't move again.

I was inside for eighteen months, he told her.

You told me.

It nearly did my head in.

I didn't mind it. It was made bearable by the woman who ran it. She was called Ana Gonzalez. She was the first person I really admired. She had great courage and energy. She loved all of us and tried to make confinement as painless as possible.

You were lucky, Kader said. Ours was called Delorme. What a cunt. He used to strut around pretending that he was keeping an eye on things. Working for change, he'd say. He'd write down complaints like: We're fucking four in a cell built for two, in this little notebook, and he wore caps. Fucking tweed caps. What a nerve. He paused and she knew his memory was conjuring the smells and colours of prison. But go on, he said. I want to hear about your time.

Mine was quite comfortable, she said. We all had a cell to ourselves. It was a new prison and it was built with that in mind. It was like a beehive with tiny geometric cells, about two metres square, where we slept and washed and crapped. The cells all stank, some more than others, but in the end you didn't notice it.

Kader stroked her hair.

Luxury, he said.

For the first six weeks I did nothing but watch.

I did nothing but fight, he said.

Every afternoon we were locked out of our cells and I think that's what I hated most. I didn't like being locked out of my cell and I didn't do any of the activities.

Nor did I. What did you have?

Hairdressing, cooking, theatre, art. I didn't want to do anything but I liked to go and sit in the art room. I liked the smell. I hated the kitchens because they stank, and the smell of nail varnish in the hairdressing salon. I've hated hairdressers since then.

It shows, he said, clasping a handful of her hair. Look at this stuff.

Astrid smiled. She knew that she was experiencing a reprieve from her own nature and she did not expect it to last.

I liked the art teacher, she said. She was a big woman with a thick Galician accent. She stopped asking me if I wanted to paint and just let me sit in the corner.

What I hated most, Kader said, was time. Time in prison is fucked. Every day it crawls and when visiting time comes around it fucking races.

Ana had no clocks in her prison.

Good woman.

She was.

There was a pause.

Tell me, he said. Is there a lot of . . . you know . . .

Sex? Yes. There was frenetic erotic activity. In my first weeks I watched so many couples form and break up. I'd see the first flush of love. Girls would pin up their hair and show off their love bites. It always involved the same people, though. You were either part of it or you weren't. People fell in and out of love very quickly. When there were fights, they were usually about love.

Were you part of it?

No. But I suppose I was in love.

Who with?

With Ana.

What was she like?

She was tiny and she smoked all the time. She had a deep, gravelly laugh. I looked forward to her visits. Everyone did. When she came on her rounds, she always had a flock of women walking with her for as far as they were allowed to go. They'd all speak at once, like children, and she'd keep walking, answering gently, always with a smile on her face. Her one flaw was that she loved one of the prisoners, this woman called Gaia. It was a mystery to me. Gaia was a gypsy from Malaga. She didn't love anyone. Except for her dog. She had photos of him all over her cell. He was a boxer with pointed ears called Cal. Short for *calcetinas*. Because he had white socks. *Calcetinas* means sock in Spanish.

I got that.

Gaia was like a stray dog herself. She was hungry and grasping. There were two groups in prison. Those who wanted money and wanted to work and those who didn't care. Gaia only thought about work and she was rich. She wore tight, navy-blue overalls every day and every morning after breakfast she'd be the first in the workshop, making inner tubes.

And what did you do?

I studied medicine.

214

No shit. Fuck, I wish I'd studied.

What would you have studied?

Anything. History. The Koran maybe. Try and get some knowledge, so people can't bullshit you so easily.

If I hadn't been able to study, prison would have been very different. The other women disliked me because I was labelled a *terorista*. Then it became clear that I wasn't accepted by the political prisoners either, that I was something different. The women who belonged to the organisation stuck together. They had an aloofness about them, as if they were set on a higher goal than the rest of us. They were like nuns. After I'd been there for a few months Ana called me into her office. She offered me a filing job. I asked her why she'd chosen me and she told me that she had the feeling that I was there by accident, that she had experience in these matters and that it showed. Studying was her idea.

What happened to the woman with the dog?

She hit someone in the face with a fire extinguisher and got sent to a place that was a lot worse. I wasn't there when it happened but I was told that she nearly killed this woman. They were fighting about shifts. I found Ana in her office and she'd been crying. She looked up and smiled at me without bothering to wipe away her tears. She just said, I'm a stupid woman, and I put my arms around her. I remember how she held me as though I was the one who needed consoling.

There was a pause. Astrid watched the shadows on the ceiling.

When I got out, Kader said, I wasn't fit for normal life.

What do you mean by normal life?

Job, car, girlfriend, he said. When I came out I felt like I was invisible. It was like everyone was living their boring lives and I was this . . . this ghost. A ghost would come back and think everything everyone did or cared about was pointless, wouldn't he?

Probably.

It was like that. In a man's prison you have to be dangerous or else you get shat on. When I came out, every time I went to a bar or a club, I'd get into a fight. My friend Amadou said it was like I was trying to wake people up. He was right. It was like everyone else was on tranquillisers or something.

In my prison there was very little fighting, she said. Mostly we lay about in a torpor. Frustration turned itself into self-loathing more than anger. I got so used to the sound of women crying that I didn't notice it after a while, like the sound of rain or bad plumbing.

They lay in silence. Astrid felt a wave of gratitude spread through her like heat.

Astrid? You said you made your sister promise to stop seeing her man. I want to know if that was because you hated him or because you loved him.

It was the right question but she knew that it signalled the end of her reprieve.

She pulled free of his arms.

I didn't love him, she said. She stood up and walked over to the sink. He was ruining Lola. She turned on the tap, filled a plastic cup and drank.

Kader sat up and leaned against the wall.

How?

You wouldn't understand, she said, walking over to the window.

What wouldn't I understand?

The organisation. The people he worked for were killers. He murdered two people.

Kader kept silent. She pulled back the curtains and looked out at the moon, trailing a stripe of cloud. She wondered what time it was. She no longer wanted to sleep.

I don't know the man, Kader said at last. But I know that sometimes it's circumstances that make people kill.

I know, she said. And I wouldn't care if it were just him. But he was pulling Lola into the organisation and I couldn't bear that life for her. She started delivering pamphlets, then going to demonstrations. Then he taught her to throw Molotov cocktails, then before I knew it he had got her to plant bombs with him. She would have joined what they call a legal commando, then she would have been identified by the police and she would have had to go into hiding. She would have started killing people herself. It's always the same path. If I hadn't gone to prison, that's what would have happened to her.

You were saving her from a life of crime.

You couldn't possibly understand, she told him.

I don't understand why you didn't just tell your sister what an

216

arsehole he was to be writing to you behind her back. I'm thinking that you must have loved him, otherwise you would have told her.

She saw that he had removed the bandage from his arm. She could not see from where she stood if the wound had healed or not.

It was vanity, she said. I was vain. That was all.

Maybe.

Suddenly she wanted him out of the room.

You'll know when you see him, he murmured.

Know what?

If you love him.

I don't love him.

She stood on the other side of the room, and he saw that she was responsible for all this pain he was in.

Come here, he said. Fucking come here. I can't move.

He watched her hook a lock of her hair behind her ear and there was the same feeling, like a string breaking in his gut, that he had felt when he had watched her walk around her car on the first day. The first day. He could not remember who he had been.

I want you to look at my fucking heel. It's killing me.

He pulled up the leg of his tracksuit. She knelt by the bed to look at the wound.

It's all green and yellow, he said. It looks like the fucking Brazilian flag.

She prodded the area around the bite. The pain was unbelievable. He closed his eyes.

It's septic, she said. Is it a dog bite?

Yes. Fucking Raoul. Racist Raoul.

You need antibiotics.

I need a kiss.

She looked up. Her face was full of pity.

I can't kiss you, she said.

Why not? I've been through hell for you, you heartless bitch.

I don't feel anything, Kader. I can't kiss you.

You can let me kiss you.

But he could not move. Pain was waiting for him everywhere.

You know you smell like a dessert my mum's sister Leila used to make, he told her. It was a white dessert. I think it had almonds

217

in it. My mum kept it in a plastic box in the fridge. I used to scoop spoonfuls of it off the top, thinking she wouldn't notice. When she brought it out for lunch with the family, there was hardly any left. It tasted of cold flowers, flowers soaked in sugar.

Astrid smiled.

My mum is Kabyle, he said. She had a beautiful voice. She wanted me to be a Rai singer. Do you know Rai?

Yes.

But I wanted to be a footballer.

You said. Astrid stood up. I'm going to get you some antibiotics.

I'll come with you.

No.

I'll come, he said, swinging his legs off the bed.

The chemist will be closed, she said. I'll have to get them to open up for me. It's better if you stay here.

And she grabbed her handbag and left the room.

Kader lay on his back, ankles crossed, hands behind his head. He closed his eyes and saw his mother's lovely face floating in the darkness. She was smiling, showing the gap between her two front teeth: *les dents du bonheur*, teeth of happiness, the French called them. How, with a mother so happy, could he love a woman as sad as Astrid? Because Astrid's sadness was what made her beautiful. It hung in her eyes like a lantern, it floated on her forehead like a veil. Kader began to hum a tune to go with the words. He hummed with his eyes closed, the words forming in his mind. The smile spread on his face and his stomach filled with heat. The song began to float out of him into the room: an Arab song in French. He was an Arab, singing a French song for the Spanish woman he loved.

He threw back the bedclothes and got out of bed. He looked at his face in the mirror above the sink. It had changed. Or he had changed and didn't recognise his face any more. That face no longer belonged in Nanterre. He grinned. You're free, he told himself.

He bent over and drank from the tap. Then he went and climbed into bed. In the morning they would go and buy him some decent clothes. In the car on the way, he would sing her his song.

The village was quiet. As she walked down the hill past Txema's bar, she braced herself. This time she would not be caught off guard. She would not forgive him for what he had done to Lola. And me, she thought, feeling her hatred gather momentum as she walked. She searched for ways to hurt him. She knew that she had shaken him with her mention of their arrest. Perhaps something had happened up there on the mountain. There had been four of them and all of them had been caught or shot except for Txema. The circumstances of their arrest had always been strange, not just to her. For a short time everyone was discussing how lucky Txema had been. They had been discovered in the hills by a mobile unit of the Guardia Civil called the FAR. But while Mikel had been taken into custody by the Guardia Civil and given life, Txema had been arrested by the French gendarmerie, had spent nine months in Bayonne prison for possession of a weapon and then been put under house arrest, which meant in those days that you could come and go as you pleased, so long as you did not try and cross the border.

Why had he eluded punishment? She cursed Mikel for having taken his own so meekly.

The chemist was dark and the metal grille was drawn across the window. She walked round to the side door and rang the bell. At length a man's sleepy voice came across the intercom.

Milo, is that you? It's Astrid Arnaga. I'm sorry to wake you. I need antibiotics.

Astrid, he chuckled. Wait. I'm coming.

Milo was wearing pyjama bottoms and a string vest. He grinned at her as he scratched his side. He had not changed: still the same weary good humour.

Good to see you here, he said. At this time of night at my door. Strange but good.

When he returned with the medication, he held it out to her and pulled it back as she reached for it.

Will you come back and see us before you go?

Yes Milo.

In the daytime, he said.

She took the drugs and smiled.

And Lola? he asked.

She's here.

Good. Come back and see us, both of you. Mirabel and I have a baby boy. That's why I have these, he said, pointing to the shadows under his eyes.

Suddenly she felt tears rising. She had to get away. She squeezed his hand then turned and walked off. It was a few moments before she heard him close the door.

Kader was asleep when she got back to the room. She crept to the sink and prepared the injection.

I thought you weren't coming back, he said.

He was lying on his back with his arms behind his head.

She went over to him and knelt down beside him with the syringe pointing at the ceiling.

Show me your ankle.

Kader pulled up his tracksuit and closed his eyes.

In the morning, she said as she injected him, I'm going to drive you to Bayonne and put you on the train to Paris.

I'm not going back to Paris. I have nothing there.

You have even less here.

I can start again here, he said. That's the whole point. Back home I'll just go straight to jail.

What do you want to do here? There's even more unemployment here than there is in Paris.

Not for an Arab from Nanterre.

What can you do?

I can drive a forklift truck, open mussels, operate a crane. I can train attack dogs. I can fight . . .

There's a world of trouble to get into here unless you know how to work, Kader.

He shrugged.

You can teach me.

Astrid looked at his eyes. They were like Lola's, full of mischief. It occurred to her that Kader and Lola were the same species: unafraid of life.

She stood up.

I don't think it's something I can teach you.

Lola told me to go home too, he said.

Her face lit up.

Did she?

Suddenly Kader was sick of looking at her. He was sick of his desire.

I'm tired, he said.

Go to sleep then.

Don't run out on me.

I'm going to find Mikel, she said.

Is that his name?

She nodded.

Why? he asked sadly. The idyll was over. He had lost her already. He felt weak.

For Lola.

I can help you, he said. I'm tough.

No you're not.

You don't know that.

You may be tough in Nanterre but you're not tough here. This is a place where everyone is involved in a war that's been going on since before they were born.

Kader exhaled through his teeth dismissively.

Some war zone, he said.

You don't always feel it but when you do, it's frightening. I promise you.

He grinned.

That's what I'm here for, to protect you.

On crutches with an infected foot, she said.

I can still help you, he said. I can use a gun.

Go to sleep, she said.

Fuck you.

Astrid went and turned off the light, then she undressed and got into bed.

Don't leave without me.

But she did not answer. Soon he was asleep.

Chastel's call woke her.

What time is it? she whispered.

Six.

Have you been operating?

No. I can't sleep. I love you.

You don't, Jacques.

Don't say that! You have no idea who I am.

His voice was angry.

I'll be back for the conference, she said.

There was a pause.

You're wrong, Astrid. I do love you.

His voice had softened. He sounded a little drunk.

I'm sorry about what I said about my abortion. It wasn't your fault.

We can start again, he said.

Yes, she answered. Once again she felt the toxicity of deceit. It occurred to her then that if only she could be truthful to one person, she might be saved.

I'm going to tell Laetitia, he said.

She already knows.

I'm going to leave her.

Please Jacques. I don't want to be responsible for destroying another relationship.

What do you mean another relationship? Anyway it's not a relationship. It's an arrangement and I wouldn't hold you responsible.

It *is* a relationship. Of course it's a relationship. You've had children together.

Astrid made him promise not to do anything until the conference on 5 September, in six weeks' time. Then she hung up. The thought of the meeting of the Transplantation Society filled her with dread. It would be like attending a religious ceremony after losing one's faith. Bopp would be there with his big hands making one of his dull presentations about transgenic pigs. Since he had sold out to Novartis and its pig lobby, Bopp had grown smug when he should be hugging the walls in shame. As far as she was concerned, pigs as organ donors were a waste of time and money.

Since 1985 she had performed over five hundred transplants. Vincent, her lab assistant, kept count. She was not a cabinet maker: although she was accomplished at it, the craft itself did not interest her. The only thing that gave her satisfaction now was her relationship with certain patients. She thought in particular of a man called Romero Bazzanella who had played the violin every night in a Russian restaurant off the Champs-Elysées. He had end-stage cirrhosis and watched death approach with his brawler's shoulders set firmly against it, ready for the impact. When she told him they had a donor, he had laughed at her and told her that she could believe what she liked but he knew when the bell had rung. Bazzanella was a wonderful patient because he had not treated her like God when he woke up with a new liver. He had simply sent her an invitation to Raspoutine's and told her that he considered that they had both been lucky to get away with it.

Astrid did not have Chastel's faith in transplantation. She could not blind herself to the fact that her patients would wake up to find themselves in a small, hampered life. She had come to identify the immunosuppressive drugs that went with a graft as slow killers. When Bazzanella was told by the anaesthetist that he could no longer play the violin like a wild gypsy, or drink, or smoke, or eat like a Cossack, he stopped taking his drugs and died of pneumonia in six weeks. Others moved into flats that offered paramedical care and shuffled around in dressing gowns waiting for the slow process of chronic rejection to set in. She knew that what made her go on operating was not her belief in the magic of transplantation but the little flutter of joy when the liver set to work in its new body; a joy not unlike that of watching Reál score a goal.

Just before dawn Astrid woke up crying. Kader was beside her. She could smell the rubber smell of his skin. He was holding her and kissing her tears.

Kader could feel that she no longer wished him any harm. Heat flooded his chest and his face. Then, as he leaned down to kiss her, it became clear that he was following her. Her arms were around him. And then her small, cold hands were on his cheeks and she was pulling him towards her and they were all inter-twined and he could feel her pulling and yielding at the same time and the room vanished and they were locked together. Her eyes, her mouth, her breath came to him in strands; she was like a ribbon, slipping through his fingers, then came El Niño leaping and then the shadows on the wall behind her head, swirling like water and suddenly he felt something give inside him, like a dou-bled rope slipping through its snap hook, and he was alone and falling and she was getting further and further away.

He lay with his head on her chest, staring into the darkness. He could never have imagined that this would happen to him. To suddenly have been cut off from his desire like that, to watch it from the far side, like a severed electric cable flailing uncontrollably.

I'm sorry, he said.

Be quiet, she whispered, gripping his head more tightly. I'm happy.

He closed his eyes.

They slept and woke, slept and woke. Astrid was afraid to move. It was clear to her that this was what it was to feel held. The man was just through childhood and yet she felt safe from all harm. She was lying on her side and he was curled around her, containing her in his embrace. His arm was between her breasts and she could feel his breath on her hair.

THIRTY-EIGHT

Paco dropped her off at the entrance to the pedestrian zone and Lola ran down the cobbled street without looking back. This time the morning sun poured through the window of the shop and there was a strong smell of dust. The little man was up a ladder taking a box from a high shelf. She could have reached the box without a ladder. He only saw her as he was climbing down. He did not greet her but took the box to the counter and opened the lid. All his movements were careful. It occurred to her that he might make bombs. Lola wove through the display rack and stood before him. The box was full of white lace. He began to sort through the contents. Beneath the glass counter were different types of sewing scissors on display. She looked at them as she spoke to him, this time in Basque.

I came yesterday. Perhaps you were too busy. I'm looking for Mikel Angel Otegui. She looked up. I understand if you can't tell me anything but I would be grateful if you could give me the name of someone who can, someone with authority perhaps.

The man now looked at her. There was eczema around his mouth now. He seemed to be taking her in for the first time.

Who are you? he asked.

My name is Lola Arnaga.

He considered her with new interest.

Goyenetche, he said, holding out his hand. She shook it, feeling the chapped skin. You were in Carabanchél, he added, picking out some *broderie anglaise*.

You're thinking of my sister. But she was in Alcalà.

I see.

He unwound the *broderie anglaise* from its card spool and wrapped it around his poor, red hand like a bandage.

I'll give you a name, he said.

He opened a drawer beneath the counter and pulled out an address book. He looked up a number and copied it onto a piece of paper, which he handed to her.

This is the address and telephone number of a lawyer here in Bayonne.

What's his name?

Gomez.

His other name?

Igari. Gomez Igari.

Lola looked at the paper and nodded. Gomez Igari was Mikel's old lawyer, but she said nothing.

As she turned to leave the little man said,

You may know the man's client. He is a refugee but I can't give his name. You understand.

That's alright.

Lola left with a sick feeling in her stomach.

Paco was leaning against his car smoking a cigarette.

May I borrow your phone, Paco?

Paco handed her his phone without a word.

A woman's voice answered.

Maître Gomez please, Lola said.

Who is calling? The woman spoke French with a thick Spanish accent.

My name is Lola Arnaga. I am in Bayonne and would like to come and see him. Monsieur Goyenetche suggested I call.

The woman asked her to hold and Lola heard the sound of her heels.

He'll see you, the woman told her. When can you come?

I'll be there in ten minutes.

Paco drove her through the ugly residential district near the law courts. The frequent roundabouts were dome-shaped flower beds sprouting gaudy red and yellow zinnias.

Paco pulled into the car park in front of a block of flats and parked in the shade of a hedge with pink flowers.

Paco, thank you.

Paco leant back in his seat and closed his eyes. He did not open them as she climbed out.

Gomez's office was in a modern block right opposite the law courts. Lola pressed the bell and waited. The Spanish woman's voice came over the intercom: 'ground floor, left', and the glass

226

door clicked open. Lola turned left in the entrance hall and walked down a dark corridor patting the walls for a switch. A door opened at the far end. The woman was waiting behind it. Lola smiled at her as she stepped into a flat that smelt strongly of wood polish. The woman held out her hand. She had silver, bobbed hair and bright, powder-blue eyes. She gave an engagingly timid smile full of anarchic teeth, then quickly closed her mouth. She held on to Lola's hand and looked into her face.

I'm so happy to see you. Lola smiled, waiting for the woman to release her hand. My husband is on the phone, she said. He'll be out in a minute. She let go at last. Will you drink something? Sherry?

No thank you.

Lola followed the woman into a cluttered and sombre sitting room. Books lined the walls and spilled onto the floor. Stacks of books and magazines were piled up all around the room.

I can speak Spanish if you prefer, Lola told her.

Oh yes. I have been here so long, and yet . . . She shook her head and smiled fleetingly again. Lola was charmed. She wondered how the organisation fitted into this woman's life. She wore a long chain around her neck with an Agadez cross on it. When she saw Lola looking at it she held it out for her to see.

I lived in Africa for a long time. When we were first married. Mostly in the Sahel. I loved it so much.

I've never been to the Sahara, Lola said. I've never been anywhere really.

Oh you must. The woman beamed, holding Lola's wrist. You're a doctor. They *love* doctors.

Lola felt like she had been struck. She looked down at her feet.

You're thinking of my sister. Astrid.

The woman touched her arm.

How silly of me. You are . . .

Lola. Lola Arnaga.

Of course. But the woman's smile faded uneasily.

I've kept track of your sister, she said.

You know her? she asked.

The woman laid her hand on her chest.

My name is Loli.

Lola stared at her. It was one of the twins from Astrid's *cuadrilla*.

It was Lorea Molina's twin sister.

I'm so sorry, she said. Of course it's you.

You wouldn't recognise me. I was eleven when I last saw you. You and Astrid went off to England and when you came back we had gone to Venezuela.

Your twin sister. What was her name?

Lorea.

What is she doing now?

She hated South America. She missed home very much. As soon as she turned eighteen she came back. She lives in the village.

Lola nodded.

We have a brother too. Anxton. He's closer to your age. You may not remember him. He was tiny when we left. He's a sweet boy, but a little lost. Then she smiled. I am lucky, though. I love my husband. He is a wonderful man. Make yourself comfortable. Sit down. I will hurry him up. And she left the room.

Lola was feeling weak. She sat down on the sofa in front of an ornately carved wooden table. Who was Lorea Molina that she had sought to ruin her life?

Gomez swept into the room. He was a little old man, with wisps of pale orange hair clinging to a shining, white pate. He took off his glasses and held out his hand. His face was covered with dark freckles.

He gestured to the sofa and Lola sat down again and watched him pull a large African drum up to the coffee table. This put him higher than her. He sat on the drum with his hands wedged between his thighs. This was the man to whom Mikel had given his letters in prison. This must be the man who had betrayed him.

You're looking for Mikel, he said benignly.

She nodded.

I don't know where he is.

Lola watched his smile fade.

I don't know where he is, he went on. But I know someone who may. I can put you in touch and it will be up to him.

His conspiratorial tone irritated her.

Who?

Gomez's face lost all warmth.

A Historic. His alias is Itxua.

228

I've heard of him.

I'm sure you have.

I thought he was in jail.

He came out in 1982 and took the reinsertion programme, but the life they offered him was not suited to him.

What do you mean, not suited?

So he crossed the border, Gomez went on. And started living quietly here in Baiona. Until someone sent him a letter bomb. Gomez looked hard at her. They blinded him.

Lola had the feeling he had told this story in precisely this way many, many times.

Do you know who sent the bomb? he asked her.

She knew.

The Spanish government sent it, he told her. A group left over from the Angolan war, recruited through the Portuguese to do the Spanish state's dirty work for them. Gomez flicked his head with his fingertips. It's crazy, he said.

Lola did not answer. The idea of meeting Itxua made her feel sick again.

When can I see him?

I will telephone him.

Gomez stood up and left the room.

Alone Lola tried to focus on what she wanted. She wanted to find Mikel. She wanted something else but she could not name it.

Gomez returned and sat down before her with a new solemnity.

He will see you, he said. Today.

Fortunately Gomez insisted on taking his own car which was parked in the basement of the building. Paco turned his head and watched her drive past him. Lola wanted to give him some sign but did not. He would either be there on her return or he would not. She told herself that guilt about Paco was a distraction she could not afford.

Gomez drove with his chin above the steering wheel, peering at the road ahead, never using his mirrors. The moment they had left his flat, he had changed. His energy had seemed to vanish and he was suddenly a beleaguered old man, spooked by the modern world.

They took the express way that ran between Bayonne and Anglet. Gomez stayed in the slow lane. It was clear that he could not drive and talk at the same time. Lola looked out at the malls: Usine Center, Decathlon, Mr Bricolage, Mammouth. Gomez pulled into Zone 2 of the Mammouth car park. He drove very slowly over the speed bumps to park at the far end.

It's all so ugly, she said.

A perfectly bourgeois comment, Gomez said, turning off the engine.

Lola looked at him but he was avoiding her gaze. She climbed out of the car and walked round to his door. She watched him pull his frail body out of the car, unable to fathom his sudden hostility. As they walked towards the mall, she offered him her arm. When he took it without a word, she realised he was afraid.

They walked into the chill of the air-conditioned mall. Two small boys were playing by the doors, gliding on their shoes across the highly polished granite floor. An electronic version of 'I will survive' was playing over the loudspeakers. There was a strong smell of dry-cleaning fluid. As they moved up the escalators, Gomez gripped her arm tighter. The first level smelt pleasantly of pizza. She saw they were heading for the Mammouth cafeteria. Gomez let go of her as they approached the turnstile. She let him go first.

Itxua was sitting at a table at the back of the cafeteria. He wore dark glasses and had his chin raised. His blue Mao jacket was buttoned to the neck.

Gomez bowed slightly as he spoke.

Miss Arnaga is here, he said.

Thank you Maître Gomez. Would you mind leaving us?

Itxua's voice sounded muffled. Lola wondered if it had been damaged in the explosion.

Gomez seemed relieved to be dismissed.

I'll wait for you in the car, he told her.

When he had gone Lola sat down opposite Itxua. His hands were under the table. There was an empty coffee cup in front of him. Through the dark lenses he managed to stare at her. She imagined his chin was raised to pick up her scent.

I'm looking for Mikel, she said.

Itxua kept his black glasses trained on her. He took a packet of

Craven 'A' from his jacket pocket and pulled out a cigarette. Lola could not watch him light it. She looked down at her lap.

Will you have something? he asked her.

She looked up at him.

No thank you.

You're looking for Mikel Otegui, he said. Why?

She hesitated.

Personal reasons.

For me there is no such thing.

His bottom teeth showed when he spoke. They were badly stained.

He's my . . .

Itxua suddenly blew hard, expelling smoke from his mouth. She started. He could not see her but she felt more deeply scrutinised than ever before.

Your what? he spat. Your *boy*friend, he grimaced. Mikel is a *man*.

I know . . .

He is one of us.

He doesn't . . .

Be quiet! he hissed. He paused to flick ash onto the floor.

Lola waited, trying to breathe slowly. She realised she was clutching her stomach. She waited but Itxua just went on smoking.

What have I done?

What are you talking about, you silly woman? You are of no interest to me.

Why am I here then?

Itxua tugged open his mouth to make a kind of smile.

I wanted to see you.

This, she realised, was as close as she had ever been to true madness. Her mother's ramshackle mind was not madness, this was.

She stood up.

Sit down, Itxua hissed.

Lola's eyes filled with tears. She sat down.

She did not look at him, trying with her posture to shield herself from him. Mikel had once said to her, There's a price to be paid for seeking involvement with people who play around with

231

death. The price, she realised, was the experience of fear. She waited, listening to the rattle in Itxua's throat as he breathed.

I will leave first, he said. You will wait ten minutes. Then you will leave.

He picked up his cigarettes and put them in his pocket.

My stick please, he said, standing up.

Lola leant down and retrieved his white stick from the floor and handed it to him.

If you do find him, he whispered, his chin raised, tell him he has no debt to us.

I don't believe you.

Her own anger took her by surprise. She pulled out of his way but he stopped so close to her that she was forced to lean back against the table.

He doesn't need you, he hissed. He needs no one.

Lola watched him shuffle off then she sat down in her chair and stared at the space he had vacated. After a few minutes she put her face in her hands and waited in the dark for the fear to ebb away.

THIRTY-NINE

Later that evening there was to be a 'Show of Strength' on the pelota court. If there was one element of Euskal folklore that had always bored Txema, it was this ridiculous spectacle: two giants lifting boulders or hurling tree trunks or chopping logs at high speed. He still found himself hoping that someone would get hurt. Lorea had been behind the games, which always attracted a fair crowd and a good proportion of tourists. Txema was in his flat getting ready to make an appearance. He had two rooms above the pharmacy. The bedroom gave on to a vegetable garden at the back, planted in neat rows by the pharmacist's wife. A large, plastic doll with blonde hair and ragged clothes was tied to a stake in the centre to frighten the birds away. Txema disliked the view, which at night when he couldn't sleep became quite macabre, but he had never got around to telling his neighbours to get rid of the doll. As he was preparing to leave the flat, the telephone rang. It was Lorea.

Good news, she said. I'm coming over. Then she hung up.

Txema looked out through the open window at the doll in the garden. From up here one eye appeared to be closed. He could hear the murmur of the crowd gathering at the pelota court and the shrieks of small children. For the first time in his life, his dislike of children no longer seemed an impediment to having one of his own. If it turned out to be a girl, he thought, he would simply let Lorea deal with it.

As she stepped through the door Lorea was flushed and her eyes were shining. She threw her arms around his neck. The cigarette in his mouth singed her hair and she pulled back. But she was not irritated.

Oh Txema, she said, brushing smooth her hair with the flat of her hand. We've found him. He's working the markets on the French side. He sells brooms from a van, she said, her face full of joy.

Txema looked at her until the joy had gone.

How do you know? he said at last.

My sister. She lowered her voice. Gomez saw him. He drove Itxua to meet him.

She's sure?

Absolutely. Loli doesn't make mistakes. The name on the van is Lamarck, she said, happy again.

Txema did not feel the excitement he would have expected. He watched Lorea step over to the window and look out.

I have to think, Lorea. I need to be alone. I'll meet you later, at the games.

She turned and looked at him. A question came and went.

We'll talk about it all later then, she said with bravado. Then she shifted her handbag to the other shoulder, kissed him on the mouth and left.

Alone, Txema went straight to the kitchen area and dislodged the wire panel from the extractor fan. He reached up inside the metal box and took down his old Browning. It was wrapped in a plastic Pryca bag that was covered in a layer of cooking fat. He threw the bag away and washed the grease off his hands. He unwrapped the gun from the chamois cloth and held it. The weight of it and the grip still gave him a thrill. He pulled out the clip, then reloaded. He aimed at the centre of the clock on the far wall, both hands, arms straight. Bang, he said. He slid the gun into his belt at the small of his back, pulled on his jacket and left the flat feeling younger than he had felt in years.

FORTY

When Lola heard Astrid's voice, she froze. Paco must have felt her skin turn cold as her whole body withdrew its attention, making his touch a sudden intrusion. He pulled back.

Lola did not want to look at his face. She could feel his dejection.

I have to go down, she said. I have to face her.

Lola, Paco said. She always felt his voice should be deeper. He was a tenor, and with his build he should have been a bass. I won't come back any more, he said.

He was pulling on his white shirt. He plucked nervously at his cuffs.

I have to go down, she told him.

Did you hear what I said?

She took both his hands in hers.

You know me, Paco. You have to decide what you want.

He watched her turn his huge hands in her long, thin fingers. He withdrew them and stood up.

I've decided, he told her. You're cruel.

Then he stood up, pulled on his clothes and left the room.

When he had gone, Lola washed her hands in the sink in the corner. She looked at her face in the mirror and saw that Paco was right. She had survived, thanks in part to her cruelty. She dried her hands and held them to her nostrils. Her mother still had a supply of violet soap from England that she half loved and half hated. She put on a red dress with tiny white dots on it that she had bought when she had first arrived in Paris. It was the first summer of Mikel's incarceration and she had worn it to visit him. It was the only time he had commented on what she was wearing. The dress squashed her breasts and tended to ride up over her thighs as she walked but she liked it. That summer Mikel had been in love with her. There had been an intensity in his gaze then, which had soon disappeared. Three summers later he would be in love with Astrid.

Lola put on her sandals and went downstairs. Astrid was not in the kitchen. She found her in the sitting room. The evening sun poured through the window, lighting up the outline of Astrid's hair and giving her a jagged, bronze halo.

Lola . . .

Shut up. I'm going to talk. I don't want you to apologise.

Lola went and sat down on the piano stool. While smelling her violet-scented hands, she looked at Astrid long and hard.

She pointed at the sofa.

Sit there. I can't see your face.

Slowly Astrid obeyed. Lola watched her walk to the sofa. She sat down and rested her hands on her thighs, waiting. She never crossed her legs.

I won't forgive you, Lola said. You're treacherous. Everything about you. I can see it in your face now. I've been looking at photos of you when you were a child. I can see that there's always been something secretive about you. It's as though you've always needed to hide things. It's your way of controlling things.

Astrid opened her eyes wider. She had the feeling that the dying light in the room was affecting her vision. Lola appeared to her as she had never appeared before. She was like an exalted performer, unreachable. Astrid could only watch, and as she did so, she was overcome with a feeling of immense tiredness. She looked at Lola sitting there on the other side of the cluttered sitting room, perched on the piano stool, all in red against the emerald-green wallpaper, and she felt weak. She had watched people die while she operated on them but she had never felt as powerless as she did now.

What I don't understand, Lola was saying, is why. You didn't want him.

Astrid shook her head.

What? Lola barked. What? Are you saying that you don't know either?

Lola.

What?

Lola.

For God's sake, what?

Astrid's voice seemed to be failing her.

Please. Lola. Forgive me.

Lola stared at Astrid. She was hunched over, her head buried in her arms. Lola watched and waited. But Astrid did not cry. She just sat there in a huddle. Lola stood up, took one step towards her, then changed her mind and left the room.

FORTY-ONE

The sky was thick with cloud as Mikel drove up into the mountains. The road wound through the forest of Sara, the same forest that had hidden Txema while he was being arrested by the Guardia. It was an ancient forest. The steep slopes were scattered with grand oaks and rocks covered in lichen. Poor Txema, Mikel thought.

The sun was setting as he drove into the village. On this side, the sky was miraculously clear. The bales of hay in the fields glowed orange. He crossed over the stone bridge and caught sight of the new playground, crawling with children. He smiled at the sight and patted his dog. When he turned the next hairpin bend, his smile vanished. The green field, covered with flowers at this time of year, had been stripped bare. Nothing was left but a bald slope of dry earth. He looked for a clue to the destruction but found none.

In the old days people would turn their heads to look when an unfamiliar car entered the village. Now there were too many people and too many cars. The place had become a tourist attraction. Mikel decided to continue on foot. He parked in a new lay-by beside a large, white mobile home with German registration.

A crowd flowed up with him towards the pelota court. An orange poster with black writing pinned to a plane tree announced an evening of Basque games. The years spent in this village must have been the best of his life. They were the years before knowledge, when the joy of being with Lola in that grand house was mingled with the joy of escaping from the slums of Renteria. The place, though, seemed not to know him. He walked among faces he recognised, unseen, forgotten.

Down the hill towards him came the old man with the slack mouth who talked to himself. He had been old twenty years ago and he was still old. He wore the same beret, pulled down over his ears, and the same dark jacket, buttoned too tightly over his belly. Mikel nodded at him as the man walked by, his mouth working, the lamentations pouring forth, but the old man did not see him. Castro halted a moment to watch him pass, then trotted after his master as best he could in his infernal sock. Mikel crossed the pelota court, passing the rostrum where the evening's compère, a man of his age in a white shirt and black leather trousers, was testing his microphone. One two, one two, he boomed. Mikel walked up the steps of the town hall with Castro at his heels. Sit boy, he told him. Wait for me here. Then he stepped through the open door.

When Mikel walked through the door after one peremptory knock, Txema started to raise his hands in surrender. He even had to smooth back his hair to dissimulate the gesture, then he stood, remembered the gun at his back and the folly of allowing Mikel to embrace him, and held his hand out across the desk. Mikel walked towards him a little stiffly, Txema thought, and took his hand. Txema gripped hard, using both hands.

They grinned at each other and for a moment Txema allowed himself the pleasure of seeing his friend again. Then the mistrust returned and he let him go, patted him on the arm and said:

You're limping. What did they do to you?

Mikel closed his eyes and Txema remembered this lazy way he had of expressing a negative.

It's old age. Then he grinned at his friend. You're fighting it, I see. But you can't fool me. Your hair was never that black.

Course it was, Txema said lightly. But Mikel had turned his back and was moving to the window to watch the crowds gathering on the pelota court below.

You happy in this job?

Txema looked at his tall figure against the red sky. In this light he seemed unchanged. He was still imposing with his broad shoulders and bowed legs. Txema wished he could shoot him there and then.

It's hard work but I enjoy it.

Mikel turned.

You built a playground.

His face was in shadow. Txema strained to make out his expression but could not.

We did.

Good job, Mikel said. Then he drove his hands into the pocket of his jeans, which Txema recognised as an indication of displeasure. What happened to the flower field?

The flower field?

The one we used to walk up on the way to target training.

Oh. That one. He smiled. It's for trail bikes.

Pity.

Txema felt a flash of irritation. He sat down and leaned back into the large leather armchair but this did not help. Mikel's righteousness still galled him. Mikel sat down on the small chair opposite his desk.

The place feels busier, he said, nodding slowly. And for the first time Txema saw the change. What he had at first mistaken for Mikel's legendary aloofness had become something more unsettling, more antisocial. His thick grey hair was wild and unwashed and his hands, now busy rolling a cigarette, were covered in scabs. He looked unhinged.

You must be here to see Lola, Txema said.

Mikel drew on his cigarette, then spat a strand of tobacco from his lip.

I saw her, Txema went on. What was it? Two days ago. She looked well.

She does, Mikel said.

You've seen her?

I've seen her.

Good, Txema said. That's good.

I had a visit from Itxua, Mikel said.

Txema folded his arms across his chest because he was afraid that his hands might shake.

Itxua, he repeated stupidly.

He knows you've got the money.

Txema could feel the gun pressing into his back. He could not move.

What money?

What are you going to do, Txema?

Txema stared at him. All he could hear was the sound of the compère's voice, getting shrill with enthusiasm. He could not answer.

Will you go to Venezuela? Mikel was asking him.

Why? Txema cleared his throat. Why Venezuela? Isn't your partner there?

The light had gone in the room and Mikel was a shadow.

What are you talking about? Txema's mouth was dry. He wanted a drink. Why would I go to Venezuela? I've got a job to do.

I don't say you should. I'm just here to warn you not to over-react. Mikel's calm was harrowing. I think Itxua is acting alone.

What do you mean?

He may still be in touch with them but he doesn't represent the organisation.

What makes you say that?

Mikel drew on his cigarette. The smoke floated out of his mouth as he talked.

He turned up in a clapped-out motor driven by an old man. No one's behind him. If they were, he'd have a decent car and a young chauffeur making his way up the ranks. You know that.

Txema felt an urge to yield to his old friend, to break down, to hold him and help him. They had been through so much togeth-er. Only Mikel knew him. But this was precisely what terrified him. He looked longingly at him. Even as a vagrant, he was an impressive man.

He wants to blackmail you, Txema, but I don't think he could find anyone to kill you afterwards. Maybe he could but my point is that you shouldn't run scared. Mikel put his extinguished butt into the pocket of his jeans. He had me in a state, he said, shaking his head. In the old days I would have found myself a weapon and shot him before he shot me. One last action, I would have told myself, to keep the peace. Then I'll be able to live a simple life. But it doesn't work, does it?

Txema could not answer. Mikel was a charismatic leader gone wrong. He was mad and dangerous. This is what he would tell Lorea when he gave her his Browning. His heart was beating so hard that he could feel the pulse in his throat.

I have to go, Mikel. We'll talk later. After the games.

To his surprise, Mikel opened his hands.

Good, he said. But he did not move. He just sat there staring. Then he began again. I thought to myself, how can I avoid doing violence to this person who is threatening me and when I looked at it like that I saw that the threat was in reality not a threat. You just have to look in the right direction. Do you see?

Mikel. You've been away too long. The world is still violent, even if you're not.

He wants the money for himself, Txe. That is what I understood. I thought about the conversation afterwards and it was obvious.

Txema could not help himself. There was real pleasure in hearing his friend use his nickname again.

How?

Perhaps he needs the money for something.

He wants to move back to the village, Txema told him, letting himself enjoy for a moment what felt like a conversation between equals. He'll need money to pay for the retirement flat he wants. He couldn't afford it with the pension he gets from the French, that's for sure.

You should not live in fear any more, my friend.

Txema felt his throat contract. He stood up.

I have to go. But Mikel did not move.

You must give the money back. Give it back to the companies it was stolen from.

They didn't steal it, Mikel. What's the *matter* with you?

He was shouting. His throat was parched. He had to get out of this room.

Mikel held up his hands.

Give it back and you'll be free, he said. It's the only way, Txema.

What are you talking about? Txema allowed a silence. He was standing and Mikel was sitting. He was powerful and Mikel was weak. He had a gun and Mikel did not. If I give it back, he said, they'll kill me.

Mikel shook his head.

They won't know. Only Itxua knows. And me.

And Astrid, Txema said.

How does Astrid know?

I have no idea. I imagined you told her.

Mikel shook his head, unfazed.

His complacency was an affront. Txema wanted to knock him down.

We'll talk later, he said. After the games.

Mikel nodded and smiled.

Sure, he said.

Mikel held out his hand.

It's good to see you, friend, he said.

Txema gripped his hand, afraid now to let him go.

When Txema and Mikel emerged from the town hall, the games had begun. Two bare-chested men in white trousers with scarlet sashes around the waist were hacking their way through two tree trunks that lay the full length of the pelota court. Txema advanced, head bowed with the mock deference of a public figure, through the standing crowds to his place on the rostrum. Mikel clicked his fingers at Castro and they walked around the court to the exit. He would not meet Txema afterwards. He had heard the hatred in his voice, even while he had heard the love. He had done what he came to do. There was no need to stay. Castro had snarled at Txema when they had emerged from the building together, just as he had snarled at Itxua. The dog knows, Mikel thought to himself as he walked down the hill towards his van.

FORTY-TWO

Astrid had been unable to sleep. Kader had fought his tiredness and stayed awake with her. They had lain together in their hotel room talking until the streets were quiet. At last he had convinced her to go and ask Lola's forgiveness. He had made her believe that it might be easily won. But now, as she walked through the deserted village, she understood that she had ruined her sister's life and did not deserve forgiveness. She understood that what she had believed to be love for her sister had driven her to seek control over every aspect of her life and for this she would be punished. Perhaps now she could start loving Lola. But from a distance.

The day had been long. It had reminded her of the early days of prison; a day over which she had no control, a day that had simply occurred. Kader had held her all night and she had woken in his arms to such a sense of dread, of the contrast between the comfort of being held and the knowledge that she was alone, that she could hardly breathe. She could not cry either. While he went out to get breakfast she lay there in the blinding sunshine, afraid to move.

She blamed their mother. Margot had abandoned them. She had let her own misery overwhelm her and had vanished into it with no thought for her children.

Astrid walked along the narrow alley and through the wide stone arch where she and Lola used to play cards in the summer. They liked the spot because the air was cool here while the flagstone where they sat, the only place in the sun, was hot. Beyond the arch was the path with the grass verge running down the middle. As she walked she listened to the sound of the long, yellow grass whipping her calves and caught the scent of cattle on the night breeze. Josu, she thought, had abandoned them too.

She saw the dog before she saw Mikel. It was lifting its leg on the fountain where a man was once drowned in front of the whole village for stealing someone else's wife. Mikel was standing a little further down the hill, whistling for the dog. He too must have known the story of the fountain and, perhaps out of respect for the dead man, did not want his dog pissing there. He looked so steady, standing on the hill, calling his dog. Astrid watched him, feeling a little envious that after only a few days of freedom he could appear so at ease in the world. Then he saw her.

Neither moved. It was the dog who picked up the connection between the two of them, seemed caught for a moment in the strings that ran between them. He turned on himself, bounded towards Mikel, then halted, turned and looked at Astrid. He appeared unable to tell if she were a friend or an enemy.

Mikel started up the hill towards her. At arm's length from her he stopped. He raised his hand to touch her, then changed his mind.

Mikel, she said.

Then she looked down. She was ashamed to use his name. She looked at his old boots on the tarmac and found them reassuring. Then she looked up.

Can we go somewhere and talk?

As soon as she had spoken these words she wanted to take them back, but Mikel was looking about him, then putting out his arm and gingerly, without touching her, urging her forward with him down the hill.

They did not speak until they reached his van. They stood in the stark light of a street lamp. Mikel drew the soles of his boots back and forth in the loose gravel.

Is he your dog? Astrid asked.

Yes. This is Castro.

Astrid held out her hand for the dog to lick. Then she patted him and stroked his soft ears. At last she felt strong enough to look at Mikel. His dark eyes were set more deeply and did not shine as they had. His cheeks were marked, each with a single vertical line, and his mouth was thinner and more sharply drawn. His thick hair was all grey. She felt a sudden tenderness towards him that she knew was not limited to his person.

Lola found out about your letters to me.

He looked at her. He did not appear to want to speak.

I didn't tell her, she went on. I couldn't. I wish I had. I wish you'd never written them.

He kept on staring at her. She tried to read his expression but could not. All she saw was tiredness. He looked very tired.

I wish I had told her about the first letter and put an end to it, she said. I was mad. I *am* mad.

She realised that she was talking to herself. She turned on him.

Why did you do it? It was so selfish. You didn't love me. You didn't even know me.

I know you as well as I know anyone.

You don't. You know Lola.

Mikel looked down at his feet, began to shuffle them again. Astrid was grateful for his silence now. It would have been an affront to hear him talk about Lola.

I don't know you, she said, softening a little.

No, he answered. He was still looking at his feet. I've led a bad life. She detected no self-pity in his voice.

Good and bad, she said.

I don't see the good.

You've paid.

He looked up. She flinched as he reached out and tucked one of her escaped curls carefully behind her ear. She found herself holding still as though he were a madman. She was full of anger at the idea that she had let herself be drawn into his fantasy. That she had allowed it to exist at all proved that she was as mad as he was.

All I can offer to the world, he was saying, is the promise that I will try not to add to the sum of its suffering. I realise that I can only begin to do this if I stay away from you and from Lola.

Not from Lola! You must *not* abandon Lola.

He was looking at her with a kindness that she had not seen in him before.

Will you forgive me? he asked.

Astrid had the feeling that something was slipping from her grasp. His anger had vanished. He had changed. She was filled with panic.

She should have turned and left him there in the cursed village. But the old habit of control made her seek a solution.

FORTY-THREE

Txema smoked and looked out of the window at the macabre doll in the vegetable garden. Occasionally he would look over at Lorea, fully dressed and sleeping soundly in the ugly armchair she had given him. He had told her at the games that he thought the time had come to act and she had turned and smiled lovingly at him, setting her silly, chandelier earrings swinging, and he had been appalled by the realisation that this woman was the price he must pay for his peace of mind.

After the Show of Strength, they had walked in silence back to his flat. At home she had said simply, I need a nap, and there she slept, free of torment.

Txema marvelled at her poise. She was a machine. Her brother, Anxton, was to ride the bike. Although Txema had shied away from getting him involved, it was a good idea to use a stolen bike.

Anxton had located Mikel's van. He was parked near the entrance to the village. As soon as Mikel moved, Anxton was to telephone them, let it ring once and then hang up. Then he would come and pick Lorea up on the bike. Her leathers and helmet were ready by the door.

Do the helmets have tinted visors? Txema had asked her before she fell asleep. He had hated himself for the anxiety in his voice.

Of course they do.

He's not to bring a weapon.

He won't.

He'd better not.

He won't Txema.

If he can screw it up, he will.

Wisely, Lorea did not respond but closed her eyes.

Txema now started at the sound of the phone.

Lorea stood up immediately and went straight to the bathroom. Anxton would be downstairs in three minutes. As she looked at her reflection in the mirror, she told herself that she would never again have to worry: she would never have to fuck

Txema again. He could find someone else for that. What mattered was that she was to be universally acknowledged as his wife.

When she stepped out of the bathroom, he was sitting in her father's chair. Her poor father had watched TV in that chair for the last years of his sad life, while her mother was having it away, sometimes in the next-door room, with a wall-eyed, Venezuelan meat packer. When Lorea had come home to the village she had brought nothing with her but her clothes, her make-up and that chair. She had given it to Txema without explaining its origins, because for some reason it thrilled her to see him sitting in it.

She stood above him so he could look and admire. She wore her tight jeans and a T-shirt with a black-and-silver leopard on the front that she had bought in San Sebastian only the day before. She stood with one foot extended, hip askew.

Txema's Browning was waiting in his lap. She leant down, kissed him on the mouth and took the gun. She turned it appreciatively in her hand and held it out as he had taught her, closing her left eye because she led with her right. They both knew she was now a better shot than he was.

Get him on the road, he told her. Preferably on the other side.

Lorea laid her hand on his cheek.

Don't fret.

Txema allowed himself to close his eyes. After this, all between them would be doubt and mistrust.

Thank you, Lorea, he said.

Thank *you*, Txema, she said.

And she was gone.

FORTY-FOUR

Kader hobbled up the path to the sleeping house. He knocked briefly on the back door, opened it and stepped in. The kitchen was dark. He walked through into the entrance hall and called up the stairs:

Lola!

He waited, listening to the ticking of a big clock, then called again.

Lola!

A door slamming, then stamping. Lola was at the top of the stairs, flaming angry.

What is it? My mother's asleep.

Astrid's disappeared.

I don't care. Will you please go?

Kader found himself short of options. Violence, abuse, charm, his usual weapons were inappropriate here. He stared up at her, open-mouthed.

Lola stormed down the wide staircase towards him.

For God's sake. She's gone back to Paris.

Kader shook his head.

She hasn't.

She stood, one step above him, towering over him.

She's unhappy, he said. She came to see you, to ask your forgiveness. I said I'd wait for her at the games. She never came back. All her stuff is at the hotel. Her car's still here. I've looked all over the village. He gripped his throat. I'm hoarse from yelling.

Lola stepped down to his level. She looked into his eyes. Hers were icy blue.

She'll hurt you. Whatever you do, she'll hurt you.

She didn't mean to hurt you.

Maybe.

She loves you.

Lola tilted her head slightly to one side. She had a strange look on her face: part amusement, part anger. Kader wanted to step back.

Who are you, Kader? she asked coldly. What are you doing here?

Kader opened his hands.

Look. I was hitching. On the wrong motorway as it turned out, and I fainted. Your sister picked me up. I'd been in a fight. It *was* a knife wound.

I knew it.

She was upset. There was something about her that made me want to help her. She made me want to be strong. She was going to see you then she changed her mind. She dropped me off at a gas station and went to see a colleague at her university. It was on the way.

Orsay.

Yeah. I followed her there. Made her take me with her. She'd changed her mind and was going south.

To see Mikel.

To see Mikel. Or to see you. I don't think she knew.

She's probably with Mikel now.

Kader shook his head.

She doesn't love Mikel.

How do you know?

She told me.

And you believe her.

She loves me, he said, holding her cool gaze.

Lola laughed. Kader saw that her incisors were sharp like his. He wanted to hit her. He didn't move.

Why are you laughing?

She stopped and looked at him. Kader felt as if she were suddenly far away and out of reach.

You think she loves you? That's what you think?

Yes I do. She cried in my arms. I held her all night.

Lola tilted her head again. She reminded Kader of old Arnaga.

And now she's gone, she said.

Kader seemed to be trying to drill the crutch into the wooden floor. At last he looked up and said,

You know, I don't care if she doesn't love me. I love her.

Then you're as sad as I am, she said.

250

Come and help me find her. He looked at her shameful night-dress. Get dressed and come with me.

To his surprise, something made her obey. As she turned and ran up the stairs he thought it must have been his own belief, or perhaps sympathy drawn from somewhere deep inside her. He sat down on the stairs to wait.

FORTY-FIVE

Castro sat between them on the bench seat. Mikel was talking with ease about the satisfaction his job brought him; the interaction with people, he said, especially women, did him good. He had talked of the pleasure his dog's company brought him, of his contentment at being on the French side, where life seemed less of a struggle. Even the light, he found, was different. He had told her what a joy it was to drive again and had apologised for the poor quality of the headlights, even on high beam.

Astrid listened, full of anxiety, trying to gain some footing in the sliding scree of his thought processes. How could Lola be happy with a man like this? He was broken.

Then he said,

They want me back. They want me for the Refugee Committee. He glanced quickly at her over his panting dog. I wish they'd leave me alone.

Get out of here, she said. Take Lola and make a life somewhere. A simple life.

She looked at Mikel's profile. There was still something grand about him. Lola had said all other men seemed pale in comparison Astrid stroked Castro, dragging his silken ears through her hand.

Have children with her, be happy. Love her, she said.

I would if I could, Astrid.

It's the least you can do! she said, striking the dashboard with her hand. She clutched her stinging palm. Take me back to the village.

He slowed the van and pulled over. They were at the entrance to a forest path. A sign warned of the danger of fire. Astrid sat rigid as he reversed the van and drove back onto the road. The light of a motorbike blinded them both for an instant before it sped past.

They drove back to the village; Astrid silenced by her despair, Mikel by his shame.

FORTY-SIX

At the wheel of Astrid's Volvo with Lola beside him, Kader had an unfamiliar sense of purpose. He felt useful, perhaps for the first time. Even in football he had always believed that his position was expendable. The only experience that had come close to this was being pushed around the supermarket in a trolley by his mother, who had been given a list by her employer that she could not read. At six he could read all the words on the list. His mother had been so proud of him.

He opened the window as they drove out of the village.

Don't you love that sound? he said. I heard it when I came in. Is it a waterfall?

Just a fast stream, Lola said.

They drove over the bridge.

Astrid and I got trapped down there once by a herd of cows. They crowded round us and we thought they were bulls. I got stuck hanging upside down from a branch over the river. Astrid had to wade in and rescue me. When she put me down I kicked her.

Kader smiled. He spoke without looking at her:

He's working in a village called Sara. I remembered the name because one of my aunts is called Sara.

He could feel her excitement.

How do you know?

Astrid told me.

He told her, she said, her voice bitter.

No. All she knew was that he worked in the markets on the French side. She found out that tomorrow morning the market's in Sara.

What's he doing in the markets?

Selling brooms.

Lola was staring at him.

How did she know that?

He left her a number on her mobile. I was with her when she

called it. A friend of his told her about his job. She wanted to find out where he was so that she could tell you.

Why *didn't* she tell me?

Kader was scanning the road.

I don't know.

After a while Lola sighed.

I didn't let her, she said. I wouldn't let her speak. I was so angry.

Kader was enjoying the drive. He suddenly wanted Lola to enjoy it too.

I made up a song for her, he said. Do you want to hear it?

Before she could answer he began to drum a rhythm on the steering wheel. He sang and Lola listened. When the words didn't come he used Arabic, any word he could think of: the words for beans, pasta, couscous, auntie and goodbye, because they fitted with the tune which came unhindered from somewhere so deep within him, he thought it must have been there before he was born – when he was inside his mother and he could hear her own voice, distant and ghostly, from the old land. When he had finished Lola was silent. Then she said,

That's beautiful. She's lucky.

Kader glanced at her. There was no sign of bitterness now.

You can't lose each other, he said. It's the strongest kind of love.

Lola looked at him and smiled. This time her blue eyes were warm.

I know that, she said. I do know.

FORTY-SEVEN

Mikel had started humming. It was an old habit, Astrid could tell, so ingrained that he probably did not know he was doing it. They were on a stretch of road that had been stripped of asphalt. The irregular motion made Castro jump off the seat and settle at her feet. Mikel was looking in his rear-view mirror.

That bike, he muttered.

She thought he must be so used to solitude that he could settle into it even when he was not alone.

He glanced at her, then back at his mirror.

Put your seat belt on.

Astrid looked.

There isn't one.

Then crouch down there, he said.

She caught sight of the glaring light in the wing mirror.

What is it?

Get down.

She heard his command and at the same time saw the bikers, level with his window. They looked like a pair of coupling insects, one higher than the other, bodies concave, their black helmets almost touching. She crouched down in the footwell with the dog. Mikel was accelerating and the engine was screaming, then he braked suddenly and the bike disappeared. Astrid watched him in the light from the dashboard, his teeth clenched, the veins sticking up on his neck. She had an obscure feeling that her safety was in his hands and she watched him like a child, free of all responsibility and fear, only a vague anxiety: would the wall between her and danger hold? His head was cranked round and he was reversing at high speed. Her safety now seemed to be tied to the ascending pitch of the engine. Suddenly he braked hard and she was thrown against the seat, her head whipping back, then forward, and she huddled closer to the panting dog, knowing, more than ever, that her body was nothing but a fine membrane.

Then there was a shot, an explosion as the windscreen shattered. The van swerved once, then again and she heard herself scream. Castro was barking and Mikel was trying to run them off the road.

Who are they? she screamed.

Keep down! he commanded.

This was Mikel, she thought, hugging the dog. This was his element, the element she had sought to protect Lola from all these years.

There was a moment of calm and she looked up to see that the bike was there again, at his window, the engine droning. Castro began to bark wildly. She put her hands over her ears and looked straight at the gun. Mikel swerved into them and she buried her head in her arms and she heard a noise like a grunt, a noise so rudimentary and forlorn that she knew he had been shot. She looked up and saw his body slumped over and she sprang up and grabbed the wheel, hauling him towards the window for protection, but she could see nothing through the frost of shattered glass and the pitiless grinding of the engine was in her ears and she heard the shot and felt the impact of the bullet and the warm blood trickling down her neck and she had time to wonder where they had shot her and see the precision instrument removing the bloody bullet and then she saw the blanched trunk of the tree, close, close as salvation and the car seemed to swerve again and she was not in control, she had let go of the wheel and she was floating even while she was aware of the gun aiming at her and she could feel their concentration, their keen intent and she heard the second shot, so loud and so near that it closed her eyes and everything slowed and she understood nothing.

FORTY-EIGHT

Kader sat on the bench in the long corridor and stared at the red lino floor. Reflected in the floor were the neon strip lights in the ceiling, like the broken white line in the middle of the road. Beside him Lola lay asleep with her head in his lap.

In three different languages they had told him that Astrid was dead but he still didn't appear to understand. In the end they had got someone to come and tell him in Arabic. He didn't tell them that he didn't really speak Arabic. Then two doctors, a man and a woman, came to ask Lola if they could turn off Astrid's life-support system and Lola had said, No.

Both Mikel and Astrid had been shot in the head but the fools had managed to miss Mikel's brain and so he was still alive. Kader had begun to laugh when he had heard this. He had laughed until tears had poured down his cheeks. Lola had held him, her body shaking with his, until he had stopped.

Later, the two doctors came back. Astrid was brain-dead, they explained . . . Kader remembered her talking into her tape recorder on the way to Bordeaux. Brain death, she knew all about. He wished he knew. He also wished he could have found his tongue. Instead he had sat there dumbstruck while they convinced Lola to let them turn off the respirator. Astrid was breathing but she was brain-dead. Kader still did not understand. He watched the luminous lines on the floor and found he still wanted to laugh.

The killer had turned out to be a woman. They must have crashed trying to get away, the police said. Kader imagined the felled bike, the woman's body sliding across the road like a puck then wrapping itself around the tree. He had seen her body as they drove away, her arms flung out at an odd angle and her head in its helmet, all cranked back. The driver was not dead. He was in the hospital. The police said he was a car thief, that he was the woman's brother. They were waiting for him to wake up so they could question him. Kader wanted to find the brother in the hospital and unplug him.

257

He looked down at Lola's sleeping profile. She had a swollen bruise on her cheekbone. She must have got it when he had slammed on the brakes at the sight of the crash. Lola had begun to whimper as he climbed out of the car. I know it's her, she said. It's her, she kept saying, over and over again, and Kader had run to get away from her, headlong into the carnage. When he saw Astrid he had opened the door, carefully, so carefully, and reached past Mikel's body and wrapped his arms around her. He had held her for too long, covering himself in her blood, while the dog howled. Then Lola was at his side, screaming about ambulances, yelling but touching him gently, purposefully, talking about phones and hospital. And he had watched her take control and discover that they were both still alive.

He now looked for Astrid in her face but could not see her. He looked at the pale skin, the tiny lines in the corner of her eye, the silvery-blue skin beneath, the freckles across her nose, and he knew he had to leave. It was quite clear to him that if he stayed to look after her, he would be in the wrong place.

Lola would wake to find him gone. She would be distraught but then she would wait for Mikel to recover and they would either be together or they would not. Kader felt a wave of repulsion for the woman in his lap. For some reason she had survived to give her permission to let Astrid die.

Your sister was a surgeon, the doctor reasoned. It's what she would have wanted.

Even so, Kader knew that he would not be able to forgive Lola. Perhaps he would go and find René the knife-thrower and the evil Raoul. He would not go home.

Carefully, he lifted Lola's head from his lap. He eased himself out from beneath her and laid her head gently on the bench. As he straightened up, his joints clicked and she opened her eyes.

Where are you going? she whispered.

He still could not kneel so he bent down and smoothed her hair from her face.

I'm just going to stretch my legs.

You will come back, she said.

He kissed his fingers and laid them on her bruised cheek.

I'm just going to get some air.

And he limped off down the corridor and disappeared through the swing doors.

Outside, dawn birds were singing. Mikel's dog was sitting at the bottom of the concrete steps. Kader bent down to pat him.

He found that patting the dog made him want to cry again, so he straightened up and walked on. When he stepped out of the car park onto the street, the dog was following him. Kader halted and waited for him to catch up. The dog stopped, sat and looked about him nonchalantly. Kader crouched down and looked at the metal disc at his neck. Castro, it said.

What's this for? he murmured, touching the dirty sock on its paw, and he found that talking to the dog made him feel a little better. I'm going to take it off and have a look. OK? The dog panted. You don't need this. Kader removed the sock, stood up and hurled it into some bushes. For some reason the act of throwing triggered his tears again, so he called the dog and they walked on together.